T

THOMAS KENEALLY was born in 1935 and educated in Sydney, Australia. He trained for several years for the Catholic priesthood but did not take orders. His previous novel, *Bring Larks and Heroes,* won the Miles Franklin Award for the best Australian novel of 1967; *Time* called it "as lovely and spare as a falcon stooping."

Also by Thomas Keneally

THE PLACE AT WHITTON
THE FEAR
BRING LARKS AND HEROES

THOMAS KENEALLY

Three Cheers
for the Paraclete

NEW YORK · THE VIKING PRESS

Copyright © 1968 by Thomas Keneally

Published in 1969 by The Viking Press, Inc.
625 Madison Avenue, New York, N.Y. 10022

Published simultaneously in Canada by
The Macmillan Company of Canada Limited

Library of Congress catalog card number: 69-15651

Printed in U.S.A.

Acknowledgment

New Directions Publishing Corporation: Ezra Pound,
The Cantos. Copyright 1937 by Ezra
Pound. Reprinted by permission of New Directions
Publishing Corporation.

Second printing March 1969

To Derek and Alison Whitelock

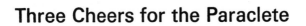
Three Cheers for the Paraclete

1

One Saturday evening, Maitland had to say Mass on a headland for a guild of graduates. The occasion had been arranged
in the heat of early March, but on the afternoon itself dusk
was all cold light and fierce winds. The altar cloths had to be
tacked down, a truck to be driven to the weather side of the
altar lest the chalice and chalice veils blow away. The Mass
proceeded under a sky dark as plums. The sea raced in
obliquely, breaking on his left, and wraiths of spray infested
the hill. He enjoyed the occasion and was happy when turning
to speak to these people who half-lay to hear him. They re-
clined on rugs and ground-sheets as if they might well be preparing to drink coffee from a thermos or make love. This
somehow gave him the sense that what he performed had an
affinity to the earth and the elements and the blood. So that,
for the first time since coming home at Christmas, he did not
feel an alien.

In view of the elemental air of the place, he changed his
mind on what to say to them. He began by telling them that

he had been prepared for a picnic ground with silver garbage tins. He said that what he had expected were those pixie-hatted picnic huts which record that Bill loved Olive at some stage and that Olive's small brother had learnt there his first four-letter word.

Laughter moved among the young men and women, reclining hip and shoulder on the earth among grazing Lambrettas and cars nicely blurred to soft animal shapes by twilight.

He began again.

"Christianity gave Eros poison to drink, says some German or other. Eros is the name of love between the sexes. Is the German right? Yes, he is."

The trouble was that he sounded like a fashionable priest, the glib kind. Perhaps his hearers had never felt, as he did, that they and he had been separated from their origins in the earth, and that the hill, the sea, the dark and the wind encouraged a tracing of the tragedy. He traced it badly, with a hateful facility.

"There are historical causes why European Christianity gave Eros poison to drink, took a confused view of him, placed him under a subtle ban."

He said what the causes were, he touched lightly on centuries and found them pliant to his touch. It was a false pliancy.

"Of course," he said urgently, "anything I say does no more than give hints of the way the truth was lost. We know only that the truth *was* lost, that Eros *was* poisoned."

It was warm in chasuble and alb and the rest, but he was cold to the calves in his thin, wet shoes.

"What have you been told from childhood, again and again? You've been told that Eros is a source of danger. So he is. Yet it must have seemed that if he did not have a hand in the propagation of little Catholics, he wouldn't be given standing room. For Eros is a filthy little pagan with dirty habits. One comes to see that he has been maligned. His presence generates in a person those decent human enthusiasms without which life and even religion are lost. You complain of the pallid cast of soul of this or that priest? But he lacks the self-

2

surrender imposed by Eros to help men to enthusiasm. The priest's way is harder because he does not have this ready means of keeping his personality malleable. As you pity all sapless humans, you must pity and have understanding for the sapless priest. For some of us have been betrayed into a frame of mind that is justly expressed in the saying: 'Because they love no one, they imagine that they love God.' "

After the Mass, a fire was built in one of the groins of the hill. It was made of a dead acacia-tree pulled whole out of the ground by men and priest. A fireplace was built of rocks, a wide, crafty oven worthy of the context, of men sacrificing, foraging, feasting in a gale. A first waft of wood-smoke stung the young women waiting with plates of meat in their hands. They began to talk together as if some doubt had been soothed. Flame rose and made the last light irrelevant. Finding another dead tree, men were content only with uprooting it. Meat fried on a griddle, blood fell into the fire, flame entered the eyes of the women, the slim and inviolate ones, the ones taut with child beneath their plaid coats.

It was like a rite.

The priest heard a voice at his elbow say, "Dr Maitland? Dr James Maitland?" He turned to the voice with a wad of red meat in his hand. There was a young man with a piqued, satiric nose and a forty-inch waist. Beside him stood a soft, shy girl whose scarfed head looked Slavic in the firelight. She seemed irradicably old-world and knew her place before a priest. As well, she was appallingly lovely.

"Dr Maitland," the young man said, "I'm your cousin Brendan. This is my wife Grete."

"Brendan. Brendan Carroll?"

"Of course."

They both laughed at once and shook hands emphatically. The girl waited without reproach for them to cease exulting as kinsmen-strangers always, on meeting, insist on exulting.

"This *is* a pleasure," said Maitland. He had heard of these two. Aunts and uncles who had known depression and wars, yet had won through to an Axminstered haven close to shops and bus, found lovely Grete and flabby Brendan a scandal.

3

"You know," aunts told Maitland, who had been in Belgium for three years and needed to be freshly enlightened on *The Family—Its Heroes and Apostates*, "they both got honours at the university. He was offered a job with the State Planning Commission. She could have got a job on the university staff. But do you know what they said? They said they needed time to digest whatever it was they'd learnt. *Whatever it was!* After four years' study and all those sacrifices by Madge and Charlie, he still didn't know whether he'd learnt anything. Anyhow, they went off travelling like the people in the Depression. They worked as housekeeper and handyman in country pubs. Once they worked in a cannery and a bauxite mine. As far as I'm concerned, they *deserve* a taste of the Depression."

"Perhaps they're just rounding out their education," Maitland vainly suggested; and angry avuncular feet shifted on the hard-won carpet.

"For what it's worth. You know he's *supposed* to have published a book of poetry. I mean, you'd think if he had it would sell, wouldn't it? There hasn't been any poetry since Lawson and Wordsworth and all those. Poetry's a novelty these days. So I keep on asking for it down at the newsagent's. But they've never heard of it."

Someone else said, "Charlie told me it sold five hundred copies. They live like tramps and all that comes out of it is a little book of poetry. *And* bad teeth."

Someone else again: "What would have happened if she'd fallen pregnant is what I always wondered."

Here were the two ramblers now, in the firelight. Their teeth were perfect and they showed no sign of parenthood.

"I've been told so much. . . ." Maitland said. "The family is particularly proud of your book of verse, Brendan."

The large young man closed his eyes and savoured honestly his literary kudos.

"It sold five hundred copies," he explained. "That makes it a verse best-seller for this country."

The girl said, "Anyhow, fodder, most pipple read verse by borrowing from libraries. All dose who should know say he's der major poet of anodder twenty years."

4

"I thought you were both on the road," Maitland told them. "We've settled down," Brendan announced. Both he and Grete found the idea funny. "We settled down when the North-west mail brought us in this morning. We've been respectable for the last thirteen hours." The two of them laughed. "I'll get a job with superannuation and Grete is starting Monday week in the German department of our old degree-shop. Grete's really first-class on German literature. She ought to be. She's a bloddy reffo." He glared at Grete. "Bloddy reffo!" he snarled, and she giggled. "I wish I could bear the children. I've got the right hips. And you can write verse in a labour ward if put to it. But you can't teach German."

Grete and Brendan had been brought to the Mass by a friend who had done his duty by his degree and had a sedan as evidence of it. When tea had been drunk and the fire winked out, the same man packed the priest and Grete and Brendan into the back seat of the car and carried them back to the city in the sweet reek of new upholstery. Grete slept. Though they were wanderers, her soft dozing body seemed to suggest that all their arrivals were homecomings.

"Where are you staying tonight?" Maitland asked.

"We know a fellow who owns a flat."

Brendan's friend looked sideways at his own wife in the front seat and said, "If it wasn't that Helen's parents were staying with us. . . ."

In the city, when the poet sat forward, Grete's head fell against the seat, the chin lepered by the blue light of car showrooms. Still she slept. It was this docile exhaustion and her refugee air that helped bring Maitland to a decision later in the evening.

Under Brendan's sporadic directions, the car left the lolly-water ambiance of the big streets and found its way among terraces. They saw little corner pubs, strewing light at intersections, reach closing time and spill their fixed clientele out of doors. Brendan stared. Perhaps the aunts were right about him, since he obviously had that poet's derangement that kindles to the grotesque and lets the familiar—Grete—go hang.

"That's the place," he called. At that, his wife roused herself and swallowed and looked instantly capable of greeting a new host, making a new home.

The place was a terrace with all its lights on. Three men were lowering a made-up bed by ropes from the top balcony to three others on the pavement. Two girls with that streaky hair and those narrow cheeks derived from too much claret-bibbing and Camus, watched from the rim of the pavement. It occurred to everyone in the car that the bed was being moved as some ultimate domestic expedient, that the house must already be full.

"Grahame!" Brendan hooted at one of the downstairs men.

Grahame came, yelling "Whoa!" to those upstairs. The sight of what he called Brendan's poxy old face caused him terrible joy and terrible contrition. "Christ," said Grahame, "any other night, old son, I really mean that. But it's this party. I've got dozens of people staying, even married ones. Respectable as all get-out. . . ."

Grahame stood back laden with the functional dolour of a hotel receptionist. Behind him the bed nosed the stonework like a small craft washed high by flood.

The car went forward then in a dubious gear to an area of bond stores. There was another place, Brendan said, but it would probably be better if he and Grete were let out at a corner. People didn't have as much pity for you if you arrived in a car.

Grete sat still and blinked with an awesome placidity at everything he said.

"Here," Brendan commanded sweetly after a time. "This is the corner."

They got out. There was no sign of disquiet about them as they made their very pleasant good-byes.

"Are you sure you're going to get in?" Maitland asked them.

Brendan said they were. Even if the tenant was out, he knew where the key was kept. He began to wave them on their way. It was clear that if the car stayed to see them safely off the street he would take it as an intrusion.

What happened was that they spent the night in Maitland's

room at the House of Studies where he taught, while Maitland spent it in a bed in the infirmary, thirty yards down the same corridor.

Maitland had left the car after a short way, and found them chatting equably in the doorway of a warehouse. Here they might have meant to wait out that passing phenomenon called night, an arm around each other. When Maitland arrived, Brendan was actually shaking open an anthology held in his left hand. He could not have read it in that dark; perhaps the grain of the pages brought back whole cantos to him; perhaps he was searching for an address.

He was angry at being caught underneath the arches on a night in an age of plenty. But his cousin was a priest, and anger against a priest had shades of sacrilege. The facts were that they had a dollar between them, he and Grete, their luggage was at the railway, their money in a country bank, their parents in another city. Since Dr Maitland had taken the trouble to come hunting for them, he might as well know these things.

"Come on," said Maitland. "My room's just slightly more comfortable than a warehouse door."

While in Belgium he had lived haphazardly in a two-room flat in Louvain, had been free to entertain vagrants if he wished. Now, as they walked a mile hunting a taxi, he had leisure to remember that he was not in fact giving Brendan and Grete the hospitality of a two-room flat but of a house for the training of priests where his own writ did not necessarily run. He had leisure, too, to feel a meddler, to assure and reassure Grete that she would not be driven out with incense and aspergillum, and to telephone the president of the house without having his call answered.

Close to midnight, a taxi took them to the side door of a grotesque stone bulk growing from the earth as emphatically as a cathedral. Maitland had a key and let his cousins into this cavernous symbol of his unhappiness. It went by the name of St Peter's House of Studies. Here Maitland had studied years before, and now that he had returned to teach, he caught constant echoes of the years of his first immurement. These gave new proportions to the fatuous, funeral-hall look of the corridors by night. Brendan and Grete, failing to see through the fatuity, were impressed. They would have laughed to see the staircase, its one bulb throwing a fuzz of luminosity down the wall, in a Boris Karloff film. But this was a priestly, solemn, celibate place; so they did not laugh now. Maitland led them upstairs, turning to see Brendan unwontedly timid for a best-selling poet and Grete, still in her scarf, as terrified as any pneumatic refugee in a Hollywood blood-and-luster. Upstairs another dim light, in a swan's-neck fitting from the days of gas, hinted the way down two corridors.

Maitland led them to his room and pushed open the cedar door barbarized with bulk varnish. "Welcome to *Mon Repos,*" he said. "Here is my ante-room and through here is my— rather, *your* bedroom."

The room was untidy and furnished with historical biography and memoirs. In the corner stood a three-quarter bed embattled among the gossip of the dead.

"Beyond that door is the balcony and over here is the wash-basin." He found them a clean towel. "Please don't be overawed by the house. It's just flatly horrible by daylight. You'll be quite safe."

Brendan followed him to the door, out of Grete's hearing. "We're more grateful than we can hope to tell you."

"It's not the Ritz," said Maitland. "If you can be comfortable on that sofa of mine that's redolent of old prelates, you're welcome. Good night."

Outside, the light was out, meaning that the president was in and would have to be approached. Maitland first carried what he had in his hands, his breviary and the old shorts and beach shirt which did him for pyjamas, to the infirmary. Here Hurst, a nervous student perpetually brought down with boils, viruses and impetigo, wrestled angels in his sleep and snuffled at the job. Maitland dropped his goods on a bed and found blankets among old books in a cupboard. They smelt of mould, but Maitland cared too little about that sort of thing. Besides, he felt nervous of waking Hurst.

After a little time, he went to Dr Nolan's office at the

bottom of a windowless anabranch to the main corridor. The president could be seen through the partly open door, extending one foot at a time towards his radiator and listening to his expansive deputy, Dr Costello. Maitland knocked. As he went in he was watched by Costello with an irony that seemed mainly to emit from the rimless crystals the man wore on his nose, and to be therefore mainly the fault of an optometrist.

"Like your blonde," Costello said. He was a princely man, even when in cardigan, black trousers and slippers (which shone like dancing pumps), even when holding a towel and a little bag of toiletries.

Maitland sighed and hit his forehead. "You haven't *found* them?"

"Sit down, James," Monsignor Nolan said. The president himself was seated, still in a long overcoat. In so many ways, he and his house were kindred. His conversation had a dated air that proved contagious, Nolan reducing both parties in any interview to a heavy idiom which Maitland thought of as Edwardian. In his overcoat, which was also on Edwardian lines, he looked very like a parson in a *Punch* cartoon. Across the saddle of his half-bald head he had six long hairs combed straight, and parallel from temple to temple, in what had once been, perhaps, the priestly equivalent of waxed moustaches. "Sit down," he repeated, a little too much like one of Lord Lundy's uncles.

Costello began to chat.

"I've just now met your cousins in the corridor. Charmers they are, but a bit of a shock when seen by one of those forty-watt globes economy forces on us. Anyhow, it turned out you'd forgotten to show them where the washroom was."

Seated, Maitland swatted the arm of his chair. He'd forgotten that they might need toilets. He'd thought that, once installed, Brendan and Grete would remain a secret Dr Nolan could be admitted into at everyone's leisure. Yet Costello had found two strangers so well entrenched as to be seeking a bathroom, and this before Maitland had even approached the president's office.

As Maitland explained himself now, he was disturbed at

how pained Nolan seemed. Something less shallow than a
sense of slight made the man's stubble-grey cheeks typify, of
all things, bereavement.

"I wish you had asked me first, James," Nolan said; and
Maitland found himself abject enough to suggest, "They're
both absolutely respectable Catholics."

"Where do *you* intend to spend the night?" Costello asked,
as if he'd isolated the very point at which the project touched
absurdity.

"I've set myself up in a corner of the infirmary."

"Good God. Who would have thought of the infirmary?"
Not Costello, for one. "You'll catch a neurosis from Hurst."

Yet, from Monsignor Nolan's general air of deflation, one
would have thought neuroses were nearer to hand than that.

"I didn't think I could let them spend the night in a warehouse doorway," Maitland explained again. He hoped that
the warehouse doorway, with its overtones of the thirties,
might penetrate the old man's imagination. "They had no
money, neither did I. I felt I could either offer them my room
for one night or stay there with them till morning."

"You're a rare one," Costello amiably took it as his right
to say. "You spend half the night buggarizing around a
headland and crawling round the slums, and then forget to
tell your cousins where the toilets are. Isn't your own bladder
subject to the strong east wind?"

In view of Nolan's sustained air of tragedy, it was not a
question that warranted answering.

"Perhaps it would be best if I went and joined Hurst."

"I'd be grateful if you stayed a second," Nolan said.

Costello yawned. "Well. Back to the washbowl." He was
listed to preach at the cathedral the next day; he was a popular preacher with a standard to maintain and, like a surgeon
or bomber pilot, needed his sleep.

When he had gone out, the monsignor said, "I'd have pre-
ferred you hadn't brought them, James." His eyes moped
across a letter fixed waist-deep in his typewriter. Maitland
could see a Latin sentence beginning, "Therefore, Most Holy
Father, I humbly crave. . . ." What? Some liturgical privilege?

A new dogma? A statement on contraception? Or the "I" might be a nun or brother wanting to be dispensed from vows; needing Nolan to frame a petition in that involuted Latin which atones partially for the defection of woman or man.

"They travelled all last night?" he wanted to know.

"Yes."

The old man breathed resignedly, his sinuses grating. He appeared to have been done irremediable damage. He blamed no one. But he was remotely angry with Maitland.

"You know James, I don't even let my sisters stay in this house, though they're both widows. I have them stay up the hill at the convent."

"I can understand your feeling insulted," Maitland assured him.

"Can you understand my sorrow?" Nolan said, and smiled in pain.

"To be honest, I find it hard. . . ."

"Can you understand you have introduced something new into this place?" Nolan played with the roller of his typewriter so that whoever's humble petition it was trembled and bowed.

"But worse than new. Alien."

Maitland came too close to smiling.

Nolan went on. "This has been a celibate house since its foundations were laid. That is a matter of eighty years."

"Monsignor, aren't you overestimating the importance. . . .?"

But beneath the clerical scalp conviction was impregnable. "I think that given the fact that they travelled throughout last night, and given their youth and various other condign circumstances, then we must make certain assumptions, James."

Maitland squinted at the sad, pale eyes.

"Monsignor, we're not Hebrews. There isn't any ritual uncleanness involved, no matter what assumptions we make."

"You will see to it that your sheets are changed tomorrow, won't you, James?"

Without thinking, Maitland stood up. "I'm sorry you feel this way, Monsignor, because it's so unnecessary. I have broken the laws of good manners, but I haven't broken any mystical rules of house purity. If I have, I'm willing to take any consequences on myself."

Nolan said bleakly, "You haven't lived here as long as I have."

"I would be more concerned about real matters if I had. Hurst, for example."

"There have always been sick young men here. It's the will of God."

"So is—so are other things."

Without any warning the monsignor lost his temper and typed a violent line of the petition. "*Alii situs, alia licita,*" he told Maitland and frenetically planted a colon on the sheet. "In other words, there's a time and place for everything, Dr Maitland."

The young priest had no answer, so said good night. As he left, Nolan called behind him, "The sheets, Dr Maitland, don't forget."

Maitland lay distracted by the old man's celibate pride for about an hour. During the hour his aim was contemplation. But he frequently heard Hurst, and beyond Hurst's bed the long frosted windows now held a glacial and insomniac moonlight.

Tonight and every night, as he futilely attempted mysticism, he dreamt that God had been reduced to a luminous surgical trolley on which he lay with his feet in cold blood, his own. His bloody hocks and bare shoulder-blades embraced the canvas cover of ultimate reality with a dreadful fervour, making so strong an affirmation and subjection that he writhed. He thought that this dream was merely a gauge of his fears on departing from the traditional God in whom he had been raised, the lee-shore, safe-as-Lloyds God he could no longer believe in. So he suffered the cold of the trolley with some detachment, knowing that men who are in transition between gods must expect unquiet rest.

He woke when Hurst said, "Unbelievable as it may seem, I find it hard sometimes not to run wild at table."

12

He found that he needed another blanket, he would cough for days if he didn't get one, but an etiquette of souls made him wait to be sure that Hurst had nothing more to say. In the end he slid from the high bed and found the cupboard. The cold fust of old books assailed him in the dark; devotional books, Dublin 1913, a good year for unalloyed faith. Why couldn't he have been alive and priested then? Saving up indulgences, averting tumours of the throat with a St Blaise candle, uttering arcane litanies; going off to the holocaust the following year to be outraged at the intemperate use of the Holy Name by the men in the trenches; dying in 1924 of dropsy, rosaries, and the certainty of Paradise.

Maitland hunted then, among the devotional excesses of some of the Irish Catholic Truth Society's most popular writers, for a blanket, and found one reeking like a brewery from mould. As he arranged it on the bed Hurst said a second time but more emphatically, "I know it sounds mad. But sometimes I find it hard not to run wild at table."

"It embarrasses me to confess this," Hurst had confessed to Dr Costello a week earlier, "but sometimes I find it hard not to run wild at table. A bread-and-butter knife can put me into a sweat and it's impossible to eat."

This was on a close night in Costello's bedroom study, and one of the vast windows stood four or five feet open. Beyond it some crickets could be heard mourning the cooling season. Costello wore languorously his black cardigan, a purple confessional stole and a pursed-mouthed brand of sympathy.

"It's so ridiculous, but I dread meal-times. A bread-knife is the worst. It ties my soul in knots, it really does. As soon as anybody begins to cut bread. . . ." The crucial word *cut* put the slight young man's teeth on edge. "It always seems to me I'm only a hair's-breadth away from grabbing the knife and doing the worst I can."

Costello smiled at this so patently gentle boy, at the unlikely temptation. Hurst did not see the smile; his bent head continued to wag and agonize. He kept his mind's vigilant eye

13

on the child-braining, man-gutting barbarian who dwelt in his belly.

"I don't see," he said, "how I haven't consented, in the mind, to mutilating other people. How guilty am I? What am I bound to do about it? Am I mad? Do you think I should surrender myself to an institution? I simply don't know any of the answers."

He knelt still, though the fingers of his right hand raked a skin blemish on his chin. He did not open his eyes, but could feel Costello's placid aura. Behind Costello, on the desk, as everyone knew, were the proofs of the man's *Praelectiones de Codice Legis Canonicae*, the codified certainties of his life of study, soon to be published in Rome. On the wall stood Costello's crucifix, below it Costello's white tumulus of a bed.

These things Hurst apprehended even with closed eyes, and envied as sources of plenitude, as if the priest had charged them with his own tranquil success.

Costello said in the end, "You are in no way guilty. That much is certain, my son, *in no way guilty*."

And if that sounded theatrical, Costello was not disquieted, for the sacrament itself had dramatic quality, and he had given and received it innumerable times. Neither did he rush. He breathed amply, having been taught by an elocutionist at three dollars a lesson the use of the breath as a weapon of reassurance or censure.

"It isn't a general sort of violence, is it, that you intend towards people? You don't simply want to put the knife anywhere? It always has to do with this one . . . area."

"Yes," Hurst admitted.

"And you don't have anyone in particular in mind when this compulsion strikes you? I mean, you feel you'd willingly attack anyone at hand, friend or enemy, anyone at all?"

Hurst covered his closed eyes with a hand. "I have no enemies. Anyone at all."

Costello stared at him through the glinting sanity of those rimless glasses. "Let me tell you, these movements of violence, these compulsions, everyone suffers from them. We are not long out of the forest, really. What? Two thousand years? Less,

14

in many cases. Some European races were barbarians until eight hundred years ago. And eight hundred years is no time, no time, a relative instant. So there is that part of us that wants to return to . . . well, to the forests where it was happy under the law of blood. These compulsions of which you speak, they're no more than an indigestion of the spirit and aren't to be taken seriously. Now you have taken yours too seriously, you have been too easily shocked. For your soul's sake you must not be too easily shocked in future. Put your trust. . . ."

He listed a number of supernatural agencies.

"Relax too," he said, and exhaled. "Panic is what kills. Consciously control the breathing, which is a gauge and determinant of normality."

In some crumbly fox-hole beneath his skull Hurst shuddered and called, "Christ, my Christ!", and his breath slopped in and out.

In the meantime Costello squinted out of the windows at the darkness plangent with insects.

"Do you think I need to see a doctor?" Hurst asked.

"I don't really think so. Faith is what ultimately cures. The doctors themselves will tell you that. And faith is merely a highly informed form of relaxing. Put it thus." Costello drew himself up in his chair and extended both hands, clenched to represent that both horns of the young man's agony were in fact padded.

"Either you will succumb to this compulsion or you won't. If you succumb, you will be no way guilty, because you'll have gone mad—an impossible contingency: even you can see that. If you don't succumb, then the compulsion is what statesmen call a paper tiger, and the question arises then: Why in the hell all this anguish?"

"I see," Hurst said, opening his eyes, but there was so much doubt ingrained in the corners of his mouth.

"Now these psychiatrists are not altogether reliable. They have a smattering of theology and tend to pontificate. In the end, all they can do for you is give you sleeping-pills, and I have some of my own here that I'll give you in any case."

Hurst said, "Thank you, father". But he had hoped he was sick enough to need a battery of doctors, for if he wasn't, then this was normality, and if this was normality, he wanted to die.

Then Costello questioned him about the origins of his compulsion.

"It is all part of the same—" Hurst's open hands considered such words as *demon* and *torment*, but he did not, before this priest breathing so episcopally, have the courage of his own bitterness—"thing." He explained how he had begun by feeling liable, in God's terrible eye, for all the corner-cutting, jay-walking, bus-hanging and variously endangered humans of that city. He had once pulled the emergency chain on a ferry because children were running around the decks. Not that he thought of their lungs bursting fathoms down in the bay. But he was convinced that *he* was liable with unlimited liability. Under God.

"Scruples," Costello said perfunctorily. "Some of Europe's greatest souls have suffered in this way."

Hurst raised frightened eyes to the priest. They slewed away like gulls at the sight of the white coverlet. An expanse of white could provoke the barbarian as an expanse of canvas provoked the artist. "Then the foulest blasphemies began to rise in my mind," he went on. "Chapel became a long battle to keep the lid on these ideas. The—*thing* always picked what I feared most and played on it. It used my eyes and my soul to choose what it would torment me with next. If it had been a Communist interrogator, it could not have—"

"Don't be melodramatic," Costello told him. "The *thing* is *you*. Well, there's every good chance that it's you. I sometimes think that the battle with oneself is harder than the battle with any prince of darkness. None the less, there's never any excuse for hysteria."

Hurst gave up, covered his eyes again. His complexion was streaky white and remote from the ruddy mania that absorbed him.

Costello demanded coolly, "Then how did this preoccupation with castration arise?"

16

"I was reading about the Indian wars in the Rockies," explained Hurst. "It was not a pulp work. It was researched, a bona fide history. I read what the Indians did with the corpses of American soldiers."

"Let us into the secret," begged the robust Costello.

Hurst grimaced. "They mutilated them and forced the results into their mouths."

"Of course they did. What else would any genial savage do in war?"

The young man shook his head.

"Now listen, Hurst, you are a man of faith. You have the barbarian beaten. These are his death throes at which you're so alarmed. Hurst, I tell you as your confessor, summoning all the special graces of the sacrament to my aid, that these are its death throes and that the very presence of these compulsions may be a sign of how far you have advanced towards perfection. Not that there is ever reason for pride. . . ."

Hurst, his face no more than quiescent, showed, in fact, no glimmer of conceit. He explained, "It's just that if I ever made that simple movement of picking up the bread-knife, I would not be stopped until I'd done what I had in mind. I *know* that."

"You'd have to catch your victim first."

"Not necessarily." He took a supreme risk and said, "I always have myself at hand."

"What rubbish!"

Outside, somewhere on the umbrageous stone façade, pigeons, as if stung by the priest's electric anger, began to troll.

Costello said, "It's cowardice to think that way. It is pride to think that you should be exempt from our native insanity, and cowardice to take the compulsion seriously."

And anger, being so therapeutic, did the trick. Hurst began to show signs of assent and reason. Costello rose and found a phial of white pills on the table, among the galley-proofs. With his confessional-stole on, and as if it were all part of the sacrament, he extracted two and gave them to Hurst. Then he sat down to absolve.

17

2

Grete and Brendan were present in the side chapel where Maitland said Mass, both young people seeming appallingly certain of what the rite meant: *His* actual and offered flesh, *His* actual and offered blood. Seeing his two kinsmen, Maitland was assailed by a nostalgia for lost certitude.

He remembered a young priest with whom he had shared a meal in France.

"Of course," the priest had told him, "I don't believe that the substance of bread becomes the body of Christ and the substance of the wine becomes . . . well, you know. I mean, that was a suitable way of expressing the Mass in the Middle Ages. But the words of truth change from century to century. Old formulas of belief go out the window the same way old chemical formulas do. Or rather, they should. You know that; you're a historian."

"I know that," Maitland admitted. "Well, what do you think this rite we perform means?"

"I'm working on it."

18

But Maitland, studying for his thesis, had never had the time to work on it. Now he could only close his eyes and pray on into the thick of the mystery.

After unvesting, he went back to the infirmary, looking for his breviary. It lay in the nest of tangled blankets where he had spent the night. The ruins of his bed and of Hurst's were bad testimony to the peace promised him in his youth as emphatically as trainee teachers are promised a superannuation scheme.

Hurst entered then, limping because of boils. His bedevilled eyes blinked *good morning* at Maitland, and he raised the infirmary window on the unbedevilled morning. Maitland could see, beyond and below the boy, the beach empty except for someone middle-aged walking dogs. On the balcony of a de luxe flat behind the promenade a man in Bermuda shorts watched the sea and enjoyed his corruptible lot a sight better than Hurst seemed to enjoy his incorruptible one.

Then, his blankets put away, Maitland searched for matins in his breviary. He wondered what to begin to say to this young man and stranger. During his uncertainty, the student who tended the infirmary came in with Hurst's breakfast. He frowned, seeing Maitland.

"Pardon my using your sick-room," Maitland called to him. "I had visitors using my quarters."

"You're very welcome, doctor," the student said with warmth and some irony. Enough for the priest to see that probably no other teacher or doctor of some sacred science had ever given up his suite (to an itinerant poet or an itinerant anyone) to doss down informally with the sick. Never in all the years the house had stood making priests and providing bishops from its staff and breeding demons in men of Hurst's kidney. And it was not necessarily a virtue to introduce, into a house that wasn't his, a late streak of softness for the destitute. His three-year casual occupation of Belgium had taught him a nomadic insouciance which was also not necessarily a virtue. Finally, he thought, inspecting his drenched soles, I must buy new shoes.

"Steak this morning," the student told Hurst.

Maitland left, reciting matins soundlessly with his lips. He heard Hurst claim with some urgency, "No, I just don't need a steak-knife."

In Maitland's bedroom, Grete and Brendan browsed timidly among his books. The bed had been made; he suspected that Grete had even tidied his desk and found a broom and besom and garnished the place. He couldn't be sure: he had a bad memory for the disorder he made there each day.

They put the books down quickly. Both of them looked well scrubbed and were dressed ready to go. Just inside the door stood Grete's large hand travelling-bag, to be gathered up in passing.

Brendan said, "We'll be going, father. Our sincerest thanks."

"Fodder, you saved us from a terrible night," Grete told him softly.

"I hope we haven't put you in a bad light, father. We met a colleague of yours in the corridor—"

"You haven't had breakfast yet," Maitland said. "And where will you stay tonight?"

"We have so many friends. We'll ask them straight out, too. Tramps' pride."

Somebody knocked on the outside door. Conspiratorial or timid. Since Maitland was not on terms of conspiracy with anyone in the house, he went through to forestall whoever it was that was timid.

It was a nun with folded linen in her hands.

"Doctor, I believe you needed new linen."

She was middle-aged, too old to be running Dr Nolan's funny errands.

"No, sister. There must have been a mistake."

"Oh," she said. She regretted, therefore, the stairs she'd just climbed. "Monsignor Nolan sent a note to the laundry."

"I'm sorry you've had the trouble, sister. Look, leave the linen here and I'll take it to the laundry when I go down to breakfast."

"No, doctor. Every man to his trade. Good morning."

He called to the two inside and told them he had to see the

monsignor for a second. But he did not rush. He waited in the corridor under a picture, so evocative of the awe-struck religion of his childhood, of Ignatius Loyola taking God by storm at Manresa. When he had decided what to say, he went downstairs to the refectory. But, of course, Monsignor Nolan and the students were at breakfast, still stirring tea and listening to the reading. If anything, their massed serenity fed his anger, and he turned into the kitchen and feverishly gathered boiled eggs and sausages for his guests' breakfast. Once he had juggled their ill-assorted trays up the narrow stairs, he found that they were gone. They had left a few atoms of face-powder on the cover of a book on Hapsburg policy in Bohemia. Also, more deliberately, they had written an apologetic note.

His loneliness exposed by the presence of the two breakfasts, he sat down. He thought, "I must see more people and find some of my old friends. *Because they love no one, they imagine that they love. . . .*" But he found it too hard to imagine what he did love.

Later in the morning, when Maitland entered Monsignor Nolan's room, he found him singing, "Good morning, James!" as if the house's supposed taint were forgotten. The president was in fact ready, in piped soutane and purple sash, for the Solemn Mass held every Sunday morning in the chapel.

Maitland said, "Monsignor, if you ever again interfere in my moral or physical health, I'll consider it a serious insult."

In the interests of sweet reason, the monsignor began to spread his hands in peace, as pontiffs do for photographers from *Life*.

"I recognize," Maitland continued, "my unforgivable bad manners in bringing them here. However, once they were here, you should have realized I wouldn't let them be insulted."

"Insulted? That's hardly fair."

"I want to assure you that I *will* be able to use the furniture in my room without catching from it either hydatids or damnation."

"Oh," Nolan murmured, extending towards Maitland the

meritorious black sleeves honoured with purple buttons. "James, you neglect yourself. I'm sure you never fed yourself properly in Belgium. Perhaps a tonic, James. . . ."

"Perhaps. But on the point of injury, we both owe each other an apology. I've given mine."

"And it's heartily accepted, James. By the way, you are rostered to preach in the cathedral on this day fortnight. If you could have the text of your sermon with me by Wednesday week."

"Do you mean to say you censor all cathedral sermons?"

"It's customary," the monsignor said genially.

"Dr Costello's?"

Nolan's hands ran like mice into one of the half-opened drawers. He tugged at a fat manila folder which contained the credentials of his life-span. He tossed a chancery document, twenty years old, to Maitland.

"I am deputed censor for all cathedral sermons, among many other things."

"But do you ask to see the sermons of other members of the staff?"

"You are in no position. . . ." said Nolan.

And this was the truth. He had let his anger over bedsheets spill into the question of a cathedral sermon.

"Very well. I mustn't keep you from your Missa Solemnis, monsignor."

"*Our* Missa Solemnis, James," said Nolan mandatorily. "I always like very much to see my staff there."

Maitland, who did not own a biretta and had hoped to get some work done, strewed the corridor with French obscenities and prepared to have a shave.

3

There were five of them in the sedan, returning from a death and happy as larks. It had been the quiet and ideal death of an old scholar called Monsignor Cairns, and Dr Costello had given well-timed and sonorous last rites. Now he drove, perhaps adventurously, the conversation holding its breath at crossroads. This was after all not a lasting city whose corners, blind with pubs and glossy chemists' and surgeons' high fences, he managed, scarcely braking. Yet he loved it and knew that he might be one day its archbishop. Therefore he enjoyed his nascent affinity with all those people who burst from between parked cars to chance a foot towards the flow of traffic. He wished ecstasy on the long-legged girls. On the dark ladies, carrying Balkan delicacies under their arms and frowning towards their six-o'clock stoves seven rivers of traffic away, he wished serenity; and such unlikely fates as love and mysticism were what he wished on the successful men in crisp suits and briefcases fat with devious commerce.

Monsignor Nolan sat beside him. In the back Dr Maitland,

warmly pressed by Nolan to attend the death, sat tight between the profuse hips of Monsignor Nolan's two widowed sisters, Mrs Clark and Mrs Lamotte. Both ladies were secret claustrophobes and liked to have a door each and the air on their faces. Maitland suspected that they both intended to leap out if a collision seemed likely. Their eyes constantly assessed the traffic and the side-streets, and Mrs Lamotte sighed quietly in moments of risk. Even though Maitland sat forward, both their gusseted flanks rasped slightly against him.

Costello drove downhill through an avenue of camphor-laurels. Between blocks of flats, the bay showed to Maitland raw-blue and sub-tropic, alien to the priesthood he shared with the two men in the front seat. He had missed an afternoon's work by going with Nolan, and the loss made him angry. His backside itched on Costello's synthetic upholstery.

What had already been said on the journey vouched for what he had assumed two months before, that he was numbered among Nolan's staff not because of any merit there might be in what he had learnt in Europe but for purposes of safe-keeping—fatherly safe-keeping, the Nolan brand. So that he could hardly see why he shouldn't scratch like a tom and end without equivocation his career as a priest-teacher-of-priests.

Mrs Clark had said, some minutes before, "They tell me that you're a great favourite in the confessional, Dr Maitland."

Maitland would have liked to believe that the topic had been instigated by Nolan. Yet he knew that the male ethos of the priesthood mattered too much to the president for him to give his sisters a part in chastising any priest.

"It's all the one absolution, Mrs Clark," he said with an orthodox smile. Besides, in the suburban confessional where he spent four hours each Saturday, he had not been aware of any milling of penitents.

"No. You're very popular with the young people. We knew a few who travel some miles to confess to you."

"Helen Simmons," Mrs Lamotte reminded Mrs Clark. "Four Caesareans and the doctor wouldn't take responsibility for the fifth. . . ."

"Oh, yes," Mrs Clark pursued. "Well, you put her mind at rest. The right thing, too. The commonsense solution. No claptrap."

To the experts in the front seat, *no claptrap* meant permission to use regulating drugs. Mrs Clark was a vigorous girl to have come from the same loins as the pallid theologian, her brother.

"I see," Maitland said. He tried to sound like a rough-shod confessor. "But one can't give the *happy* answer every time, you know."

Nolan remarked idly, "There's so much discussion drummed up these days on questions such as *that*." Meaning by *that*, his sisters' friend who had had the four Caesareans. "Telling people that they are still bound by the same laws as ever is a marvellous reassurance to them."

It had to be noted, in justice, that the monsignor seemed to want that to be the final word. If Maitland was a moderate, that is, a heretic, on some questions, the issue was too delicate to be argued between seats in a fashionable sedan.

"You polyglot idiot!" Costello yelled at a fruiterer's truck, and the danger to Maitland seemed past.

"The same laws as ever," Mrs Clark harked back. "Since all the doubt began—"

Nolan gave a small litigious giggle. "No doubt has begun. The Church's stand on these issues is identical with its stand in the first century A.D."

"Oh, go on!" said Mrs Clark, whom Maitland was beginning to like. "The Pope's waiting to make up his mind. How can anyone have a stand in the first century on drugs that weren't discovered till the twentieth? I *ask* you."

"The Pope is not waiting to make up his mind as if he weren't sure where the truth lay. His Holiness is making an attempt to reconcile extremists. Whether the attempt is wise or not, history will decide. For my money, I'd rather Popes didn't make apologies for their authority but simply imposed it."

Nolan had become so humourless that it was clear how often he and Mrs Clark must argue about dogma and morals, the lady debating without regard for her brother's status as a specialist. Yet the monsignor was not necessarily a humourless man. He taught a rigid moral theology, based on immutable first principles, within whose framework he was a man of wit. Accept my first principles, he virtually said, and their application, and I shall laugh with you. I shall laugh with you if you accept, for example, that direct killing is always wrong but that indirect killing can be right. See therefore that even in its most harsh applications—the garotting of a criminal for the good of the whole, the death of a mother because a therapeutic abortion cannot be allowed—it remains immutable, and we are brothers.

Students of a particular cast of mind suffered considerably in his lectures.

"Anyhow," Mrs Clark was saying, "a lot of priests are confused these days." She appealed across Maitland's lap to her sister. "Remember what that priest told young Cath Doran."

"Oh yes," said Mrs Lamotte, interested enough to stop looking up side-streets for death.

"What?" Costello asked. He was a friend of the family with the right to be blunt.

"A woman's matter," Mrs Clark said chastely.

Costello laughed, the back of his neck creased into three olive bolsters of flesh.

"Anybody who doesn't enforce the traditional morality in the confessional would want to watch out," the monsignor announced. "There's no future in chaos. I am sure His Grace is about to step heavily on the so-called moderates in this matter." He turned to the back seat. "This is confidential, of course."

Maitland said, "I never repeat anything unless it comes from an official source."

"A good rule," Costello called over his shoulder.

"He'll have a fair bit of heavy stepping to do," Mrs Clark decided, meaning the archbishop.

"Don't you think His Grace's word should be final with all his priests?" Costello asked her light-heartedly.

"I suppose it would have to be final," admitted Mrs Clark.

"The archbishop *is* the archbishop," said weighty Mrs Lamotte.

"Exactly."

Yet Maitland regretted that such robust polemics as Mrs Clark's were to be so meanly squashed. He said, "That would simply mean that a given woman would be refused a permission in one diocese that she could probably receive with ease in the territory of some other bishop. That would make—" he was forced to old-fashioned words—"would make salvation and damnation a matter of diocesan boundaries. I think we must find a better solution than that."

The front seat held silence.

"*There's* an argument," Mrs Clark was confident.

But Nolan laughed spaciously then. "I hardly see that you, Patsy, whose specialty is sponge-cakes, nor you, Dr Maitland, whose specialty is history. . . ."

He could not finish questioning their credentials. A woman in a little British car was confronting Costello to the left and flourishing her raffia-slippered foot at the brake. The foot skidded out of the slipper, flush onto the accelerator.

Mrs Lamotte squealed on Maitland's left, but Maitland and the combative Mrs Clark did not see the impact. They were aware only of the sedan, unaccountably full of grey air, rising sideways and turning over.

Maitland forgot the ladies as ladies. He remembered and could feel, all the same, that he was closeted somehow and that it was unspeakable to be so closeted; while the car came down on its roof and the widows' handbags split like gourds either side of his head. Both his hands warded off the crumpling roof. The car continued to bounce and the roof to buckle. A compact flew before his eyes, spilling powder across the roof. He had time for contrition, but it would have been a futile formality—like filling out customs papers when you know you are carrying contraband and know that *they* know it. So he gave up all his time to terror. At last the roof struck him on the head.

He woke in quiet, seconds later or hours. They all sat inverted and in perfect order and silence. Dr Costello still had the wheel by one hand. Nolan leant towards him on the verge of advising. Nothing was said. Around their heads were strewn breviaries, saccharine bottles, lipstick cartridges. A capsule of hair-dye near Maitland was marked *Tahitian Amber*, and Maitland could see it even though his vision broke continuously into yellow clefts. Beside him, Mrs Lamotte's exposed suspenders and unhusbanded white flank seemed unconscionably sad.

"Do you think we should try to get out?" Maitland asked the lady.

Costello told them all, "We had the right of way."

The engine was silent. Beyond Mrs Lamotte, Maitland could see sunlight and bitumen.

"Do you think we should get out, Mrs Lamotte?"

The lady pulled her skirts up around her knees, coughed and jiggled the handle.

"It's stuck," she told him. She had all the lassitude of a survivor, and felt through the squashed and diminished window, the air on her face.

Outside, somebody began to haul at the doors. Maitland further found that he was impinging on Mrs Clark's lap. He moved away, as it seemed to him, into a cold sweat and an area of nausea.

"Put that cigarette out!" Costello was roaring out of his window at someone coming to his rescue. Using both hands on the roof, he turned his large shoulders towards the back seat.

"All well? Ladies? James?"

"Dr Maitland's head is gashed," Mrs Clark said, though her own hands were bleeding.

"So it is." Costello took a more strenuous look. "Nasty, James. Bloody woman from the left."

Maitland put his hand on his scalp and found the short, reddish hair sticky with blood.

"I'm going to be sick, Mrs Lamotte," he said by way of edging past her earth-mother bosom and out of the window on his belly. He had just had the supreme emotion of his life. The years he had put in and the meals he had been fed to prepare him for the sublime, and when the sublime came, it was not the vision of truth, it was a sublime fright. Soon he would be ashamed beyond words. At that moment, what most actively occurred to him was that Costello used hordes of students to give the car a bi-weekly clean and would not readily forgive a man who sicked up in its back seat.

In the sunlight, people took him by the arms, talked about luck and providence, invited him to take lottery tickets with them. They put him on a fence outside flats and wrapped his head in a towel.

It seemed to be immediately that an old lady served tea and gem-scones to all the victims and to some mere bystanders as well. He saw Costello actually accepting a cup and chewing a scone as he chatted with a constable. Farther along the fence, the woman in raffia slippers, so narrowly saved from being a mighty slayer of priests, would not be comforted by police or beverages.

"I'm sorry," she yelled across the crowd whenever she sighted one of Costello's party. "I'm sorry," she called down the fence to Maitland.

At one stage he was sick.

When he felt better, there were the three Nolans standing around him, all with blood-tacky hands, the monsignor's cheek grained with blood. These were people he had forgotten. Their concern put him to shame. An ambulance came, and Mrs Lamotte collapsed. Knowing that she had become dizzy on her way to ask him how he was, Maitland knelt by her and made a bad attempt to find her pulse among the yellow, speckled clouds of his own concussion. All the time, a blue beach towel remained on his head. He could smell its cool, well-laundered cupboard smell. It was very likely, he thought, that that smell was Europe's or any one's prime contribution to civilization, since all other contributions—law, religion, literature—had so often become such bad jokes. An ambulance man came and took Mrs Lamotte's wrist from him.

It seemed to him then that they *descended* into that demi-monde which is the back compartment of an ambulance. He sat on one stretcher berth; Mrs Lamotte lay prostrate on the other. At this stage there was a swab on his head and antiseptic savaged the edges of the wound. Through the open doors he could still see Costello's sedan on its hood in petrol and glass. What a burnt offering it would have been had he and the Nolan girls burnt together without room to writhe—fat to fat, bone to bone, ash to ash. Unholy priest and holy widows wed in one excess of flame. The poisonous thought went through his system with that false methylated coolness peculiar to fevers. He stared at the sedative, smoked windows. Outside, Monsignor Nolan convinced Mrs Clark that she should travel in the front with the driver. Costello raucously swapped addresses and insurance companies with the raffia-slippered woman and was trailed to the very doors by her.

". . . absolutely nobody's fault. I'd be most angry to know that you blamed yourself. No special crime in running into us. We're just blood and gristle like other people." In fact, he carried a gob of blood on the tip of his left ear. "After all, *we're* supposed to be ready to go. Understand?"

She would have understood the Trinity had he asked her to. Her husband was also there, hanging onto her elbow and full of a baffled pugnacity.

Costello and the attendant mounted to the ambulance. He said, "James, your poor head. Mind if I sit here?"

The doors were closed.

"Isn't that woman coming to the hospital?" Maitland asked.

"Stupid bitch. She's going by taxi. All this black cloth would make her hysterical or something."

Costello raised his voice to a picnic-bus level and asked of the population of the ambulance, "Who remembered to give absolution while we were all sitting there upside down?"

Nolan said pitifully, "I tried to give one as we rolled over." He shuddered and sucked his blue lips. "But everything was so incoherent."

"Never mind. I got you all with a general and conditional absolution just after we landed. And no doubt James here did something similar."

But Maitland's priesthood had never been as reflex to him as that. "No," he said. "I'm sorry."

"Good God, that means you would all have died shriven except me. You'd all have been absolved except me, the absolver. In our next disaster you can all go hang."

Nolan, Mrs Lamotte, even the attendant, all laughed dutifully. Outside, the city was going home in its first two gears and the simper of brakes. No doubt there were cursing and impasses at traffic lights. But in that capsule of satin glass it all sounded homogeneous and very sweet, and sharpened one's sense of having survived.

Monsignor Nolan became ardent without warning, saying, "We could all have died. At least some of the doors should have flown open and thrown us on the pavement. The petrol could have ignited. I am convinced of a divine intervention."

Even concussed, Maitland blushed for the attendant.

"Of how direct a nature?" Costello asked.

"Of as direct a nature as is needed to keep four doors shut when some at least should have opened. As direct as is needed to bring us safe out of such wreckage."

"Our old mother was looking over us," Mrs Lamotte told Nolan. But he frowned: ancestor-worship was not among his crimes. He was a strict theologian, and he knew that Aquinas cast doubt on the idea that the departed have any knowledge of our affairs.

"It was almost like a parable," said Nolan. He laid his chin for some seconds on his purple stock, while Maitland sat pressing his fists into his cheeks, trying to soothe the scalp from a distance; Mrs Lamotte rested; the attendant was an outsider. Only Costello was capable of presiding and looked chairmanly.

"It happened because James was with us," Nolan proclaimed, unspeakably certain.

Given Costello's off-hand driving, Maitland blinked.

Costello laughed. "I'll tell the insurance company."

"It is exactly like the Jonah story," the monsignor told them all, beginning again to shudder. "The point is, James, that a Jonah has ultimately more chance of life and a sublime destiny than the rest of us. That is why he is always a source of storm, because he is in flight from God, he is a fugitive. As you are, James."

"Quieten him down," Maitland told Costello bluntly.

"It is exactly as if the traffic cast him off in the same way that the ship's crew cast Jonah off," Nolan said to the others. "The organ where he has been hurt is very significant."

"It's hard to agree altogether," said Costello.

The president raised his head and extended his cock-robin ecclesiastical breast towards Maitland. "James, I shall not rest until I have done what can be done to make you the priest you should be."

"I think you have had a bad shock," Maitland was able to say.

"You have been saved to serve, James. Your head has been gashed and bled to signify that up to the moment you have been headstrong and in contempt of authority—"

"To signify that Dr Costello," Maitland insisted, "was driving too fast. To signify that I was so crushed in the back that I was closer to the roof than the rest of you to begin with—"

"Calm down," Costello said.

Nolan stood up, crouched but anxious for dominance. "The archbishop will descend like a hawk on all those who do not enforce the traditional—"

But Maitland was continuing, his head whirring so hard he had to shout to surmount it.

"—to signify that I had work to do this afternoon and that when I want to be taken to an exemplary death I'll ask to be and that—"

"Don't worry, James," Nolan promised him. "We'll forgive you whenever you wish to make your apologies."

"He's sick," Costello said in extenuation.

Monsignor Nolan nodded like a judge in a dream.

Half an hour later, when he lay half-etherized in a hospital cubicle, they forgave him without apologies, as he forgave Nolan. Costello said, "It was all the result of shock", and all parties voted for the proposition.

32

4

One night early in the following week a plump-hipped, sandy-haired priest visited Maitland. This was Dr Egan, Nolan's assistant in the teaching of moral theology, *defensor vinculi*—defender of the bond—in the archbishop's marriage court. A capeless student soutane gave him a defined, self-contained look that matched what Maitland took to be his impregnability.

The dumpling figure moved fastidiously through the province of dust that was Maitland's ante-room and book depot. The bedroom-study had disarranged itself that night with particular malice.

"First time I've been visited by a *defensor vinculi*," said Maitland. "In fact, first time I've been visited by anyone on the staff. Except Costello and Nolan. And I suppose it's *their* duty."

"Well, it *is* time we got to know each other," Egan asserted. He, like Costello, had been to an elocution teacher, but it had done him more permanent harm.

"I thought I mustn't be using the right soap or something."
Maitland's eyes sought the second chair, finding it by the
wash-basin. He removed some suds-stained memoirs from it
and placed it for Egan. "I suppose you've all been very busy."

"It's been a very busy season in the marriage courts.
Mainly—" Egan swallowed—"mainly impotency cases. An interesting Petrine privilege case, too. That has to go to Rome, of
course, but Costello and I have to do all the spade-work. And
my job is to make sure that the court takes as much time as
possible. I'm the nigger in the woodheap." He chuckled like
an insurance man. He must often have used this piece of
whimsy on star-crossed spouses who wanted their marriages
annulled. "In any case, we're very busy."

"Fascinating stuff, canon law. I'm afraid I've forgotten most
of mine." Picking the *defensor* for a teetotaller, Maitland
said, "Like some whisky, doctor?"

"No thank you, doctor."

The little priest looked as if he knew he'd be given the
drink in a glass streaked with toothpaste. This Maitland was
very glad to decide. "James," he insisted.

"James. It's very kind of you, but I'm a teetotaller."

"I would never have picked you for one."

"Wouldn't you, doctor? James, I mean. Please feel free. . . ."

"You're sure you won't?"

Egan was. On his knees, Maitland enjoyed hunting down
some White Horse under the bed.

Egan continued, "People get so resentful about our work.
You know, one night a gentleman whose plea failed tried to
assault me."

Maitland, finding the bottle, groaned.

"Make unto yourself friends of the mammon of iniquity,"
he said.

"Oh, of course," Egan agreed, thinking that Maitland was
approving whisky with a text.

"No, I don't mean me. I have already more than fulfilled
that glorious old saying. I meant the marriage court. From
what I can remember of canon law, the court moves in gentle
channels. I was thinking that if you employed a detective

34

agency you'd soon scotch half these pleas for annulment on the grounds of impotency. I don't suppose His Grace ever considered it."

Egan became very still. "I don't think anybody has ever been temerarious enough to suggest it."

Temerarious, thought Maitland. It was an adjective worthy of conversation in a home for retired civil servants.

"Well," he said, "I think there's a great future for some temerarious cleric. It would be no different from employing professional fund-raisers. Private eyes are often used by jealous mothers, and I don't think Mother Church should be out-jealoused by any fleshly momma."

Concluding at the sink, he let a drizzle of water into the whisky. "Well," he called as he turned, "here's to Dr Egan. May he prove *defensor* of a successful quorum of *vinculorum.*"

Allegory of the mystic courting the divine fires, a brown moth fried itself against the ceiling light. Light fell on the defensor's dark hair kept counting-house sober with coconut oil. Tomorrow's beard showed faint purple under the white cheeks but had no future in such a neat little man.

Egan said painfully, "Are you trying to make fun of me, doctor?"

Maitland threw his untasted whisky down the sink.

"I've been here for two months and have received no more than a hullo from anybody."

"Perhaps no one has received more than a hullo from you."

"It's not my place to make the move. I'm the outsider. I'm doubly the outsider because I've had too much freedom in Europe and freedom is dangerous in my case and I'm here for some form of rehabilitation. I don't want to force myself on any of you if I'm likely to become an embarrassment to you. But two months is a long time for two priests in the same house to be merely nodding acquaintances."

"As I explained, I've been very busy," the blue-white jaws enunciated.

"I believe that if you meant to speak to me you would have. I'm sure that if I went to your room I would find all your books under proper regimen, a year's lecture notes in your drawer, a razor in your cabinet that a surgeon could safely operate with. Your pyjamas would be in creditable creases under your pillow and all your dirty socks in a linen-bag. If you had wanted to see me you would have. You would have to leave excuses about being busy to people like me."

"You have too high an opinion of my orderliness, Dr Maitland. My lack of organization, like other people's, calls out to Heaven for vengeance. I should have been to visit you earlier than this. I hope you are happy here and that you won't find it necessary in future to poke fun at the work of others."

The little man then risked offering his hand. The way it was done was suddenly a hint of integrity utter within its limits. Maitland shook the hand and sat down.

"Thank you. But I'm under a style of house arrest."

"That's a bit exorbitant."

"I suppose so. But what I mean is that the monsignor is taking trouble with me. I suppose you know that he dragged me away the other day to attend an exemplary death and we nearly died an exemplary death together coming home from it."

"Monsignor Cairns," Egan said like a judgment.

"Yes, I shouldn't be flippant. I'm not a busy priest at all, in any real sense. But I'm getting my thesis together for publication. For once, I couldn't afford the time or the split skull."

"Of course not."

They exchanged names, Maurice for James. Maitland was suddenly very willing that over the rubble of scholarship on his table an improbable friendship should grow. Only now that it began to lift did Maitland feel the full oppression of the Grete-and-Brendan business, of the Manichean quality of Nolan's injunctions on hygiene at that time, of the veiled accusation before the accident that he peddled oral contraceptives in the confessional, of the accusation afterwards that he was spiritual kin to Jonah.

Before friendship formed, however, and while there was still time to deal unscrupulously with the little canon lawyer, Maitland got in the question, "I wonder could you tell me how long before the Sunday do you have to submit the text of a cathedral sermon to Dr Nolan?"

And like a practised canon lawyer to whom time-limits are the expected thing, Egan speculated with some assurance, and the lips trembled on a number—but did not say it. He frowned.

"I beg your pardon?"

"I thought cathedral sermons had to be scrutinized by the monsignor."

"No," Egan said, putting an explanatory hand on the table. "It would be a sad day when they weren't able to trust the preaching of a member of this staff. Even one under house arrest."

Maitland saw that until then his guest had kept both hands clasped on the left hip and that now, as a pernicious silence grew, they fled back there defenceless as sheep. This disposed Maitland to suspect a number of things, among them that Egan might sometimes find his quarters immaculate with the same dismay as Maitland found his own to be a shambles.

Egan chirped suddenly, "Speaking of censorship, James, have you ever heard of a book called *The Meanings of God?* Its author is a man called Quinlan, a Catholic priest, according to the publishers."

"You *are* the complete canon lawyer," Maitland said after a silence. He stood again. "*The Meanings of God.* So they've found out about that?"

He could remember meeting a cerebral young English publisher nearly three years before in Ghent. As people do to friendly publishers, he had shown the man a very ragged manuscript. He had said, "It's a history of the idea of God since the eighteenth century. If Tillich speaks of a God beyond God, this is a history of the God who is somewhat this side of the unknown God. It is a history of the God of the institutions, pulpits, political parties and wreath-laying generals. It is a history of the abuse of the notion of God and of its place in the motives of modern man." He could remember the publisher arriving in Louvain by Volkswagen and running up the stairs to his, Maitland's room, shouting praise and royalty percentages. He had wanted to publish under a pseudonym, using his mother's maiden name. His motive was stage-fright, not fear of a dimly remembered Church law by which priests were meant to submit whatever they published to censorship by their superiors. Just the same, he thought that the spirit of the law would be satisfied by a pseudonym. Apart from that, his was intended to be a historical study, even if it did not permit the same type of ordered treatment as would a life of Garibaldi or Lola Montez. If there was a difference between what God was and what man, at this or that stage, thought God was, then this was a work of history and not of theology.

He published it. It went into two editions. Historians were diverted by it although, as they all said, it was not, could not hope to be, definitive. Most theologians enjoyed it. The young publisher had not been able to afford a third edition, but he had sold it into paperbacks, and Maitland had received the cheque for this sale a month after coming to the House of Studies.

Now he walked without anger to the balcony door. Like every writer who ever published, he said, "What else can a person expect in a country like this?" He added, "In a Church like this?"

"I beg your pardon."

"Did Nolan send you to see me?"

"Monsignor Nolan is not my keeper."

"You found out yourself."

"No. The Grand President of the Knights of Saint Patrick drew my attention to it, and we thought you might be willing to study the book. Being a historian, you see."

From the balcony door Maitland watched car lights blink and shift behind the beach in pin-points and beams and smudged radiances that brought the message home to him. Egan was not exposing him, but merely talking about books.

He turned back to the *defensor*.

"Forgive me, doctor. I misunderstood you. . . . I don't think we're speaking about the same thing."

"I'll show you."

Egan offered Maitland a page of Sunday paper which had

come from his pocket. Maitland saw Miss Associated Canneries abundant in a two-piece and "90 Year Old Sires Twins".

"The other page."

The other page asked "God: Is He A Political Hoax?" Among the normal Sabbath melange of misquotes, Maitland saw the names *Mark Quinlan* and *The Meanings of God* honoured in italics. A publisher's agent had seen that the book, filleted for the press, had that same appeal which, at first sight, only Miss Associated Canneries and potent ancients possessed.

"The secretary of the Knights," Egan explained, "who fancies himself as an apologist, bought a copy of this book, took some of his sick-leave, read it in two days, and then wrote a letter to the morning papers. Now it appears he used the name of the Knights without authorization. The next day a ferocious letter appeared in the press, written by a university man who admired the book." Maitland raised his eyebrows. "This man cited the letter from the Knight as an example of the general anti-humanist tendencies of the Church. It was at that stage that the president of the Knights telephoned and asked for help in the dialogue between the Knights and the scholar. You see, the secretary was silly enough to reply to the scholar on the third day."

"Armed with quotes from such high sources as the *Sacred Heart Recorder*, no doubt."

"Perhaps. Now it's a very scholarly book and a dangerous one, mainly because the public won't be able to see that when Quinlan says God he doesn't mean exactly God in any pure sense."

Maitland smiled, too proprietorily. On one level, it was impossible not to be as gratified as a schoolboy.

"What did you have in mind for me to do?"

"The Knights have voted to print a pamphlet refuting both the don and, if possible, the book. I want to know whether you would consider reading the book, as an expert, and advising the Knights?"

Maitland became immediately afraid of the farcical possibilities of the affair. "But I have already read it, Maurice," he said, and eliminated from the words all irony of the type that comes home to roost. "I own a copy, in fact. The hard-cover edition." His eyes hunted the shelves, and he could have been simply looking for yet another book worth keeping. Not that he did know exactly where it stood; still, it held the essence of the freest years of his life, it was a young man's book written happily, and the memory of having produced it was a vintage one. "I can't find it," he said. "But I have to be honest, I suppose. Maurice, I found very little to challenge in it on the level of history; and on the level of theology, well, it simply doesn't make direct judgments. Perhaps it is a dangerous book for the general public, but it was not written for them, and if they buy it, they won't read it. As for the Knights, I'd advise them to lick their wounds and forget the business. I think Miss—" he squinted at the paper—"Associated Canneries is a far more meet matter for the secretary to take his sick-leave over."

"You wouldn't consider re-reading it? I know it's an imposition. But the Knights do so much good. And I feel a responsibility. I'm their chaplain, you see."

"You do move in powerful circles, Maurice."

Maurice shielded his eyes from the irrelevancy.

Maitland repented. "I'll read it again, certainly."

"Only if you have the time."

"I have."

"If there's anything I could do in return. . . ." Egan glanced shyly around at Maitland's pylons of books with the look of noncommittal pain peculiar to his plump cheeks. And though he *might* have meant that he would be willing to put Maitland's suite in order, it was more likely this implication was an accident arising from a discomfort that remained no matter how easy their talk became.

"That's very kind of you. I'm fairly well settled in now."

"It's a good place to live," Egan told him, a man reciting a creed quickly as a substitute for belief. "So close to other priests."

Outside, the big loveless corridors creaked and headed for that deep midnight when even those nominal lights now shining would be out. Every hour or so, a priest or a student walked down the waste of hallway under those myopic bulbs that give each figure in black a meaning close to symbolic. *So close to other priests. . . .*

Maitland told Egan, "I hope you'll call in whenever you'd like a talk. I *mean* the invitation."

Egan seemed very pleased for a moment. His bright man-of-commerce face made Maitland think of commercial analogies, this time of a records clerk with a chance of burning the invoice file.

"That would be pleasant some evenings," he said humbly. "There's very little of that sort of thing, here."

Outside, bound for his room, Egan passed a student called Hurst who was returning from another absolution. They said good night. The corridors being so allegorical, and the mean light pretending to possess dimensions not its own, the passing of these two pale men was like the passing of the *Rachel* and the *Pequod*. Within a second Hurst had Egan quartered with a panic-stricken glance, then shrugged on his customary pelts of guilt and went upstairs to take a tablet Costello had given him.

An hour or so after Egan left, Maitland came to the end of redrafting the second-last chapter of his thesis. The idea of the last chapter lay idle and pliant in the bottom of his mind. Five thousand words were implicit in it, two or three days' work if he were allowed to do it. The task of writing a cathedral sermon frightened him more, and he would not be able to begin it until the Thursday at the earliest. He knew what was required. In his case in particular, something fit, grammatic and vapid would be the ticket, something to assure the citizen, chancing an eye towards the sermon section of Monday's paper, that God, like Jupiter and Mars, like abstract art, the United Nations and bank interest, had not swung loose from His established path. He was brooding on rhythmic boredom and how well it went in cathedral sermons, and was promising himself aggressively that it was the one thing of which he was incapable, when he remembered his night meditation and came to the prie-dieu.

His rule was an hour's meditation each night, his aim the scalding sight of God which disrupts the network of senses and rearranges them on a higher level. His chances were small, this proved by his having to time himself. One could no more travel the distances involved by making oneself available for an hour, timed by travelling-clock on the mantelpiece, than one could write a sonnet taking sixty-divided-by-fourteen minutes for each line. Sometimes by emptying himself of impressions, seeing himself an island eroded by a black surf of nothing, he became aware of the underlying astringency of an *Other's* existence, you could call it. At your peril. Words were the trap, for the same words that fakers used of psychic indigestion, fakirs used of God.

The Other's sting was never strong enough to clear his resentments or even to keep him from dozing. Often he was distracted by vanity at some of the better passages in *The Meanings of God*. He no more remembered these word for word than the salmon knows the fall drop for drop. But he remembered with pleasure the colour of its ideas, the contours of its language. They recurred of their own accord, as if their place were threatened by the Other, as it may have been.

This night he fell asleep, and Egan and Nolan, the publisher and God-as-a-trolley moved like crayfish in the shallow doze. When he woke, it was past the hour. His token siege of the citadel had ended.

5

Maitland entered the refectory five or ten minutes after the beginning of breakfast. The students ate at long tables either side of the aisle. They were silent and appeared to be listening to a reader on a rostrum above the steaming teapots. At the top table Nolan ate and *did* listen to the reading, taking that funny care that worried over broad vowels and misreadings yet allowed Hurst, watching demons flicker down the quicksilver length of a bread-knife, to go to hell unsupervised. Costello ate, Egan merely sat. There was no other priest at table. As Maitland sat down, Egan rose and said a Grace to himself. His small white flippers worked throughout the prayer to rid the front of his soutane of suspected crumbs. Then Maitland could hear him breathing fervidly at his elbow.

"More letters in this morning's paper. About the Quinlan book. Some nasty things about the Knights and about the Church, by implication."

Egan stopped, for the reader had lost his place and was too new to the House of Studies to know that he could safely have begun again anywhere in the book. When he did find his place and began again, so did Egan.

"*They've* had all the scholarship so far, all the scholarly jargon. If you *could* see your way, you'd be the man to alter that."

Before Maitland a breakfast of devilled kidneys waited, the same breakfast that stood that morning before most commercial travellers and resident schoolmasters throughout the land. Yet, in his discomfort, he stared at it with a notable air of discovery.

He said at length, "It's very difficult."

Egan inhaled in a way that left the floor still open.

"It's no use fault-finding just for the sake of fault-finding," Maitland explained. "The Knights would do better to forget it."

"The Knights may, but no one else is willing to. The book and the dilemma of the Knights and the rantings of the history department of the university are all given extensive treatment in this week's issue of *Forum*."

Despite years of practice in the confessional, Egan reached such a pitch on this last whisper that Nolan threw a glance of warning down the table.

Maitland turned his listless fork in the kidney gravy. "I'll come to your room in about ten minutes."

He found little Egan behind a cedar door in the same corridor that held Costello's suite.

Within, the study had just been visited by the nun who did the bed-making and dusting. Pines shone beyond the windows as if someone's solicitude extended to them also. All was properly aloof from all else—the bed moored in the corner by a sheepskin mat; the prie-dieu hung with purple stole; the desk on an isle of carpet in the mists of polished floorboards; the bookcases with a crucifix, centrally placed, consecrating all the dull suburbs of Egan's learning; in one corner, a Latin Quarter of paperbacks with scenes from the recent film on their covers.

Egan came to the door carrying *Forum*.

44

"Did you know that this Mark Quinlan unequivocally claims to be a priest. Or rather, the publisher claims it." Egan was all elation and no anger.

"So you told me. There's no reason why he shouldn't be, Maurice. He's no heretic."

Egan thrust the journal into Maitland's hands and conducted him to a chair.

"But the things he says about Pius the Ninth. . . ."

"He says nothing against Pius as a man of good faith. But there have been such things as disastrous papacies."

"Yes, but poor old Pius the Ninth!"

The *defensor* sat at the desk, which seemed too big for him. He may have been five and a half feet tall, but his schoolboy build seemed to take inches off him.

"Anyhow," he said, "the book carries no bishop's imprimatur and that means that if Quinlan is a priest the book was published without his bishop's approval. And it's not likely that even the most radical priest would do that. I'm more than toying with the idea, James, of writing to the editor of *Forum* and outlining the canons regarding permission to publish and, then, censorship—canons which every priest in union with his bishop knows and respects."

Maitland had not read beyond the first line of the article. He had been frowning at the line drawings that decorated it, a rusty knight bearing a standard with a triple-tiara and poking a mailed fist towards a ferocious young humanist. Now he transferred to Egan some of his chagrin at them.

"I wouldn't do that, Maurice. You shouldn't make the mistake of thinking that all priests remember their canon law. There may even be places where restrictive canons like that are treated as a dead letter."

"Never without perilous results, James. *Vide* Father Mark Quinlan, if he *is* Father Mark Quinlan."

"*Perilous results*," Maitland said, condemning the term.

There was a small hiss of embarrassed laughter from Egan. "Yes, perilous results," he contended. "Where is the sense in maintaining purity of doctrine for all these centuries, keeping

45

a strict watch on heresy, if we let the entire system slip in these latter days for the sake of the Quinlans?"

"But Quinlan's book does nothing to anyone's ancient purity. As I told you last night, it's an historical study, using historical methods."

Egan's hand advanced for the journal. There was an incisiveness about him arising from his affinity to the law, the Pope's law that had once made emperors truckle. He kept eyes on Maitland that were going to make a point. They made Maitland very angry.

Egan read from the article, " 'While the book deals directly with the crucial meanings God has had for some of the most prominent men and institutions of the past two hundred years, it raises by implication the question of whether God can be known in any of the traditional ways.' Even the heathen hack can see it."

"Then the heathen hack is bloody-well up a tree." Yet he was shaken. He said, "Look, Maurice, maybe the book does of necessity make a few theological judgments, but they aren't the point of the thing."

Downstairs a bell was rung, the type still rung in schools that cannot afford an electric one.

"Twenty to," Egan said as it lulled.

"Court this morning?"

"Some paperwork. Also, I intend to recommend to His Grace—"

"If you recommend anything to do with this *Meanings of God* affair, well, you put me in a position of extreme embarrassment to begin with. I'd prefer not to have to argue it out with a prelate, thank you."

Egan's face formed itself in invincible areas of plumpness around a tiny tight mouth. Somehow Maitland felt vindicated, thinking, "As soon as I saw him I knew he had it in him to look like that."

"Extreme embarrassment," the *defensor* quoted. "Because you agree with Quinlan? I find it hard to see how you could."

"A person isn't necessarily brought into the world to be seen through by canon lawyers."

46

Maitland excused himself and went. Ten minutes later, dressed in street clothes, Egan knocked on Maitland's door. He stood improperly childlike, his contrite hands held before him. This, anyhow, was the way he was discovered by Maitland. A second later he coughed, and veils of adult and discrete flesh seemed to overlay the child's face.

He said, "James, controversy provokes me. Please forgive me for insulting your honestly held view of the matter."

Maitland said that, as a matter of fact, it was his own arrogance that required forgiving. . . .

"I keep on forgetting," Egan protested, "how unfit I am to judge, to judge anything. As for mentioning it to His Grace, which I might have done in good faith, well, the older I get, James, the more I begin to see that friendship is a primary duty and. . . ."

"That's very gracious, Maurice." Maitland was half-amused by this duologue as mannered as Nolan's haircut.

"Well, I must go," the little priest said, and bared his wrist. A navigator's watch sat there tocking with utmost dedication and no sense of unfitness at ferrying Egan across seas deadly but allegorical. So he was off, on the way to defend the bond, carrying a pork-pie hat so spotless and an ox-blood valise so lambent that nobody would ever have suspected he wasn't arrogant.

6

It happened that Costello and Egan were the archbishop's representatives on the judging panel of the Couraigne prize for religious art. Their work was to prevent the blasphemous or obscene from winning, for Mrs Couraigne had been devout, a painter of saintly apotheoses, most of them now distemper-coloured and hanging in the corridors of the House of Studies. Knowing that all talents but one in a million date and become distemper-coloured, Maitland was saved from resentment of Mrs Couraigne, though her work heightened the spiritual flatulence of life in Nolan's house.

The prize-winners were named in a bank foyer on a Friday evening. Here Mrs Couraigne's latter-day sisters, in body-stockings and zebra trousers, had taken the hanging area and the catering arrangements by storm. Tediously messianic men in net-singlets and jeans recurred every few yards. Of course, there were artists who had found favour with judging panels or who taught technique and, become respectable, did not need to dress aberrantly or rampage through platefuls of

48

savouries. And then, the public servants of art, gallery people, trustees, entrepreneurs; and the press running down notables in the corners, running down Egan and Costello who, as comptrollers of the distasteful, were said to have vetoed a number of entries. And as guests of Egan and Costello, Nolan and Maitland sat on the fringe of the excitement, holding sticky sherries.

It was almost impossible for a painting to win the Couraigne prize if the archbishop's two delegates debarred it, but they could not debar a painting from being hung. Costello had meant to be vocal about a number of those hung, about a St Paul who looked like Benito Mussolini, about a Senator McCarthy Moses moving in on the Golden Calfers, about a gentle Judas quavering before a feral Christ. So he and Egan were soon chivvied loose from their chairs and washed on strong tides of controversy down the length of the room.

Maitland and Nolan sat alone.

"Strange crowd, James," said Nolan. "Aren't they?"

"Yes. Black predominates. I wonder why."

Nolan couldn't say. He forwent the second half of his sherry and pushed his glass to the far rim of an occasional table. "I knew Mrs Couraigne, you know. She was a daily communicant. I don't think she would recognize this." He pointed to the hanging area. "Look," he went on, counting through his programme, "there are four, five, seven—*seven* of those messes called 'Epiphany', and one, two, three, four called 'Nativity', and you could label all the Nativities 'Epiphany' and all the Epiphanies 'Nativity', and they'd still mean as much or as little. My heaven, look at that."

Across the room, a vegetable prophet, growing out of rock and blossoming into flowers sable and gold, affronted him.

"That mess, James, is actually called 'Isaiah after the Rain'. And they've got clean away with hanging it."

"Perhaps the flowers are symbols of spiritual growth."

"That's the trouble. They get away with blasphemy under the name of symbolism. By the way, when am I going to see your sermon, James?"

Maitland maintained the even rhythm of chat. "I didn't

49

intend showing it to you," he said. "It seems that you don't ask to be shown the sermons of other members of the staff. I think that if you distrust my orthodoxy, it would be better to take me off the preaching list."

"It must be obvious that you are not exactly in the same position as most of the other members of the staff."

The young priest stared at the gloss of the new shoes he had remembered to buy. "But don't you want us to test you for a fractional fit, father?" the appalled salesman had asked him. "No thanks," he'd said. "My feet have no responsibilities, except to themselves."

Now he admitted, "I realize that. Most of you have managed to convey the idea that my position is different."

"Don't blame the others. You haven't sought them out. They are, taken all round, as fine a body of priests as it could be any other priest's privilege to share his life with."

As evidence, Costello's robust laughter rose at the far end of the lobby.

"Not everyone has it in him to establish himself with others from a position of disadvantage. It's a matter of temperament."

"In your case it's a matter of self-pity. I honestly believe that, James."

"You're right, monsignor. But self-pity is a matter of temperament, isn't it? I feel that all your priests are established men, with niches on committees sacred and profane. It's not my place to do the approaching. I have no right to make you people welcome in your own house."

"This," Nolan whispered, for a young waiter in cutaway coat and bearing a tray of tiny beers was dancing towards them, "is all part of a false judgment you persist in making between us others and yourself. As far as I'm concerned, James, you are part of the *us*."

"The fathers haven't got anything to drink," said the waiter in full voice, and fluttered his eyelids, knowing an impropriety when he saw one, the impropriety being that priests-forever-according-to-the-order-of-Melchizedek should go without sherry when the body-stockings were nearly reeling with it. He

50

was, very likely, a satiric gent and a rampant anti-clerical.

Both fathers shook their heads at him. Maitland lied, "A priest always finds wine too evocative to be enjoyed." He wanted to hurt Nolan, for, as he knew, Nolan felt a spouse-like identity with the Mass, whereas he himself felt only a custodian, performer of someone else's fantasy.

Maitland succeeded too well. Nolan would be as angry as an old wife within ten seconds and use all the old-wife's sharp practice, but for the moment the mouth opened, an old man's head of pallid teeth could be seen, and the point of the bottom lip rose to cover them. It was a glimpse of age and its vulnerability and it made Maitland properly ashamed. The cutaway coat cut away, tittering.

"So this is the way your resentment works," the monsignor decided. "To pretend to those who have nothing to be proud of that we are of the same ilk as them."

"I'm sorry. But let's have no more cant about my belonging in your house."

"And you wonder why you don't belong in my house. After that."

"I'm not an outsider because I used a waiter in argument. I used a waiter because I'm an outsider. Give a dog a bad name. . . ."

"A priest is a man of lonely trials. If you didn't like that idea, you should never have let yourself be ordained."

Maitland repeated this adage about lonely trials beneath his breath as a form of capitulation. Axioms paralysed him; he could not prevail against them. Rather than try, he watched the room. Even on such miserly liquor, the crowd had begun to blend. Egan was making his points to the creator of Mc-Carthy-Moses, and a gallery trustee laughed and patted the skin-tight back of a bone-tight girl.

As if to himself, Maitland said, "Apart from a misbegotten account of some young matron's confession, had from your sisters, I wonder just what it is that you find substandard in me."

Spittle was flying from the perfect teeth and fury of the painter of Senator Moses. Before these forces little Egan stood, patience entrenched, ticking off his arguments on the plump fingers of his left hand. That degree of patience was a provacation, Maitland thought, and one of the panel thought so too, and moved in to soothe the artist.

Nolan was explaining coldly, "I take no cognizance of women, not even of my sisters, and I give them no place in the government of the Church when I am in my right mind. I would have thought you had the kindness to believe that I was not in my right mind on the afternoon of our accident."

Meanwhile, at the passionate end of the foyer, the painter's girl slurred Egan. It seemed so lively that Maitland regretted Nolan and himself were off after hounds of their own. They could see, though Nolan hadn't yet, that some notable was protecting the little priest with outspread arms. Then the artist and his girl stood back, chanting, "Oh, angel of God, my guardian dear, to whom God's love commits me here", and so on, as if they were reciting Egan's code of art. People faced in upon the priest's discomfort and wore their humanist half-smiles like the worst sort of cruelty. Maitland was about to excuse himself and perhaps go to his friend's help, when the incident, too rugged a growth, faded into the synthetic bonhomie of four or five converging officials.

The monsignor had not been distracted. "I was alarmed, so was His Grace, by an article of yours in an English review. I don't want to be offensive, but I have to say that it's an indication of the Church's peril that this article was ever published. I say this, James, though I realize what pride scholars take in what they have had published. None the less. . . ."

"The article on Luther?" Maitland suggested.

"That's the one. Now I know little history, Dr Maitland, but it seemed to me that you were saying Luther and Aquinas were in agreement, that the Supreme Pontiff fell into a trap in condemning Luther. Is this a correct reading?"

"Not exactly. I claimed that they were in agreement on the basic question, which was the nature of the Redemption. As people like to say these days, it was a question of semantics."

Nolan's hands began to shake in a small way. They savaged the cellophane from a pack of cigarettes.

"And you still believe this?"

"I believe that the gulf between Luther and the traditional doctrine was not such as to warrant excommunication, schism, war and so on."

"A question of semantics." Nolan struck a light to his cigarette in a near-frenzy of rightness. He smoked it held between his middle fingers, as many women who learnt to smoke in the twenties do. His reason was different to theirs— he saved the index and thumb for the usages of the altar. Yet he did look like an angry refugee from an age of du Maurier and post-impressionism. "Luther's denial of tradition a matter of semantics? Luther's attack on the doctrine of the Incarnation and on the Sacraments?"

"Yes. Of course, the rift became greater once Rome and Luther had divorced each other, but there was nothing in Luther's early teaching that need have caused the schism. However, all those qualifications are made in the article itself. If you didn't accept its drift in print, it won't do us any good if I detail it here."

"I never thought I would hear such hogwash from a priest trained in our House of Studies," Nolan said and crushed out his cigarette.

Confused by anger, Maitland took out his handkerchief and was constrained, seeing it in his hand, to blow his nose unnecessarily and with adenoidal caution. "Oh, orthodoxy," he muttered then. Nothing more necessary, nothing more inconsequential. The world keeps to its stale or knowing ways, no matter what. Pride of the eyes prevails as surely on most canvases, pride of life holds up the walls of banks and puts the pillars in and the loveless furniture from Scandinavia. Just as surely, hands of influential men feign fatherly interest on the waists of artists' molls who breakfast, come rain, hail, predestination or signs in the heavens, just as surely on methedrine and cornflakes.

"How do I know what you might say from a cathedral pulpit?" Nolan wondered.

Maitland said, "If you wished, I could give you some sort of promise." He had lost interest in Nolan's demands and in what the programme described as "one of the art events of the cultural year in this country". It was apter than Nolan suspected that the president of a House of Studies for priests should be here on the outskirts of the event. For the priests pursued their orthodoxy and the artists theirs, orthodoxies alien to each other, orthodoxies in conflict with society at large, orthodoxies prolific in closed minds. Of which his was one, but could not challenge Nolan's.

A woman of dark, gangling and slightly speckled beauty was speaking now to Egan. She had a long, very special neck rising from a cowled dress of the same colour as the monsignor's stock, and she bent to Egan who was three inches shorter and whose lips were, at that moment, compressed toutishly as if he were giving the inside story on something.

Orthodoxies prolific in closed minds.

"You could ruin your career with a rash sermon. I'll preach myself if there is any doubt about yours. His Grace and I both consider it necessary to know *exactly* what you intend to say. The main danger of our not knowing is to yourself, James, and it's no small danger."

Now that drinks had been had and the crowd were familiar with the form and colour and even the texture of all the visions hung there, a general listlessness seemed to have come down on the occasion. This and Nolan's speech were both broken in upon by some dutiful hand-clapping. Like a master-stroke of ennui, a vice-regal party made an entrance and speeches began. Under this cover, Maitland excused himself from Nolan and crept across the room. When he was obscured from the monsignor by thickets of art-lovers, he stood on his own, applauding the awards.

As soon as the speeches ended, a very elegant young man assailed him from the side.

"Father," he said, "you've seen that fierce-looking Christ over there?"

"Oh, yes."

"Don't you think it improper, honestly, that an interpretation like that should be actually hung in an exhibition of religious paintings?"

54

The young man squinted at the painting and turned a geometrically barbered neck on Maitland. He seemed to be possessed by a strong sectarian anger.

"It's sad," Maitland was willing to say. "Christian mystics are overwhelmed by the very opposite of that." He nodded at the picture. "They're impressed to gasping point by his—what?—elected defencelessness, you could say. That sort of thing over there hurts. On the other hand, it should make us wonder what we've done to earn him so much hate."

"What we've done?" the boy echoed. "By *we*, do you mean priests, father?"

"Priests among others, perhaps."

"You wouldn't see that painting then as the work of the forces of darkness?"

"Not altogether. We've done a lot to make Christ seem anti-human. And anything that's anti-human ends up hated by people who can't be said to be the utter dregs."

"There seems to be a strong element of hatred right through the exhibition," the young man ventured, and spent some minutes depressing Maitland with an interpretaion of some of the dingiest paintings in the hanging area. At length Costello loomed and made signs with his eyes.

"Excuse me," said Maitland. "It's time for us to go, I think."

The haranguing boy said, "Certainly, father," and vanished.

"Wanted to deliver you from that fellow," Costello explained. "Bloody old woman. What was he on about?"

"Just orating about some of the paintings that gave yourself and Egan trouble."

"I'm sick of all this carping, James. You know, every one of these bloody artists, emotional creatures and all as they are, accept the decisions of the other judges as final, but annually the art community drops garbage on little Egan and me from a great height. Why? You're a wild one, James—now, no blushing. *You* tell me why they can't see that bad religion can't be made into good religious art. Where's Egan?"

Egan was still speaking with his dark lady.

"See that woman with Maurice?" Costello asked. "Very statuesque. She's an old client of ours in the marriage courts.

I don't suppose it's a breach of ethics to tell you that. It's good to see her looking well. A person gets to know these people very well despite the requisite aloofness. She was in a very poor state by the time her annulment came through."

"She seems friendly enough to Egan, even though he must have been the villain in court."

"Egan's a very kind little chap though, very kind. If you didn't know, you'd think a *defensor vinculi* would be the most hated of men. All the marriages he defends are putrefying on their feet by the time they get to us. But there they are, Egan and the Tully woman, polite to each other. Not that they shouldn't be polite. It's only good sense."

Maitland waited while Costello went to collect Egan. He saw the woman give Costello the curtest of greetings and stand back. As the two canon lawyers came back across the floor, Costello could be heard asking, "What's the matter with her? A man only does his job."

In the House of Studies, Saturdays were normal working-days. Yet there was always a Saturday feel about the light, a feel of Saturday-morning big spending, of the Saturday bounty of gardens, of the drama of blossoming premierships and enterprises on the totalizator, all of it subtly transmitted from the town below. So, as Maitland came down to breakfast, the grains of the ether seemed to indict him with being an alien.

Within the refectory, the priests at table appeared to have complaints against him. Not just Nolan and Costello, who held their heads up and stared obliquely as judges; but Egan and three other priests, who had till then treated him with that quaint inadvertence that comes from being too long resident in closed community, watched him from beneath their eyelids. As he said a Grace and sat, Costello sopped his mouth with a napkin and rose.

"What price solidarity?" he hissed in Maitland's ear and placed under Maitland's nose that morning's paper, tortured open at the magazine section and folded in two. It was a standard article about the Couraigne prize, salted with precious little headings such as "Sacrilegious?", "Fascist?" and,

56

worse than any, "Earn Him Such Hate". Here were manifestoes by artists who said they'd been misunderstood or worse by Egan and Costello, both of whom were then amply quoted on distasteful art. Finally, Maitland's statement, spoken to the young man, was set down, and a pernicious sentence began, "This, coming from a colleague of Drs Costello and Egan, raises the question of responsibility for the estrangement between established Christianity and the arts. While churchmen squarely blame the arts and the arts squarely blame churchmen, Dr Maitland's statement is properly self-questioning. . . ."

Costello murmured, "*You* would have no idea how hard it is for Maurice and myself on that bloody committee. We're not utter fools, you know." For some reason his hand went out over Maitland's shoulder and placed a sugar-bowl with precise anger. "What I resent most is the reference to you as a colleague. I will in future consider you as a colleague only when it cannot be avoided."

Then he began what was intended to be a march with intent, a march that would be a withdrawal of any brotherfeeling from Maitland, and would be remembered by the students when the story of Maitland's treachery became known to them. He took the first step and then almost fell. Maitland's hand, concealed beneath table level, had him by the skirts of his soutane.

"Listen to me," Maitland told him so loudly that Nolan gave up his bogus enthrallment in the reading and glowered down the table, crooked horns of light from the windows taking the forefront of his head, making of him a prim and institutional Moses. "I didn't know that slimy boy was a journalist. I'm not that much of an utter fool either."

"Are you going to let go of me?" Costello roared.

Nolan, his cheeks blue with reproach, had no choice then but to ring the bell before him and put an end to the reading so that Costello's high temper could be drowned out by conversation.

"I'm sorry," Maitland said, and handed back the newspaper. "But I didn't know."

Costello marched out, more or less as planned. He had become very large and even more barrel-chested with anger.

At the top table, Maitland had stood up and was edging behind Nolan's chair to speak with Egan. The little priest received the explanations at worst judicially and at best sunnily. He said, "But you have to be particularly careful with strangers, James. You have no idea of the number of people on and off the panel who consider it fair sport to prey on Dr Costello and me. It worries Dr Costello."

Yet it didn't seem to find Dr Egan home at all. Propriety alone seemed to motivate him towards the grave or genial acceptances he kept giving to Maitland's story. He was impatient for Maitland to finish, and closed the topic with one sentence: "Just let me warn you, James. Suspect any stranger who so much as mentions the Couraigne prize to you." This said not nearly so urgently as the words themselves demanded.

Then Egan lowered his voice, his eyes wavered in such a way that he could have been a travelling salesman telling about the farmer's daughter.

"Did you notice? More letters about the Quinlan book. And a review in the book section. Pity you can't join the fray."

"I wish I could," Maitland lied, beginning to see that his friend was an anomalous sort of man. Egan was concerned with blasphemous art and radical opinion in the way that an idle woman is interested in her neighbour's sins, but honesty and lassitude both kept him from taking the shrew's overly moral tone. It was possible to believe, comparing Costello's wrath and Egan's unsurprise, that Egan was the one who might well be frying bigger fish of unknown and unexpected species.

Maitland kept to the point of his betrayal. "I don't want to offer this as an excuse for being a Judas, but I was in an anti-clerical mood, having just finished an argument with the monsignor."

Egan's boyish hand raided a silver dish of marmalade. There was no doubt he was feeling well today.

"That's funny," he said. "You think of yourself as less of a priest than he is, and so you think that a word against the priesthood is a word against him." He went out of his way, by

58

grinning, to imply that this reflection was curious, not moral. "Don't let the monsignor give you a sacerdotal inferiority complex." He made a gesture of amplitude with his bread-and-butter knife. "It's everyone's eternal priesthood," he said. "You surely can't have anything more eternal than eternal."

"Even the way that man does his hair reminds me of the everlasting hills. Never mind."

"You mentioned an argument, James."

"Yes. Over my sermon. I'm rostered to preach at the cathedral tomorrow. The president wanted to censor my sermon."

"The cheek!" Egan beat the table with his furled serviette. "I've never heard of such hide. As if anyone can hear what you say in there anyhow. It's for all the world like one of those old-fashioned railway terminals. It isn't exactly Wittenberg Cathedral in 1517, is it?"

"I hope to heaven not."

His breakfast eaten, his students' breakfasts eaten, Nolan remained, not willing to ring the bell, aware that Maitland was at work on explanations and not wanting to break their rhythm in case there were any for him. So in the end Maitland came and stood by the back of his seignorial chair spired like a cathedral.

Nolan said, hearing Maitland's defence, "I realize, of course, that the newspaper came accidentally by what you said. I never imputed malice to you, James."

Maitland knew that he was meant to say, "Thank you." He discharged that duty.

"The trouble is that you only speak with any confidence to outsiders. *Externs.*"

Maitland flinched at the narrow word he had not heard since student years.

"I'm not under suspicion from *them*, monsignor."

"Yes you are. The whole world fails to understand the priest and therefore suspects him. One who pretends to be *of* them, *like* them, they simply despise."

"I see," said Maitland, attempting to skirt irony. "Might I assure you that my sermon of tomorrow will be so much *like* this House, *of* this House, that no one need hang his head?"

Nolan chose to make a small gratified noise and reached for the hand-bell.

"That's very wise, James," he said. "Anyhow, it's hardly worth saying anything revolutionary in there; it's an awful place for sound." He even brought his left hand across to pat Maitland once on the wrist. "If you're bent on becoming a famous heretic, James, I'd like to see you begin your career to more effect than that."

Perhaps this warmth was merely a face-saver for Nolan, who was not, after all, going to see a draft of the sermon. Yet Maitland found it peculiarly welcome, like the one card—and that from a business firm—that the lonely get at Christmas. Upstairs, he soon forgot the raw blue sea and the Saturday sun now making a short incursion across the balcony he never used. The drumming-up of a sermon to fit the peculiar needs of that Sunday engrossed him. He began by accepting Egan's and Nolan's tenet that a cathedral sermon could do nothing for the commonalty of man. Therefore it must do something for the man who spoke it. It must be both honest enough to allow him to keep his self-respect, specious enough to woo the respect of the Nolans and Costellos. And, *Il faut intéresser*, as Flaubert says.

So well did he enjoy working by these imperfect or even indecent standards that he spent the whole day on the exercise, forgot his dinner, and postponed all morning turning on the heater in a room where the cold hung like wet clothes from April to September.

Years before, he had written an article comparing the religious perceptions of a number of modern novelists with those of some of the mystics. He had meant to point to the meeting-place between humanism and religion. This morning he decided to make this the basis of his sermon, accepting the immense young man's abstractions involved without too much discomfort. It would all go down very well after his Friday-night treachery.

So he dipped all day in broken-backed Penguins, in St John of the Cross, Tauler, Teresa of Avila, Blaise Pascal. He allowed himself, without any cringing at all, to write such sentences

60

as, "However doctrinally misled the great Frenchman Blaise Pascal may have been. . . ." As if he valued anathemas more than the vision of God.

Altogether, he had a day's good reading and easy writing.

There is something unique and even narcotic about the way of Gothic with light; even of neo-Gothic; even of the bad neo-Gothic of St Kevin's Cathedral as Maitland came forward to preach. Over the Celtic mosaic of the sanctuary floor lay a sharp pattern of light, gold streaked with the red refraction of the wounds of the martyrs in the rose-window, gold blotted with the blue virtue of Virgins and the dappled authority of Evangelists. From the brow of the pulpit, the illimitable nave looked like a steppe, and the clusters of worshippers were scattered over it as if symbolic of towns on a great plain.

All this made it somehow appropriate that he should shuffle his manuscript lightly like a born Rosary Crusade preacher and fix the people with the eye of a priest who is onto their pettinesses and evasions. Twenty feet up, he did all this not merely because no one could see the nuances of his eye and hand, but as revenge on a building and a sermon (his own) which were almost not spurious.

None the less, he *was* an orator. He felt very professional with knee-length stole round his neck, and the insipid innocence of what he said so well lay warm beneath the heart. As well, his thorough-going cynicism was in the nature of a busman's holiday for him. He glanced towards the north transept where sunlight and two late-comers stood in the doorway. Beyond them was the cathedral presbytery within which the archbishop sat with his ear to a radio broadcast of the sermon being preached fifty yards away.

Maitland closed vigorously, switched off the microphone, and went away into the sacristy. He doffed the surplice and stole at the long vesting bench and found the lavatory near the outer door. This was of hewn rock, with a cedar door, a lion's-snout door handle, and a bowl too fragile, you would think, to carry a Costello. Skinny Maitland, however, was well within its strength.

He was still there when someone came in through the outer door and could be heard pacing the sacristy. Maitland bet himself odds-on that it was a comforted prelate. Thinking it unworthy of the occasion to activate the crude cistern, he washed and emerged to find His Grace leaning on the vesting bench and fondling a red biretta.

"James, I must congratulate you. Very scholarly, very powerful, and couldn't have come at a better time. . . . What? Don't worry about that, we all have our day of grief with the press. They're as pervasive as the grace of God. However, this surely makes amends. Just when this whole Couraigne business has broken again, as it does most years, and then the dispute over that infamous Quinlan book going so badly, nothing could do more good for our prestige than the style of sermon you've just preached."

For more than one reason, Maitland bowed his head.

On the way to the ferry, he passed through the Botanic Gardens and was forced to confront the honest face of Sunday—lovers under a magnolia-tree, children throwing crusts to the ducks, a Calabrian family dressed in Calabrian best negotiating the alien picnic places. By the trite alchemy of such things he stood convinced that his jaunt in the pulpit that morning had been the worst mummery of which he had ever been guilty. A man of excess when it came to guilt, he stopped in a walk of tropical palms, beside a prosy statue of George V. He accused himself of being as inapposite to man as was the florid monarch to his avenue of palm-trees. This small melodrama of shame over, he continued on down to the wharf.

But, trying to come to some sense of the Other, all he could find was his own small, sharp vacancy, not unlike the heart of a municipal gesture, the grey craw of a king done in bronze.

Until dinner-time, he hid in the library of the House of Studies; and it was not until he got to table, until soup had been taken and the Martyrology read, that the unwelcome applause of the monsignor and Costello's forgiveness descended on him. Never, even as an Ishmael, had he felt so abandoned at that large joke of a dinner-table.

7

"Are you uneasy?" the genial Costello asked. "I mean, after our last drive together."

He could not have expected the truth; for though he sped downhill at sixty and more, he at the same time jabbed all the buttons on his new car and carefully made Maitland welcome to all its fingertip amenities.

Outside, it was night and the beginning of winter. The beachfront could have been the victim of an atmospheric tragedy, the pubs and cafés standing lit and empty, offering absurd summer promises to the unpeopled promenades. Yet Maitland, however uneasy, felt gay; and for two excellent reasons. He had been called, at ten minutes' notice and an awkward hour, to the cathedral presbytery, the same way that Costello, Nolan, Egan, and other priests of consequence were called. Secondly, he and Costello chatted like the colleagues Costello had claimed, a week before, they would never be.

"Uneasy?" Maitland said. "No. I'm lucky to be driven."

"Don't mention it. I have to chair a meeting in the city anyhow."

Costello, certainly, was dressed for chairing—tailor-made clericals, regal face, and dark mane flawlessly barbered. Maitland himself had shaven quickly and missed square inches of stubble, and had no time to more than rub his new shoes which were his best point. It was possible for both men to pretend virtue on account of their habits of dress; but there would be nothing of virtue in it until, for the sake of the vision of God, the slovenly man came to groom himself and the kingly man let his beard grow wild.

"Perhaps I shouldn't tell you," Costello said, "but . . . well, do you like policemen?"

"Never had any reason not to."

"Well, the chaplaincy of the guild of policemen is vacant. A real plum. You'll have traffic policemen under your thumb, which is the only place to have them."

"Why the breathless night journey if all he wants to do is appoint me chaplain?" Knowing the answer, the young priest asked the question in celebration.

"Breathless night journeys are one of His Grace's specialities. You're lucky he didn't summon you at one in the morning. It's happened, you know. It's all a matter of when he happens to remember things. Of course, I'm only guessing about the gendarmes."

Costello slowed, but decided not to stop at a halt sign. "Let not mere traffic laws hold us back," he sang, "when our prelate summons."

Maitland hardly heard, being busy with exorbitant hopes of what Nolan would call "*settling* to the life".

Towards the end of the journey they began to speak about books. Costello's *Praelectiones* was due to be published within weeks, and Maitland was known to have sent his thesis off to the publishers the week before. There the comparisons ended. Costello's work would appear in four dowdy volumes of Latin, pages uncut. Italian publishers let a book on the sacred sciences stand between grey endpapers and on its merits. Yet it was unlikely that a man used to Anglo-Saxon, cut-throat methods of book production, and proud of his heater-demister, would allow his books to appear between cartridge-paper covers. Maitland had heard that, at Costello's own expense, covers featuring Pius IX speaking with some of the Fathers of the first Vatican Council had been printed locally and shipped to Rome.

Maitland's own book, jollied up by the publishers to look like prime reading, welts of abstract red and blue and yellow streaking the engraving he had suggested for the cover, would find its way in small numbers into popular bookshops and be bought by random people who probably had little use for it. In fact, Costello's book and his own would reach about the same number of people, one coming with honour into the libraries of monasteries and houses of study, his own outsold and outdisplayed in bookshops of high- or middle-brow.

In any case, the book talk dear to the hearts of all authors occupied them as far as the city. In time they saw the cathedral rise beneath low cloud and in a remarkable wash of reflected light from the neons and pleasure palaces—strip-tease, disco-theque—half a mile farther on.

Costello let him out in the presbytery yard. Maitland found the porch and the electric bell. In stained glass above the panelled door, one word, *Sapientia*, shone dimly like an adver-tisement for an Edwardian soap. He did not ring a second time, although he was left unanswered for half a minute. At last one of His Grace's secretaries swung back the door. The hall was revealed, lit with acanthus-leaf light-fittings and hung with religious art, all of the Couraigne school. The secretary shook Maitland's hand and brought him past a number of parlours to a room which, large as it was, seemed nearly all oaken table and seignorial chairs. Besides these, the room accommodated a fireplace set with haunches of hardwood and burning on a large scale, four chinoiserie book-cabinets, a prosperous layman, and His Grace.

Maitland knelt to kiss the prelate's ring—one of those Oriental tests of submission a man should perform without thinking too well of himself.

"James," His Grace muttered as Maitland rose. "Dr Maitland," he said more loudly then, and indicated the layman. "Meet Mr Des Boyle."

Both Maitland and the layman considered shaking hands across the table, but its width defeated them.

"Des is the president of the Knights of Saint Patrick," His Grace was happy to say, "and a chartered accountant of the first rank. Sit down, James."

Both subjects, however, waited to sit until the archbishop had outflanked them and taken the chair at the head of the table.

"Winter beginning to close in, Dr Maitland," Boyle said and raised a face, now forty years old, which Maitland had seen as a boy by two's and three's in nearly every class at R——— Street Christian Brothers'—head long and plump, hair breaking in a straight mound from a high forehead, nose bulbous, skin firm and tending to shine. One of the prides of Erin. Such faces led classes, played in the forwards, were head altarboys at Corpus Christi, and habitually won scholarships.

"You should have worn your overcoat, James," the prelate told Maitland.

"I left my overcoat in England, Your Grace. I'd forgotten we had winter here."

"Yes," said Boyle. "On nights like this in Europe you remember only the sunshine."

"True," decided His Grace, laying the word like a paving-stone on that particular subject. "James, Des and I need your help. You would have heard that Des's organization has become involved in a running fight over a book you may have read."

On the word *book*, Boyle lifted Maitland's paperback onto the table. The discretion of his hands and of his lowered eyes allowed His Grace to speak on.

"The wisdom of starting the fight in the first place may have been questioned, but starting it wasn't Des's doing." Des straightened the lie of the paperback in an acutely acquiescent manner. "As I said to you on Sunday, James, the other side seems to presume they have all the enlightenment on their side and, as you probably know, I usually dissuade priests from

66

writing to the secular press. So the Knights have felt rather on their own."

It behoved the president of the Knights to smile painfully on one side of his face, the smile fading to a businesslike grimace as he tabled a manila folder beside the book.

The archbishop went on, "I'd be most grateful if you read this book, James, and then said your say about it in a magazine article or letter-to-the-editor. I should have mentioned this to you on Sunday, except that at that stage it hadn't occurred to me how desirable it would be to have you take a hand. I've had my secretary reading it and getting a précis ready for me, but neither he nor I myself is what you'd call a historian."

"The controversy is still alive," Boyle explained. "I know for a fact that if *Forum*, for example, knew that you wanted to put the Catholic scholar's viewpoint. . . ."

Maitland said throatily and without hope, "I see. But I thought Quinlan claimed to be a Catholic, and as for scholarship, the book *has* been taken seriously in scholarly circles."

"Unfortunately there are Catholics *and* Catholics these days, James." His Grace began to fondle his episcopal ring, as all bishops ultimately do in conversation, displaying thereby a habit of status. "And there are scholars and scholars, I suppose. No, I won't say that I suppose anything. I know, it's a simple fact, that there are Catholic scholars, to be found close even to some of the Princes of the Church, who would make any real Catholic's blood creep. So would Quinlan, apparently."

"He attacks all the Popes, Dr Maitland," Boyle explained. "He attacks Pius the Ninth in particular, whose reign was one of the richest in the history of the Church. And one of the most heroic, too."

Maitland began to suspect Boyle of belonging to the species *terrible Catholic*, but would have to wait for him to call Pius "a prisoner in the Vatican" to be sure. Akin to the Knight was the chinoiserie bookcase beyond, made to be stocked with belles-lettres, loaded instead with the awful vellum-bound certainties of theologians whose names had peppered the textbooks when Maitland was a student. Both Boyle and the book-case could be seen with the one glance, and the same unease derived from each.

"I thought Quinlan merely pointed to the place these men, Pius in particular, held in the history of modern religion," Maitland suggested.

"You've read the book, James?" His Grace asked.

If you can get this crusader out of the room, Maitland thought, it will be time to tell you I wrote the thing.

"Yes, Your Grace," he admitted, but turned to Boyle, who had brought a businessman's tenacity to the meeting-table and would not easily be beguiled into leaving. "You must remember, Mr Boyle, that Quinlan is not passing judgment on Catholic dogma, only on the performances of some of the Popes. Now this is something all of us, preferably after some study, are free to do. In many ways, it's healthier that *we* should do it—like a body that heals itself rather than wait for the doctor."

Boyle said evenly, "Pius the Ninth was responsible for defining the doctrine of the Immaculate Conception. In his reign Our Lady appeared at Lourdes and the doctrine of Papal Infallibility was proclaimed a dogma. The Pope became a prisoner in the Vatican but turned his loss into a triumph."

"Quinlan attacks none of this. He *does* say, I think, that the definition of Papal Infallibility was a misguided tactic, but he doesn't deny the dogma itself. He certainly doesn't mention Lourdes."

"Des's point surely is, James," His Grace mediated, "that no Catholic could possibly be right in passing a generally unfavourable judgment on a man who had given such great doctrines to the Church."

"I think," Boyle decided, "he could have mentioned that Pius was responsible for that much."

From the way the man said it, lightly, with deference to the clergy, you could tell that he believed His Grace and Maitland would think so too. Maitland was too brusque in disillusioning him.

"He could have mentioned too that while Pius was a pure

and reverent man, he had an unordained Cardinal-secretary with enough illegitimate children to fill an orphanage. But he doesn't write this down because it doesn't apply. He isn't writing either a theology book *or* a scandalous biography."

His Grace frowned and continued to finger his ring like a ritual sore. Beneath the ruby lay a supposed fragment of the supposed true Cross found by Constantine's mother seventeen hundred years before in a Jerusalem cellar. Regaining balance, Maitland thought that it was not easy to be a Catholic.

"Could you possibly help us in the way His Grace suggests?" Boyle asked, politely enough to cause Maitland remorse. "When I ask this, I'm thinking of the part the Knights play in charity, a part that is crucial to philanthropy in this country. We cannot afford a bad name, even in regard to this Quinlan's book."

The Knight dropped the pseudonym as discreetly as a sociologist uttering other people's graffiti in the name of science; and Maitland wanted to be angry again. He was distracted by the hymn from night devotions emerging from the cathedral and muted by the wind out of doors. The emulsive tune repeated itself sharply in his stomach and, like the bookcase, whetted his improper annoyance at Boyle. The Knight had none the less committed no sin other than calling Pius IX "a prisoner in the Vatican" and being secure in the faith—having the security, that is, of being utterly secure. Which was another thing from having the security of being utterly insecure but not caring.

Between both these havens but belonging to neither sat Dr Maitland, saying tentatively, "The point is that Quinlan didn't write his book for the general public. Within the sphere of history—of which I know very little in any case—but within that sphere, his conclusions seem fairly valid and certainly not in bad taste. All I can do is say that as far as I know the book is not poisonous and that if it was ever meant to cause a furore, which I doubt, it was intended to produce it in academic circles, where it created none. The one sort of furore a serious book doesn't want to produce is a hoo-hah in the popular press."

His Grace said ruggedly, "This is beginning to look very like a knock-back, James."

And Boyle lowered his eyes, as if not to intrude on the prelate's disappointment.

Maitland gazed full ahead. "It's no great book, but I find myself in general agreement with it." He sat forward, sighing with tact. "I'm very grateful for the opportunity of taking to print. But I'd only bring ridicule on our side by attacking without believing in the attack."

All the time he had been speaking largely in Boyle's direction, in hope of clearing him from the room. But the layman, not presuming Maitland's concern, now sat withdrawn though not idle. The contents of the manila folder were being scanned. Meanwhile, some nod good as a wink from within but of unknown source seemed to tell Maitland that it might not necessarily be the best thing for His Grace and other parties to be told who Quinlan was. He wished for time to examine the bona fides of this tip, but found that Boyle was quoting from the folder.

" 'Pope Pius the Ninth confirmed the spirit of stagnation that dominated the corridors of the Vatican for the greater part of the next hundred years,' " the man read. "Any Catholic is surely on safe ground protesting against that sort of thing."

His Grace, very straight and chin up, the *zucchetto* riding his scalp as if it had been there from birth, frowned even more and needed to be answered.

"Your Grace," Maitland began, "the idea could be more happily put, but the sentence Mr Boyle has taken the trouble of reading comes from a section where he—Quinlan—complains that the Church has tended to look on truth as something static and unchangeable both at the divine end of things and at ours. I believe there's a document of John Twenty-third's which warns against this very tendency. I agree the use of the word 'stagnant' is a little emotive, but—"

"You can't see your way clear to write this article, James?"

"No, Your Grace."

His Grace nodded like a gentleman.

"It would do nobody any benefit," Maitland amplified.

"But Dr Maitland," Boyle said, "what benefit will *this* do?" And he began to read some more Quinlan, for, though neither a fool nor arrogant, he had simply never met a priest who let a Pontiff be impugned.

" 'While truth itself remains constant, the human perception of truth must grow and change or else become a cipher. The Church was sure that it had the great fish Truth firmly held for all time in a mesh of theological formulae, that neither the fish nor the net would ever grow and change, or appear to grow and change. That being so, it enforced on its subjects the study of the strands of the net as the only safe way of holding the fish. And the fish was, ultimately, God.' That struck me as rather a sacrilegious figure of speech. However. . . . 'As the Church's primary system of thought calcified, God became more and more rationalized, more and more finite, more and more only a part of a supernatural cosmos. The movement known as modernism was an attempt—', and so on. The rest is in praise of the modernist heretics of the late nineteenth century. Enough said."

In the silence all three held, a last dribble of organ music stirred beyond the window, which was St Sebastian prickling with praetorian arrows. The sound and the stained glass spoke of the happy days when right stood out as sharply as the stuck limbs of the martyr, when all the clergy were tediously orthodox, when minds roamed free of the influence of mass media, and none of the vagrants who knocked at presbytery kitchens had heard of Marx.

"He writes very strongly," Maitland admitted, a little amazed despite himself. "All young men write vigorously and overstate their case."

"He's a *young* man, is he?" His Grace asked, not altogether with sympathy.

Boyle went hunting for a potted biography at the rear of the paperback.

"It doesn't say anything here, I don't think."

"Oh, it's a young man," Maitland insisted. "A person can tell from the style. Besides, the idea isn't original. It's surely stolen from Tillich, the theologian."

71

"Tillich," the prelate wondered. "I'm not familiar. . . ."

"He's a Protestant, Your Grace."

"My God. Oh well, the world's opening up, I suppose." His Grace suddenly went sour at the corners of the mouth. "Come on, Dr Maitland, surely you can help. Catholics are Catholics, all of one mind. Des and I are Catholics and we ask you, a Catholic, for assistance. Surely that's easily enough given. I *could* demand it, you know."

Now if he did, a voice that was wisdom or sense or fraud told Maitland, a clean breast would be the only possibility. But he's too genial for it to come to that.

"I know, Your Grace," Maitland said.

Boyle announced softly, "I can't help but admit it's a disappointment."

"We must all bear our crosses," said Maitland, incipient irony having, as yet, merely made him paler than usual.

But Boyle was provoked back to his notes, finding it hard to believe that Maitland *was* properly informed on Quinlan's full range of malice. " 'Whilever the Church—'," he read.

"Mr Boyle," Maitland called to him, "if you continue to attempt to embarrass me in front of His Grace, I'm sure to lose my temper."

"James, there's no need. . . ." said the archbishop.

With a small chirping noise of regret, Boyle tidied the pages and cocked an eye at the top of page one. Then he closed the folder and placed the book on top. The front cover creaked open and revealed paragraphs underlined in red and marked with symbols, each symbol meaning a distinct grade of heresy.

"I mustn't keep you, Your Grace. I think that's all we wanted to discuss."

"We'll have to let the matter lie, Des. I suppose we can't win all the arguments."

But Maitland was damned if he was going to be shamed, though his hands trembled slightly.

"May I say, Your Grace, that if we persist in starting the wrong arguments, we'll never win any."

The ringed hand bunched itself. "Come now, James, you

mustn't expect men of good faith not to protest when they see need of it."

"I don't want to seem arrogant, Your Grace, but it's possible that Quinlan is a man of good faith protesting where he sees need of it."

"Without ecclesiastical permission?" asked His Grace, and Maitland shook his head and hung it. "Could you stay a moment, James?"

Slowly and as if coerced to it, Boyle was drawing on a thick overcoat. As he buttoned it, both the archbishop and Maitland rose, and he genuflected and cursorily bussed the ring. As president of the Knights, he was accustomed to this exercise.

"Des," His Grace told him, "you know how much I respect and value the support of the Knights. As I say, though, perhaps we must let the fight die out now."

"Nothing else for it, Your Grace," Boyle said, rising.

"I'm sorry I can't help," Maitland told them both.

"It's no good unless your heart is in it, Dr Maitland," the layman announced, and seemed to imply a fault of the heart.

"That's right," a very bluff Maitland agreed.

"You mustn't think that the Knights would carry any sort of spite or that you wouldn't be as free as any other priest to ask our help if it were ever needed."

"I always presumed they didn't carry spite, especially without cause."

His Grace confessed, perhaps not guileless but at least attempting to seem so, "I don't know what I'd do without them. And what is most blessed about them, they don't let their right hand know what their left is doing."

It would have been perilously easy to say that if the left were writing unauthorized letters-to-editors, the right had better make a point of knowing.

So Boyle left, giving Maitland the minimum farewell a Knight could in honour give a priest. Maitland preceded him down the room and held the door open for him. Passing through, Boyle left behind a carping breath of Californian Poppy.

"Are you over your peevishness?" His Grace called down the length of the table.

"I'm sorry, Your Grace. But it's not the Knights' business."

"Who says so?" His Grace seemed jaunty, but wanted answers and reassurances. "What sort of stuff do you teach the students, James?"

"Simply history, Your Grace," Maitland told him, thinking in cowardice but perhaps also in wisdom that if the book remained an issue, a fortnight's time would be time enough to confess; that if the issue died, wasn't he entitled to keep his one wild oat secret to himself?

"*Church* history," His Grace amended.

"Yes, Your Grace."

"Well?"

"Well, the Church can stand up to its own past and beside the pasts of other bodies politic."

"I suppose so. But be careful."

Frowning, the prelate shrugged and rang for supper, rang with a bell-pull plaited from wool in all the liturgical colours. In the long distempered room, near the wide fireplace, gobs of light from the chandelier resting with the tranquillity of drowned moons on the habitually polished table, he looked like the Bishop of Artois or Autun on a cold night in a Balzac novel. It begged an act of faith to believe that beyond St Sebastian's window acquisitive fires of neon splashed the avenues and jackhammers barked on flood-lit construction lots.

"You know, James, you speak of yourself as if you were, say, a university teacher of some independence. But if anyone has independence, it isn't you. There is obedience in your case, the obedience you owe me. What if I'd *ordered* you to take a stand against this Quinlan?"

"I have to admit I would have tried to dissuade you, Your Grace. And I'd have been very confident of success because you're too wise to put your money on a dead horse."

"Am I? Well, what if I still insisted?"

"Your Grace, I certainly do believe in blind obedience as a last resort. If it were the last resort, I would obey."

A resort somewhat this side of the last would be to admit to

74

being Quinlan. But while they waited for His Grace's call to be answered, Maitland's emergent tactical streak kept urging that others might not see why he had used a pseudonym; might not grasp the genuine wisdom of not burdening a book with a real name or a real name with a book.

An Irish spinster came in. "Let me see, Molly," said His Grace. "Cocoa, I think, please. Dr Maitland hasn't got an overcoat with him."

The woman made a sympathetic mouth while Maitland said, "No, no, Your Grace, whatever you have. . . ."

"It's all right, Molly. Cocoa."

The woman gone, His Grace told Maitland wryly, "I, like the Knights, don't carry spite. But be careful!"

Waiting for the beverage, both men were largely silent and rather exposed to each other by the large simplicity of the conference table. Then His Grace asked, "Of course, you know to whom your scholarship belongs?"

Maitland came close to smiling at the pretentious word. His scholarship might perhaps have been vast enough, if he were a layman, to allow him to teach history to senior boys.

"It belongs to me," His Grace said, "as much as it belongs to yourself, and if ever there was a question of obedience, it would belong to me or my successor more than to yourself. Remember that and your safety is assured."

8

The next day Maitland had a small letter of thanks from his cousin, Joe Quinlan. "We upped and invested in some land," said Joe. "For which much thanks to you." The letter evoked summer and the day of what was for Maitland a truer home-coming than a mere disembarking onto a wharf could ever be. The day had been a Thursday late in February on which he caught a train towards those flat towns he had known as a child. The sets of lines ran out molten blue to the suburb where his maternal cousin, Joseph Quinlan, lived.

In Europe he had remembered the sun but forgotten the summer. So, as he sat through fifteen station stops and watched old men's brave morning collars travelling home sodden, the exact flavour of the Februaries of his childhood returned in a rush and remained. February, the crude exposer of the mortal and the makeshift, of the mortal and makeshift shirt and floral dress, of mortal and makeshift James Maitland, the sun boring at his left, window-side ear.

He was all prickly heat by the time a station came with Joe

76

Quinlan's address on it. Outside an empty supermarket stood the right bus. Rolling off at last, it showed him all the things he could have predicted. Down flat streets jury-masted with power poles, the bus was hailed by neanderthal wives near looted phone-booths, joyless service-stations, abject corner shops.

He got out at a street of plaster-board houses. Plaster-board might have done well in dainty Japan but could assert nothing under the massive censure of this sky. On his corner in the desert, he could hear a television set promising a trip to Tahiti for the neatest correct entry opened.

Maitland could not remember the seventeen-year-old who had gone to become a priest and himself at twenty-nine; could not even remember what the seventeen-year-old had believed (though it was bound to be nearly everything). But he knew that in that young lost mind marriage had meant a suburb like this one, out of which the clean eternity of the priesthood had called him. Maitland stood a second being sad for the boy, forgiving the boy's zeal.

The Quinlans lived in 27, whose side had been barricaded with an iron gate. Beyond this he saw a fowlhouse and could hear the furtive birds. He climbed the barricade and came to the back of the house. Here a woman, hidden from him by oddments of family underwear, pegged out clothes. Sensing him, she pushed through the washing, and a small dog charged from beneath hung bedsheets.

"Oh, father," said the woman, "you gave me a scare. They've been so many attacks in this district."

She was a square, dark little woman, very tired, hardly a welcome left in her. But she had not had the scare she claimed. Maitland could tell she knew that if he were the local curate seeking money or sacrifice, she had him at a disadvantage by reducing him to a part of the general male threat.

"You should use the front door, father. I'm not to know you're a priest, am I?"

"Mrs Joe Quinlan, isn't it?"

She nodded and folded her arms, on the left of which hung

a red plastic bucket of pegs meaning that she couldn't give him much time.

"Yes. We go to Mass up here at Saint Bernard's, but Joe hasn't got the time to join societies and things."

"Don't worry about that. I'm Joe's cousin. My mother was a Quinlan. My name's James Maitland."

She said without pleasure that she was pleased to meet him.

They stood in silence. You could hear only the soft mourning of Joe Quinlan's and a hundred other fowls in other yards.

Maitland managed at last to ask, "Will Joe be home soon?"

"About a quarter to five."

"Do you mind if I wait and see him?"

"I'm Morna," she said. It seemed that someone might have told her, long ago and well, never to give direct answers to men in uniform.

"Don't you believe me, Morna, when I say who I am?"

The small dog, tensed back on his hindquarters, kept his rage close to the boil and showed Maitland yellow but functional canines.

"Oh, I know Joe had a cousin a priest. You're him?"

"Yes. I've been overseas. That's why I haven't seen him lately. There were two Christmases when we were ten or eleven, that Joe and I used to spend all our time together. My people lived on this line, only further down. Joe and I exchanged the blood-brotherhood once." He laughed.

"How do you mean?" she asked without tolerance.

"Well, you know how an Indian and a white man would slit their wrists and mix their blood and become blood-brothers? Joe and I did that once. Joe's mother beat the hide off us for it."

"If I had a boy did that, I'd beat the hide off him myself. I haven't got any time for that sort of thing. This violence on the television is why a woman can't be safe in her own yard."

Maitland coughed to acknowledge the battle well lost.

"Would you like to wait inside?" she asked.

"If you don't mind." She had her doubts, you could see. He might want Joe's time, mind, money. This blood-brotherhood business was only a way of establishing a claim—or so she feared.

"All right. The kitchen's in a bit of a mess. Roddy's in there in his high chair. Don't frighten him."

"Thank you," he said, "Morna."

She smiled briefly. At least she was sure from his long, untanned body and soapy hands that he was not some marauding piece-worker.

At the back door Maitland took off his black coat and stock. He must avoid scaring his small kinsman who had made a compost of milk and sodden bread on his meal-tray and was furrowing the mess with his forefinger.

"Hullo, Roddy," James said. "I'm your cousin. I used to know your father."

Roddy did not move. His hand remained suspended on one finger, like a stork, in the mess of his lunch.

Behind him, stew bubbled on the gas stove. Torn hollands hung above the sink and clotted fat lay on the draining-board. Farther inside the house, a television set performed to an empty room. "And how often," a professional voice asked, on a programme of live agony, "how often have these fights ended in a physical assault by your husband?"

At last Morna came in and picked up a teatowel from the floor. Her slippered foot herded dust and crumpled paper and spent matches out of the way under the stove.

"Would you like a cup of tea, father?" she said.

Suddenly the old flesh-hatred of his youth turned his stomach and he was aware of what the inconsolable sacrifice was—to live in plaster-board with such a woman.

"It's all right, Morna," he told her urgently, and took improper comfort in knowing that he would be home in Nolan's house by seven.

By a quarter to five the sunlight had taken on that level and quite stable glare which threatens never to set. Home came Joe Quinlan in his grey post-office uniform. They heard him enter as if he were in the act of taking the inadequacies of his home very much to heart. They heard him taking the barricade to heart and telling the children, for Christ's sake that was the last time he was going to tell them to leave the chickens alone.

He blinked to find Maitland in the kitchen, sitting at the table in white shirt-sleeves but inescapably clerical with his black coat hitched on the chair and his stock among a mess of children's drawings on the table-top.

Morna seemed edgy.

"This is Father Maitland, Joe," she said; and then, unscrupulously, "He says he's your cousin."

"Oh yeah," he said.

As if trapped into it by his jagged distrust of Maitland, he kissed his wife. When he held out his hand to the priest, it was like a defence. "Glad to see you again," he said; but he waited for Maitland to present the barbed demand, for piety or cash or something else beyond him. God forgive, thought Maitland, priests and insurance agents who have taught man so well that their greetings are merely feints.

"You remember me, don't you? Jimmy Maitland. I was telling Morna how we were blood-brothers. I don't think she approved."

Joe ventured a smile. "I'd forgotten," he said. He meant, that was before everything changed; it doesn't give you any claim. "That's a long time ago."

"We were ten, I suppose," Maitland supplied. Before puberty, which, in boys, voided previous friendships.

"Had a cuppa?"

"No, thanks."

"Morna, why didn't you hang father's coat up for him?"

Morna frowned. Awe and suspicion—that was why.

Maitland said, "It's all right. I have to go soon."

"You can't stay for tea?" the husband asked joyously, and sweated on the answer.

"I've got to get back to the House of Studies by about seven. It's a long way."

"That's a pity. Look, father."

"Jim."

"Look, Jim, I've just got to fix up the chooks. Do you mind? Just a few minutes."

"I'll go with you," Maitland said quickly.

Joe fetched bran from under the house. Just beyond the limits of the yard began a haze and an opalescence that gave a false remoteness to the rest of the flat suburb. Morna, seeing this, by some instinct called the children in. Joe's small girl would not obey but ran after him, while Morna yelled threats from the door. She was more frantic than angry. The phenomenon of the priest, topped by this starchy tide of heat in which her neighbours' homes rode, warned her to make her house tight and get her children in. Maitland apprehended her fear and expected Joe to turn to her. But Joe carried the bran, and the small girl trailed Joe.

She said, "Are you going to feed the chooks with father?"

"I'm going to feed 'em with bran. Can't you hear your mother? By Christ, you've been asking for it lately."

Over his shoulder Maitland saw the girl limp away with a pubescent type of disdain, ten years ahead of herself at seven. An instinct nagged him that there was something to be done with the child, something immediate that he would be able to identify if he were any sort of being. The girl, however, was quicker in reaching the back steps than the instinct was in coming to a head. It ceased to press, and he and Joe were alone then, which was what he had come for.

Maitland, outside the coop, kept the door closed while Joe went in to his birds. They rushed him, tocking with avarice, and he took offence at them and broadcast their food behind their backs and hated them even more fervently when they wheeled back to it.

"Joe," Maitland called. He looked around him for a gradual way of telling a poor man that you wanted to give him twelve hundred dollars, being your advance on the sales of a paperback you wouldn't admit to having written. You could, with ease, give a sum such as that to the Red Cross, to archdioceses or other bodies inured to thousands, who could be trusted to spend or save it efficiently. But an archdiocese did not have the pride of a poor Quinlan.

81

"Joe, I have a bank cheque for twelve hundred dollars. I wonder could you accept it from me?"

"How do you mean?" Joe said, visibly a man who had heard this sort of thing before. *How would you like to own your own swimming-pool? With every one of our $65 suits sold, we will give away free a ticket which could. . . .* Joe had never met the owner of a ticket which did.

"If you can use it you can have it."

The fowls squeaked close to the man, who aimed his boot at them without intent and began to come to his own conclusions.

"Oh, I know what you mean, father. It's kind of you to offer. But we couldn't even pay interest on it."

"I don't mean it for a loan. I mean, do you want it?"

Joe laughed through his nose.

"Who are you trying to string along, father?"

"Jim," said Maitland.

"If you *are* father, I'd rather call you father."

"Joe, please take it. If you don't, I'll have to take it to some charity."

Joe picked up the birds' drinking-tin and shook the water out. It fell like a pattern of shadow on the dust. He still smiled.

"What's wrong with that?" he said idly.

"Nothing. I'd rather you had it and did whatever you liked with it. For once."

"We're not good Catholics." With the white-hot sun niggling his left shoulder, he went further, "We're never likely to be."

Behind them, in the house, a child began sobbing while Morna said she'd told it often enough and it could damn-well expect the same every time.

"You don't understand, Joe."

"I'll say I don't, father."

"Say that while I was in Europe I did some writing and got this sum of money for it. That is exactly what did happen, in fact. Well, I don't want it, that's all. And I thought you might do me the honour of using it for me."

"Do you the honour? Come off it, father!"

"It's indecent for priests to have big sums of money, that's all. It's not a priest's business."

At least he was being taken with seriousness now. He wished to God that Joe would hurry the decision, for he felt sick from the heat, and the thick air hung as palpable as cotton wool. He heard with some longing an evening train going home on the distant line.

Joe kept arguing.

"You don't really mean that, father. Look, you might be a priest, but that's no excuse to muck me around. It's indecent for a priest to own money, you say. How many of your mates believe that?"

"You're being too hard on them, Joe. I feel I'm not allowed to keep this, the way I'm not allowed to keep a woman."

"Say I took it?"

"Say you took it off my hands."

"Yeah, if I did, how am I supposed to spend it? You don't know me. I mean, that blood-brotherhood business is a load of cock. For all you know, I might just do the lot on booze."

"Spending it is your business." Maitland took an envelope from his pocket. "The bank cheque's in there, very official, made out in your name, Joe. I took the liberty. . . ."

Joe considered complaining, but accepted the envelope instead, just for a look.

"Twelve hundred's a decent deposit on land."

"Whatever you say, Joe. It's your affair. My God, though, I'd be grateful."

But Joe was still merely considering the outside chance of his accepting the gift and had hold of it only with thumb and index finger. "There are charities," he suggested. "Why. . . .?"

"Why is my business and spending it is yours."

For Maitland couldn't say that he had felt it necessary to find someone unlovely and not blatantly pitiable nor compellingly deserving, wise or frugal. That Joe might be inept or even stupid in the spending was what made the giving peculiarly worth while.

"It's not all that much," he pursued. "It won't buy much. It might start something, though."

"I'd like some land," Joe admitted. "Sloping land with a bit of sandstone for a rockery. I'd like some trees on it, pines and gums, so you don't have to see your neighbour's house first thing each morning, if you'll pardon the expression."

"I know the feeling."

"Remember how our people had a bit of pride? If they had a door strangers could see into, they grew something in front of it, or put a trellis up. No one's got any pride round here. And the landlord's a bloody Grand Master of the Masons or something. Wait there a second."

Joe made off down the yard to fill his water-tin.

"Don't tell Morna till I've gone," Maitland hissed after him.

"I'm just going to the tap."

And Maitland could hear Morna pestering Joe from the back window, the man saying scarcely a word.

When he came back, Joe said, "What do you do with a bank cheque?"

"Just sign it. They'll show you at the bank."

"This isn't a joke?"

Maitland raised both hands to his ears and shook his head. "Whose joke would it be likely to be?"

He could scarcely believe how desperate he was to get away. If charity was an immersion in other people, he did not know how to immerse himself in Morna and Joe; but he knew as well that if he did know he would not do it, and that this was what his antiseptic bank cheque was a measure of.

"Keep the envelope!" he said.

Joe grinned. "Morna's seen it. She thinks you've talked me into joining some holy society."

"Don't believe in 'em," Maitland said.

He watched his cousin re-enter the coop and put down the can ungrudgingly.

He said gratefully, "I'd better collect my coat."

9

Now that his work had been parcelled off to the publisher, Maitland began to give up some nights of the week to having three students in his room to talk about their history or, better still, just to talk. He dreaded, as any man must whose image of the profoundest God is a surgical trolley, to intervene in their deeper beliefs and resentments. What he most enjoyed was the palliative work of making them cups of coffee and cutting them cake. Over such suppers he met nine, sometimes twelve, students each week, and promised himself that after twenty weeks he would know every student in the House.

Gaiety brews easily among monks, soldiers and all other cloistered men. Maitland had only to make it clear that they were his guests, to move the radiator closer, to produce the yellow cake-tin with its picture of the King of the Belgians, to set the odd brotherhood of his four cups ready for coffee, and these mechanical and graceless acts assured the success of the evening. Their bridegroom—the books of spirituality spoke of their souls as feminine and the Lord as their bride-groom—had not brought them to a house where all was accustomed, ceremonious; so that some of them would always remember Maitland's makeshift soirées as pleasant. Which, in itself, was some achievement for a man so unskilled in brotherhood.

After ten such evenings he felt like pleading catarrh and having the night for himself. He was still arguing the point with himself when the three students arrived. One of them was a dark man of his own age with long intelligent lips, and eyes that had ideas of their own. His name was Edmonds, and two minutes after Maitland had said good night to the three of them, turned the radiator off and taken, more than loth, to his prie-dieu, Edmonds came back to the room.

"I'm sorry, Dr Maitland. Could I have a word?"

In the bad light of the ante-room the student seemed large and coy. Light from the bedroom pointed up his remorseful ham-fists.

"Of course. Come in."

Upstairs the supper bell rang. They could hear students clumping out of rooms to the small mercies of cups of tea and biscuits. Shivering, Maitland switched back on the substantial mercy of the radiator.

"Sit down," he said; but in case the priest came to regret the invitation, Edmonds merely took hold of a chair-back with both hands.

"Were you working?" he asked.

"No. I certainly wasn't working."

"Not after your visitors, I suppose. You go to a lot of trouble to make them welcome. I hope it's worth your while."

"Isn't it?"

"Well, it's very pleasant for all parties—except for you, of course."

"Then why isn't it worth while?"

"Monsignor Nolan won't like it. He's the cattle baron and we're the beef. To extend the image a bit, he doesn't like having an outsider cut three of us out of the herd for any purpose he doesn't understand. Pardon my talking so straight. But he'll let you go on giving these evenings until he finds some irregularity he can blame on them, some breach of rules or of the etiquette due to him as number-one pooh-bah. He could use something like that to dismiss you from the service, and if you went, it'd be a tragedy."

Maitland sat down laughing. "Please. I've been here three months—under surveillance too. I've given seven plodding classes a week and I say Mass on a back altar each morning. I know one out of every six or seven students. I think my loss could be borne."

"Do you think I came back just to flatter you?" Edmonds rumbled.

Maitland leant forward on his elbows and stared at the litter of scholarship on his desk. He smiled, not too wryly, Edmonds being, at least in terms of the House of Studies, a man of the world.

"I can't imagine you did."

"Why it would be a tragedy is that you don't pretend to be secure in that old-fashioned way in which Monsignor Nolan is. Or pretends to be."

"No pretends about it. He is secure. As I'm not."

"You should be grateful. That old-time security breeds old-time arrogance. You have neither." Edmonds smiled for the first time. "You're a good example to the boys."

"Because I don't know what I believe? You can't tell me that, Mr Edmonds. And sit down when I bloody-well tell you."

Maitland was off-handedly obeyed; Edmonds was keyed for argument.

"Doctor Maitland, what do you think of Henry James?"

The priest sighed. "I don't know if he was secure and arrogant like Monsignor Nolan or insecure and arrogant like me."

"Seriously. Is he a genius?"

"Everyone says so."

"Say you had to examine the nature of his genius. Do you think you could easily sum up its nature in a few more or less scientific sentences? Do you think his genius would partake of quantity or mystery?"

Maitland scratched his head and gave the beset giggle of a

man detained too long in a pub. "Mystery," however, he said. "Definitely mystery."

"That's right. Yet there are Freudian fanatics who believe they can define the quality of the man's genius by explaining that James's dad had a leg missing and this aroused in young Henry a castration complex of the type that made him court injury of a similar nature to his father's and that all those marvellous novels are the results of a fruitfully applied neurosis all having to do with the, well, with the knackers. Do you think they're right or wrong?"

"They must be more wrong than not."

"Exactly. You can't explain something as big as James in those terms."

"No, I don't suppose so."

"Yet the men who do explain him this way are absolutely sure, quite secure in their little bits of Freud?"

"I suppose so."

To be honest, Maitland admitted, he was enjoying this grilling.

"Well," said Edmonds, "that's the way Costello's lecture notes go. I mean, if Henry James is a mystery, what about the God who breathed on Henry James? But Costello isn't dismayed. You know the way he works. Question: Is God a leprechaun? No, God is not a leprechaun. This is proved by the fact that the Council of Constance, the Council of Trent and Leo the Thirteenth all condemned the perfidious opinion that God is a leprechaun. It is proved too by something that Saint Jerome, Saint Augustine and Saint Ambrose of Milan all wrote, and then it is proved by passages from the Scriptures. And to top the proof off, it is proved by reason as cold as Einstein's, but without the same flair, that the deity could not possibly be a *little person*."

Maitland laughed, remembering that Costello had used the same blithe method for plumbing the Godhead in his own student days.

Edmonds continued, "Everything codified and as organized as a trawler master's manual. Only God is a little more intangible than a diesel engine."

"I don't know," said Maitland. "I wish I was as certain as Costello is."

His left hand had been playing with a volume of letters by an eighteenth-century Jesuit. On some off-chance, his eye consulted the page and saw "To Sister Marie-Therese de Viomenil, Perpignan, 1740."

"Listen to this," he told Edmonds. He read, " 'What I have always most dreaded has just happened to me. I have not been able to get out of accepting an office contrary to all my likings and for which I believe myself to have no aptitude. In vain I groaned, prayed, offered to spend the rest of my life in the novitiate-house of Toulouse; the sacrifice, one of the greatest of my life, had to be made. And see how visibly the action of divine Providence appears. When I had made, and repeated, my sacrifice a hundred times, God removed from my heart all my old repugnance so that I left the professed house—and you know how much I loved it—with a certain peace and liberty of spirit at which I was myself astonished. But there is more. On my arrival at Perpignan, I found a quantity of business of which I understand nothing, and many people to see and conciliate: the Bishop, the Intendant, the King's Lieutenant, Parliament, and Army Staff. You know my horror of all sorts of formal visits and above all of visiting the great, yet I find that none of this frightens me; I hope that God will supply for everything and I feel a confidence in his divine Providence which keeps me above all these troubles. So I remain calm and in peace in the midst of a thousand worries and complications in which I should have expected, naturally speaking, to be overwhelmed!'

"There, that wasn't an arrogant man, nothing like it. Yet he had no doubt that the unknown God took a hand in his interviews with the King's Lieutenant and staff officers and so on. And I wouldn't mind betting that the unknown God did." Maitland closed the letters with some finality. "It's got me beaten. One thing I'm sure of, and that is that while the arrogant priest might be an object of mockery, he's quickly becoming supplanted by his brother, the priest who doesn't know what anything means, who's a sort of humanist and in whom the only positive element is that he doesn't believe what Nolan and Costello believe in the way Nolan and Costello believe it. I just don't know," he concluded and threw the Jesuit across onto the bed.

Edmonds shook his head. "Anyhow, I don't think Christ would pass the theology exams here, because he hasn't read Aquinas and Costello's lecture notes."

"Look, if those young fellows upstairs can be as safe and sure as Costello, then good luck to 'em is what I say."

"And I say God help 'em."

"No. It's a sad life for a priest if all he knows is that the old-style religion won't wash but doesn't know yet what will. If I'm visibly that way, I'd be better off out of this place."

"It's not as visible as all that." Edmonds dropped his large jaws onto his collar and said rumblingly, lest he seem to be boasting, "I suppose I'm an expert at reading signs."

"What used you do before you came here?"

"I was a financial journalist." He winked. "Good fun."

"Are there any other experts at reading the signs here?"

"Not many."

"Thank God."

One of the things Maitland most hated about the House was that you could never speak for long to anyone without a bell ringing. One rang now below Maitland's room and above them the burr of words died and the thump of feet succeeded.

"There is an example of what I wanted—had the hide to want to speak to you about," said Edmonds. "Monsignor Nolan, when the time comes for him to present the bill to you, will complain that he never liked the evenings you held because they were the cause of keeping some students late for Compline."

"I've never kept anyone late yet."

"You're keeping me late. I know, I'm keeping myself late. But it's all the same to the president."

"Well, I'm not letting you go. I have some White Horse stabled under the bed. Are you a member of the Sacred Thirst?"

"Students are forbidden. . . ." said Edmonds, smiling. "It

90

used to be a great life with the press. You'd go round to interview company chairmen about new issues of debenture stock, and the whisky would flow like Niagara."

"All right. Stay there and I'll pour you a shaving-mug full."

So they were sitting together sipping when Egan ran in.

Egan was not breathless at seeing Maitland and Edmonds drinking together like cronies. He seemed to have problems of his own. His eyes stared above the blue third-former cheeks and he shivered.

"I have a problem I must speak to you about," he announced. "I wonder could you come to my room, Dr Maitland?"

Maitland put the drink down among his notes. But he worried now about how to get rid of Edmonds without resort to status, and in the spirit of their interview. Somehow this was the basic question. For though Egan looked like a rule-making, rule-keeping priest, and though for a student to drink liquor in this house was a massive breach of law, tonight Maurice was there not as a canonist but as a mortal, scared man, swallowing and snorting as no elocutionist would recommend. So that Edmonds was safe from all those covert penalties that can fall on the erring cleric; and safe also from the less covert one of being cast out and sent back to his financial editor.

He downed his whisky at a great pace, seeming inured to it. Maitland and Egan watched his large jaw raised for the work and his gullet joggling slowly between the strong cords of gristle in his throat. He must have decided to enter this House at perhaps the age of twenty-four. Now, five years later, he still looked like a man who knew his way around the bottles and around other things that were mystery to the two priests.

"Thank you, doctor," he said and winked. "I'll have to see a doctor about these fainting fits."

In Costello's room, Hurst confessed to being again possessed by the yen for blood sacrifice. The barbarous Hurst, too naïve and too subtle to be quashed by prayer, pressed the knife upon Hurst the neophyte, promised deer-eyed Hurst—Hurst whose face was a pale geography of nervy blemishes—quietus in the gush of blood.

"You have pandered to yourself mentally," Costello told him. "Too many high-jinx of the mind, and this happens."

"I wasn't aware. . . ."

"Look," said Costello, trying blitz methods, "you're pampered. You look pampered, you are pampered. You're the eternal pious youth. Take a pull on yourself or I'll boot you one, fair and square. You understand?"

But Hurst was too jaded to take any offence, and vapidly accepted his absolution and sleeping-pill.

Costello gave the long absolution with the special care and emphasis the words normally received only in a Hollywood piety epic. He wanted them to strike home.

Egan scarcely waited for Edmonds to be out of the room before asking, "Could you come with me now, James? I really can't afford to be away from my room for a second."

In the corridor, though, he took the time to draw Maitland into conference in the shadow of one of those terrible pilasters. Behind his head hung a barely perceptible painting of St Jerome in his cave. Its gloom seemed continuous with that of the passage where they stood, and Egan gave the essentially funny impression that he had emerged from the cave and was about to step back inside it. Yet Maitland did not for long feel like laughing.

"Thank God you're on hand, Maitland," Egan said. "The idea of turning to anyone else is impossible." He took a gulp of breath. "I have to be able to rely on your utter discretion and utter charity. And if you could see your way clear not to ask too many questions. . . ."

These demands touched Maitland. In many ways his emotions relating to friendship were still those of a blood-brothering ten-year-old.

"I'm very flattered," he said so heartily that it sounded almost like sarcasm, though Egan did not notice. "I only hope I can help."

"That's very kind," Egan told him, setting off again.

Maitland followed, thinking that this was life, that it was human relationships that perfected man; that maudlin activity called *helping out a friend.*

In Egan's spruce room, a dark-haired woman lay flushed and stupefied on the bed. Her shoes were off, and the skirt of her elegant blue suit lay crookedly on her hips. Her long legs were in burgundy-coloured stockings, one knee torn. She was whimpering softly, and looked, if anything, beautiful.

"What's the trouble with her, Maurice?"

"I did ask you about no questions," said Egan curtly.

"I'm sorry. What do you want me to do?"

"Forgive me, James. I just didn't want you to pre-judge her."

"I'm not pre-judging her. What do you want me to do?"

"She arrived in a taxi." Egan walked towards the bed and frowned down at the woman. "She's a responsible type of woman, she really is. That's why I asked you not to make any judgments. However, she arrived in a taxi, and that's scandal enough. She found her own way up to this room and wasn't intercepted."

With a peculiar and inexpert tenderness, he extended one hand towards the woman's tumid face. His arm did not reach her. Not far away the students were singing, too late to be of aid to Egan, a hymn about God protecting their house from the evils of the night; and the high notes of the song plagued the woman's ears. She rolled her head.

"I can hardly bear to think what would have happened if Nolan had met her on the stairs. I find the idea of his treating her as some sort of she-devil a revolting one."

"He would simply have said, 'My dear girl, don't you know this house is reserved to the use of celibate males?' "

"She's such a good Catholic really. It's the idea of people judging her that I find particularly hard to take."

Maitland said, "I've seen her somewhere, Maurice. Where would it have been?"

It was this question which, against the laws of logic, pre-occupied him, the woman's face evoking something both strong and recent.

"I think you must be wrong," said Egan. He began to work at tidying his desk, not as an evasion but because here was a start to many things that had now to be done. So he put his notes away in a crisp folder and recapped his ball-point as carefully as if it had been a Conway-Stewart, and returned two vagrant paper-clips to the small jar he kept sacred to them.

"I know," Maitland said. "Costello pointed out someone like her at the Couraigne prize turn-out." His memory had worked so strenuously on the girl's face that only now that it had produced an answer did he begin to see how clumsily he was behaving.

"That was her," Egan admitted without difficulty. "I suppose he told you something of her past. By that I mean her experience with the court."

"He mentioned something. I'm sorry, Maurice. I'm saying all the things you asked me not to."

"Don't worry." The *defensor* was now at his wardrobe, taking out his stock and collar. "I'm very grateful," he said, raising his chin and wrapping the collar round it. With Maitland at hand to receive orders, he was fast regaining competence. "I can't very well expect you to come into my room and find Nora in that sad state and not ask questions."

"I've asked my last."

"Well, I'll answer the one you want to ask." He swallowed and said in a lower voice, "She is—somehow, I don't know how—the worse for liquor. She is not an habitual drinker."

Maitland could tell that by her complexion, which was fine-grained and unspoiled. She must have been perhaps thirty-two or -three.

While pulling on his small bum-freezing coat, Egan said, "We have to get her home safely. Please tell me to go to the other place if you wish to, James. Do you own any sports clothes?"

He closed his eyes and, wincing and blind, adjusted the fall of his stock beneath the shoulders of his coat.

"I've got a corduroy coat I used to wear in my flat in Louvain in the winters," Maitland told him, by way of a suggestion. "I've got a pair of denim trousers too."

"Oh my goodness!"

94

"I agree. I've got an old pair of suede shoes that aren't so inelegant."

Maitland felt boyish—being in on a secret went part of the way towards intoxicating him, and that his presence had helped to make Egan look efficient again filled him with gaiety.

"Black trousers wouldn't look so queer under a corduroy coat," Egan was considering. As an aid to reflection he closed his eyes again and pinched the bridge of his nose. In the chapel the precentor's voice rose willow-thin and climbed the dark. For the silliest of reasons, mainly for his being party to Egan's plans, the chant seemed as ineptly beautiful, in this absurd building, among the Couraigne-type paintings, as it had seemed when he was seventeen.

The woman on the bed raised one lean thigh and mumbled, "It is three weeks since my last confession."

Egan's eyes blinked open.

"You see, I must take her home myself," he explained. "I'm responsible in so many ways. But more than a matter of responsibility, it would be a terrible injustice to send her home in a taxi, like a common drunk. You see?"

"Since then," moaned the woman, "I have been guilty on several occasions of criticizing the clergy. . . ."

"She lives with a sister," Maurice explained. "What I'm going to ask is so appalling that I can't ask it gently. You see, the sister knows me. If I drive her home, will you take her to the door?"

"In corduroy and denims?"

Egan's eyes dropped. "Perhaps not the denims."

"Wouldn't it be better to arrive as we are and simply tell the sister what happened?"

The little priest turned half away, snorting.

"Very well," Maitland assured him. "Whatever you like."

"You'd better wear those suedes too, James. I'm sorry for being impatient, but this is a dreadful come-uppance. To speak brutally, a man dressed as a priest or known to be one can't deliver an unconscious woman at her front door. I wonder could you wear a hat? And I've got an old pair of reading-glasses you might like to put on."

"Anything you say, Maurice. But I begin to sound like a white-slaver."

"You've every right to tell me to jump at myself. Tell me, can you drive, James?"

Egan's small car lay in the cold bay of night between the south and central wings of the house. Symbolic of its master's dilemma, it was crowded by the president's antique juggernaut of a Riley on one side and on the other by Costello's one hundred press-button horsepowers. Maitland found it hard to open the door wide. In this House, the passenger's doors of vehicles never had to be swung full-stretch to admit plump or laden wives. The narrow quarters in which the staff parked their cars testified their celibacy.

Maitland put his equipment in the back seat. The hat did not go well with the glasses and neither of them went with the coat, and as far as he was concerned, still feeling gay and con-spiratorial to the exclusion of nearly every other emotion, any woman whose sister was brought home drunk by a man wearing all three should have straightaway called for the police. However, he put suede shoes, hat, glasses, coat, in the passenger's seat and brought the car, lights out, to the main door.

There was no one in the downstairs parlour or the library. Upstairs, the washroom was empty, though the lights burned wide-awake. Maitland grinned at them as no Christian should. Eight cents extra on Nolan's electricity bill. Now that Com-pline was over, all that could be heard was the typewriter of one of the priests punching out "Tertullian's Theory of Bap-tism" or "The Meaning of *Kerigma* in St Paul" for some theological review.

The thirty yards from Egan's room to the staircase was the only danger. Maitland stood still for a second and listened a last time. It was worth it, he thought, and his heart ex-panded shamelessly with excitement. Fuelled by esoteric knowledge, the typewriter maintained speed and the urinals seethed in the washroom. On the floor above, some student avoiding starlight or a draught hauled his bed across the floor. But even this merely made the quiet more tangible.

Carrying the woman was what sobered Maitland. On the narrow stairs, he had her by the knees while Egan managed the shoulders. There was an immediacy about her limp body that made sobriety imperative, or at least fitting. Sobriety for its own sake, not for the sake of chastity. As a youth he had taught himself and been taught a series of celibate's tricks and had learnt them too well. Now he found it too easy to remember that this woman shared her species with Morna Quinlan, was mortal and menstrual, and would distend with child and decline with child-bearing. He found it too easy to remember that whoever had her had a season's fruit. Thinking so had generations of celibates succeeded at their trade. Yet Maitland knew that if he wanted the vision of God he must arrive at a more substantial purity than what was provided by these ploys of mental focus.

They wondered how they would get her into the back of the car. It was easier than they feared. After the passage of the stairs, she was willing to fall purring along the length of the seat. Egan covered her with a rug, quickly, and shut the door on her unguardedly feminine groans.

"I'm terribly sorry, Maitland," he said. "I could think of no other solution than this."

Just the same, he took unrepentantly to the wheel and drove fast and with great skill. It must have been midnight by now, but the lit suburbs and highways had not yet succumbed to the Sabbath. After ten minutes the girl woke up, calling, "Maurice I want to be sick."

"Don't worry," Egan told her gently and drove into a side-street to park.

Being uneasy for her, Maitland didn't look. Behind both priest's backs, the lovely woman retched. The cruel sound and crueller reek were terribly intimate in the little car.

She started to cry. "Forgive me, Maurice."

"It doesn't matter. But you were very foolish to start drinking."

"Perhaps," she said.

Maitland's stomach began to jump at the stench. He got his window down and, as the car moved off again, would have thrust his face out into the sweet night, except that that would have reflected on the lady.

She said unevenly, "When you're unhappy enough, you try these queer things. Whisky. You know."

"You didn't go around hotels, did you, Nora?"

"Celia's place."

"That's something."

"I want to go to sleep, Maurice."

"Before you do, Nora, I don't think it wise to tell Celia you've been to the House of Studies. You'd be so pestered. You don't mind my saying so?"

"Beg your pardon, Maurice?" she said after a long time.

"I say, we won't tell Celia you've been over to the House of Studies," Egan repeated slowly.

"No. Righto." She clearly felt much better, but not much more sober. "You're the expert on the morals of white lies, Maurice." She giggled.

"You realize, my motives aren't cowardly. But you'll be sick enough tomorrow without having Celia persecuting you. This is a friend of mine called James. James, this is Nora."

Egan spoke at top voice and could be heard panting at the end of each sentence. It seemed unfair that this dutiful little cleric, wearing on his lapel the badge of a temperance organization which the Irish pungently called "The Sacred Thirst", should have the ordering of such a crisis.

"James will take you to the door, Nora."

James is a fool, thought James.

Behind them the woman, nearly asleep, said, "Whisky keeps more people going than sanctifying grace does."

"You know that's not true, Nora."

Nora's tears began to creak out, but before long she fell asleep.

Egan and Maitland composed a story for the sister. Maitland would, if caught at the door by Celia, explain that he was an acquaintance of Nora's, that he'd seen her in this state— Egan thought up a likely locality—and brought her home by taxi; yes, taxi was what Celia would have to be told. "She knows my car," Egan explained. "Now you'll have to be firm with her, James. Simply refuse to tell her more. Pretend to be very angry at her aggressive attitude. Don't worry, she *will* have an aggressive attitude. Neither of the Tully girls has been lucky in love. Neither. Celia's separated husband, whom I met once, described her as a castrating bitch."

Maitland laughed softly at his friend's unexpected brusqueness.

"Of course, Nora," Egan went on, "Nora is a tragedy. And I just know that it will be easier for her, tonight and tomorrow, if her sister doesn't think she's been to see me. Celia will pat her shoulder and make her a cup of tea and say, 'Look what they've driven you to, love.' But if that woman—well, if *she* suspected *my* presence, that I had any part, however passive, in the business. . . . That's why I say you must be firm, James."

They were now in a slow stream of cars in the lively-deathly part of the city. Sailors accosted girls, and boys walked hand in hand, and the blue flesh of strippers simpered and risked hernia in dozens of extreme poses in the window displays.

Driving unevenly in low gear, Maurice said further, "If I am seen, Celia will not think twice of raising a riot in that street, even at this time of night. It's not easy to judge people with one adjective, but I think it's true to say she's jealous—madly jealous for her sister. She shall protect Nora, even if she protects her to death, as it were."

Frowning over traffic, Egan's face stained blue and gold and orange as the car edged. All the street subsisted in a medium of crude light, light seeming to have at its core an artist's mistake which successive layers of wash had been unable to remedy. Maitland watched faces, so unassertive under the brash assertiveness of the neons. He said, just for the sake of chatter, "All that light. Maurice. Don't you think it's a final indecency to go into the lust-rousing business and then light every doorway up like a maharajah's bathroom?"

"I suppose so, yes." But all Egan's mind was on veering the

99

car away from a white Jaguar from whose high windows Nora could probably be seen. "I beg your pardon?"

"All I was saying was that if you're going to make your living by rousing basic lusts, you shouldn't floodlight all the doorways. A dark doorway's basic enough for basic lusts. It may well be a crime above all others chief to set up lusts in one place and send them into another for the performance. You make people travel all that way thinking that they're onto the essence of things."

"Oh," Egan suggested without interest, "they probably have facilities elsewhere on the premises, upstairs." He had no doubt read of such things in the books-of-the-film Maitland had seen in his room.

There came a break in the five-ways traffic.

Egan's yellow-stained face triumphed and the car jolted away downhill. Below them, furled yachts lay on the bay, and the unsynthetic stars offered themselves for sightings to the Royal Yacht Club where a quarterly dance raged. Egan continued to coach Maitland.

"Celia will attempt to pump you, but don't let her. I believe your best hope is to skip out quick, as they say. I can't keep on begging your pardon for what I'm asking you to do, James. A person's desperation makes any fantastic scheme seem possible. I'm afraid this *is* a fantastic scheme. For one thing, why did I wear my clerical clothes?"

He slowed and began to remove them. He was handicapped by being temperamentally incapable of dragging them off. Even when he had shed his coat, he went on spying sideways at Maitland, who had undertaken to fold it over the back of the seat.

They came into a street where, Maitland thought, it would be easy to be happy. The houses were expensively unimpressive, and from gardens of long standing rose the lean sanity of pines and palms. Beyond parkland that faced the houses and stood utterly free of those white municipal threats about curbing dogs and dumping refuse, the bay was fledged with the quiet shapes of the yachts they had seen from the top of the hill. Egan parked the car.

"I can't go any farther, James. Celia's is that house there."
He pointed down the street to a stone bungalow with a terraced garden. Its lights shone. "I hope you wouldn't think I was in any sense afraid of the woman."

"Of course not."

With that, kneeling on the driver's seat, Egan began to wake the girl.

"Maurice," she said. "No, it's James," said Maurice. "He's going to take you home. Sit up, will you, Nora?"

She came halfway upright. Her hair swung in a sheath in front of her eyes, in the fashion of the movie queens of the forties. Fingering the seams of the upholstery, she was saying, "Bless me father, for I have sinned. . . . It is umpteen years since my last confession, and since then I have been sick once in a priest's car." She found this funny and adopted a solemn father-confessor voice. "That's a very gravyous sin, my daughter. Don't you know a priest's car has to operate on all six celibates?"

Maitland got out and opened the woman's door.

"Maurice?" she said again.

"It's James," Egan insisted. "You'll have to give her your hand, James. Poor dear thing."

"Here you are, Nora," said Maitland, probing his open fist towards the reek. Her hand lighted in his gently and very cold. Feeling acutely estranged from himself, he began inexpertly to pull her to her feet. Yet she seemed to rise out of the car with little effort. He helped her to take a few steps along the footpath, and felt her legs give way alternately.

Egan, considering that Maitland and Nora had been properly launched, called, "Rest well, Nora."

They hadn't gone far when Nora began to chatter. "When I used to board in the convent at W——" She said some indistinguishable native name that brought to Maitland's mind white eucalypts awash in red dust—"we used to make up silly riddles, Maurice. . . ."

"James," Maitland grunted.

"James. The parish priest of W—— always had a good car and he always told us what it had—you know, gears and ratios and diffs and so on. And I made up this riddle. I was very proud of it. I'll tell you." Maitland looked as attentive as he could with his face averted from her fouled dress. "When is a biretta not a biretta?"

"I don't know."

"When it's a car-biretta." She giggled. "I'm quite lucid now. Just a bit nauseated."

In fact she was at once sick again, making a shocking barking noise. Maitland tried to hold her by the shoulders. Finished, she remained bent forward; she breathed with an obvious sense of the goodness of breathing. Maitland's stomach began to leap as it had in the car, finding her closeness hardly bearable. So, after a few seconds, did she. In a flash, she forwent the ease of leaning forward against Maitland's bony hands. When Egan came up she had left to go and prop herself against one of her neighbours' fences.

She said, "What have I been doing, Maurice?"

"Don't worry. James was going to take you inside. But I think I should now."

Both the girl and, to his own mystification, Maitland protested.

Egan allowed himself to see reason. "It isn't that I don't want to face her," he said. "But she can be so nasty—to you, I mean."

"I'm not a prize tenant. I'll let myself in. What a dirty mess I'm in!"

She yelped and began to cry and search for a handkerchief. Her rifled handbag hung gaping on her left elbow. Maitland watched her for some seconds before remembering his own vast institutional handkerchief and pressing it on her.

"James your name is?" she asked in a stifled voice.

"Yes."

"You go back to the car, Maurice. And you, James, you just help me to the door. Maurice, you know that I have a long and close experience of shame, don't you? I mean the court and all the rest of it. I *have* a long experience of shame, don't I?"

The ovoid blue moon of Egan's face nodded. "Yes. It seems

to be the woman's lot in these matters. I wish it wasn't, Nora."

"Well, I've never been more ashamed than I am now. You must forgive me. . . ."

Egan answered gently. "What I sometimes think is that you must forgive us." His white priest's hand included Maitland in the guilt.

She began to walk away saying, "No, no, I can't have that."

Maitland turned Egan, who seemed dazed, back to the car and then followed the woman, getting to her side in time to open the gate. Red-tiled steps climbed the two terraces of her sister's garden; and once Maitland had pushed her up them, what looked like a lion but was probably a golden labrador burst on them from the blind side of wisterias.

"Sit down, Brian," Nora told it sadly, in a tone that accused it of insincere ferocity. "I'm so tired."

In a way that was still drunken, she searched for her key over her left elbow into her handbag. The porch light flashed on and discovered her at it. Then the front door opened and the fly-screen flew wide. A woman dark, bitter and tall stood inviting explanations. She was, in terms of form and composition, a vulnerable figure. Her long hair had been combed out into ropes, and this and a short quilted house-coat above thin legs and feathery slippers made her look top-heavy. Also, she carried in one dark hand a cheap novel whose cover showed a young man with paramount shoulders receding from a thin, badly-used girl. None the less, her effect on Maitland was Medusan. She too gave the impression of having been badly used, but by somebody who had not misused her with impunity.

"All afternoon and all night, Nora," she said, "and not even a phone call. Where have you been?"

Nora held her hands out, swayed and shook her head. Her handbag fell with a thud.

"Excuse me," Maitland felt bound to say with however full a knowledge of his ineptitude. "My name's James. I've met Nora casually in the past and when I saw in this state—so sick—I felt. . . ."

"Mr James," the woman said heavily, Maitland letting what

103

seemed a happy mistake stand. "I'll get your address before you go."

He blushed within his dubious combination of clothes. His one reasonable impulse was to bolt for the sake of discretion, leap down both terraces, vault the fence and hope that Egan was fast on the ignition. "Perhaps," he said simply.

"No one is going to bring my sister home half-covered with sick and get away without explaining himself. Come inside, Nora."

As Nora obeyed, Maitland swept up her bag and pressed it into her hands. She began to move—not at all pretty by the porch light. Her stockings hung so baggily on her legs that she seemed to have wasted since pulling them on earlier in the day. She smelt badly, and her clothes were draggled and soiled. All this she knew and was willing to be ashamed at anyone's beck, especially her sister's.

"Say good night to the *kind* gentleman," Celia told Nora, and Maitland saw that Egan had been largely right in predicting the woman's drift as the point of "*kind* gentleman" was aimed at him alone. On the other hand, he began to wonder whether Egan might not just as well have delivered the girl when, a second later, drawing in her breath to let Nora go inside, Celia hissed, "You've wet yourself, you fool!"

Then Maitland and the sister stood in silence listening to Nora plod around the interior of the house, sobbing so peculiarly that when she went into the bathroom they could tell by the tiled echo. Hearing the bathroom door close, they were both immediately ready to speak.

"I felt so sorry for her," Maitland said, and not for effect.

"Are you a friend of Dr Maurice Egan?"

"That's the fellow who's on the Couraigne prize committee?"

Celia flourished the book in her hands. The gesture said, "Look, save your prevarications. I've studied you people in fact and in literature, and I can tell a prevarication from some distance." The book was one of those that feature, as well as a dust jacket, an extra ration of promises printed on a belt of white paper. Maitland, who habitually stared at books, got a

104

glimpse of the words, "Classic story of the emotional exploitation of a young girl. . . ."

"He's a priest," she said. "He's a bumptious little priest."

She put such classic hatred into her plosives that Maitland hung his head.

"I know him," he conceded. "I thought he might have been bumptious when I first met him. In fact, he's very unsure and much humbler than most."

Celia came out with a remarkably whole-hearted laugh. "Where did you find Nora then?" she asked, willing to extend to Maitland's story the same suspicion she applied to his claim about Egan's humility.

Maitland told her none the less. For embroidery he said, "The taxi-driver got very angry about it. He wanted us to clean up."

"I don't blame him," she decided, while patently disbelieving in both cab and driver. "How much do we owe you in fares?"

"You don't owe me anything. I was very pleased. Listen, pardon me for saying so, but I think she should be allowed to sleep and then see a doctor. She seemed beyond herself with. . . ." But he didn't know what. "Some sort of unhappiness," he temporized.

"Now, that *is* perception! Don't think I won't consider your advice, Mr James. You see, I *do* have some concern for her."

"I'm sure you do. I'll have to go. It's so late."

She laughed and stared up and down his length, her eyes fixing on his black trousers.

"Yes," she agreed, still staring. "No doubt you have to rise early to say Mass, father."

"I beg your pardon."

"By their black trousers you shall know them. Anyhow, I heard you preach a few weeks ago. It was very pleasant. It shed no light, but at least it didn't bore. Speaking of boredom, have you ever heard a sermon from Father Egan? No. They should make you listen to each other. That would be only fair."

"I don't think we'll gain by—"

105

"No, you wouldn't. You fellows never do think anything will be gained by any argument where you hold the thorny end of the stick."

"What's the use? You have me red-handed."

"Do I, indeed?" She felt a mole on the left cheek of her ravaged-looking face. "What's your name, father?"

"James."

"James? That wasn't the name. . . . Oh, I see. We're on to Christian names, are we? Call me Celia, James."

"I would. But I have to go."

Celia smoothed down the soft floral gown as if it were a uniform. "Oh yes, you're all so busy. It took the church courts a mere four and a half years to decide that Nora's husband was impotent as a paling fence. The pace must be deadly."

"I know very little about church courts, Celia. I'm not a canon lawyer. But I know they're slow. I suppose all courts are slow."

"Nearly five years to discover that a man is impotent! It must be a record. Of a kind."

"I suspect that you wouldn't find it was a record. The Church is accustomed to take its time. We boast about that. But it has its bad aspects, I know."

"Indeed. It gives a girl, Nora, time to develop a taste for the judge."

Knowing that he was playing the game Celia's way, Maitland could still not prevent himself from saying, "Judge?"

"In the second case. No, he wasn't judge. He was usher of the black rod or defender of the seal or something. Egan."

"He's defender of the bond."

"That's it. Now, isn't that a title? Straight out of Gilbert and Sullivan."

"Let me assure you, Celia. Egan had nothing to do with Nora's state tonight."

"I know what you mean. He wouldn't have the gumption to liquor her up. He wouldn't have the gumption to sleep with her and go on being a sacrilegious priest. Damn it, it's happened to better men than he is. Virtue through lack of initiative, that's Chubby Egan for you. As if he would ever be

106

likely to do any good to anyone, sacrilegiously or otherwise."

Maitland said, "He has to be of use to himself first of all. But you know that."

Boyishness had died in him by now; this vigilant and bitter woman had given it its final discharge. He was beginning to take glances over his shoulder, niggled by the awareness of Egan's disquiet assailing him from a distance of a hundred yards or more and through a series of hedgerows. Then Nora's hollow voice could be heard, calling, "Celie, Celie!"

"Circumstances end our talk," said Celia, a sentence worthy of the novel in her hands. In her craggy frame somewhere was hidden the snakes-and-ladders-playing, dolly-tea-partying child sister to whom Nora was now calling. "But if you should see Dr Egan within the next few months, tell him it's either all in or all out. If he wants to be celibate and heroic, flog her away from him. Some saint did that, didn't he, to a medieval good-time gel? Or there's the other alternative. But that wouldn't work, despite what I said a moment ago, not with Nora. You know, she still wears a scapular. In this day and age! I'll bet you don't even wear a scapular."

Nora called again, "Celie!" But it very nearly seemed that Celia was fonder of her advantage over the enemy than of suc-couring her wounded.

"Anyhow," she said, "tell Egan it's cake or eat it. And next time to do his own deliveries."

Nora could be heard screaming.

"God bless *you*, father," Celia sang virulently and then slammed the door.

In the car, Egan sat with one hand on the wheel. He peered like a comic getaway man and took a guess. "Celia, wasn't it?"

And Maitland, so vigorously misinformed by that lady, could not help cutting Egan's apologies mercilessly short. He forgot how willingly he had joined the expedition earlier in the night and had to be chivvied into answering all the questions the little priest had to ask. By the time he had realized how unfair he was being, and how unfair Celia could not help being, it was too late to make anything but full disclosure just. So that Maitland had to tell Egan even the cake-or-eat-it message. The little priest seemed to sink in his seat.

"She's dead right, of course," he said.

"She couldn't be as bitter as that and still be right."

"You must think I'm a fine one, James. Though what any-one thinks doesn't alter things at their source, does it?"

"No. And I'm under such a large obligation to you."

"However do you make that out?" Egan said, but he didn't want to be answered, he wanted the idea to stand. "I'll have to go and see that Celia in the morning."

Maitland most dreaded Egan's excuses and held himself stiff against their possibility. But, blessedly, travelling home among late talkers and drinkers at the soft narcotic hour of two, even the *defensor* called a truce unto himself.

Egan avoided him. They passed early one morning, each on his way to say Mass at a side altar; and that was all Maitland saw of him for the rest of the week. On that one silent occasion, Egan held his head and shoulders up, as if trying to imply an impossible range of things; his neck grew cords of gristle and his frame seemed striving to say, "No, I have not desired Nora Tully nor betrayed my vow with her. I know you don't think I have, but since I am going to the altar, I want to make it clear that I'm not acting sacrilegiously. Of course, if you don't think I've considered every aspect of the problem, then I don't really care what you think. However, I know that you aren't the type. . . ." And so on.

In fact, Egan had tried to tell Maitland this in so many words, the morning after their Saturday-night stunt.

"I hope, in fact I know, that you wouldn't think I've—" He had shaken his head. "The trouble is, the words I've learnt for a situation like this seem snide now. 'Compromise', 'illicit liaison', 'entanglement'. . . ." He had begun a second time then: "I do hope you wouldn't think I had jeopardized, in any way, my vow of celibacy. . . ."

Maitland objected.

Egan blinked. "I've already said I know you don't think along those lines. Just the same, it must be a source of anxiety

108

to any priest to see a colleague saying Mass in a doubtful state of soul, perhaps multiplying sacrileges."

"It wouldn't be my business if you were."

"James, I am not multiplying sacrileges."

"Good."

But still the little canon lawyer went on compulsively explaining. For Maitland's approval meant nothing to him. By his own severe standards he was in jeopardy; by those standards he must judge himself. He wanted and dreaded the glib and final judgment he could have had only from a Costello; he wanted to be declared *not* guilty on the level of a Nolan, for that was his own level, the level his conscience had worked on since boyhood.

10

Throughout the winter no friendship other than his unlikely one with Egan developed for Maitland within the house. Just the same, since his sermon of some Sundays before, his standing with the staff had gained. With some of them he went to see a film, with others to an international football match. Early or late, though, he would be nonplussed when they boasted of their new number-two irons or discussed restaurants. His sense of fitness, being nine-tenths pride and essentially working-class, made him wonder what was the sense in risking hell or its equivalent by becoming a priest if, like everyone else, you knew what was par on expensive golf courses and commended cynical waiters on the filet mignon.

He felt cheated too when their legalism transformed them momentarily into ciphers. Such as the night Costello introduced for discussion a question he had been asked that same afternoon. A girl had been walking home the evening before when a man attacked and raped her. A doctor had telephoned to ask Costello whether a person was justified in treating the girl in such a way as to prevent a possible pregnancy.

"Of course, I referred him to Monsignor Nolan, who happened to be out. But I told him I was sure that, however unfortunately, the answer was no, he couldn't treat her in that way. Agreed?"

He made an adenoidal noise and stirred his coffee, and the gentle lighting of the parlour was trapped in each crystal of his glasses. Anguish did not penetrate their cheery rimlessness; he had no notion of the stew of heartbreak he stirred with his coffee-spoon. Like any specialist, he could not afford adverting to such things.

Some of the priests made gestures of assent. Maitland watched Egan, who merely reached for a biscuit.

"What do you think, Maurice?" Costello asked.

Maurice didn't particularly want to say. At last he did, reluctantly. "It's an unfortunate case. It's one of those border cases where to keep to principle may seem barbarous in a human sense. However, you're right. Conception could well have taken place. Just the same. . . ."

"Catholics get used to stomaching the unfortunate," Costello said, making a face as he downed his mocha. "What about you, James? You're the humanist of the group." He persisted in trying out such barely ironic phrases on Maitland, and Maitland let him, in indemnity of the Couraigne prize incident.

"I'm glad it's not my responsibility."

"But if it was?"

"I don't want to buy into the fight, thanks."

"Well, I thought I'd get a real rough-house discussion going on this. But the others could scarcely care less. Come on, James, it's up to you."

"No, I'm prejudiced."

"In what way?" Costello demanded.

"I find it impossible to believe that anything that might be there is a human being with human rights."

But Maitland's unspoken prejudice arose from his being the only one his mother did not miscarry. For all her losses, whenever they occurred—in the first, fourth, seventh month—she

111

wept, above all because they had not been baptized. He resented that her grief should have arisen in this way, more or less on the authority of theologians. Such as Costello.

"Ah," said Costello, "but it may well be a human with human rights. What is there may well have an immortal soul. No one knows just when the soul *is* infused. Who would want to take the risk on their consciences?"

"I don't know," Maitland confessed energetically and with an edge of anger. "As I say, I don't have to know, because people with a problem of this size always ask an expert. Thank God!"

Costello pushed his hand outwards and palm up. The gesture was meant to imply the artlessness of the hand's owner. "Look, Maitland, I'm not trying to rib you. Tell me what you think. It's a shame when a man can't have a spot of controversy with his coffee."

Without warning, the young priest was blind with anger at this man who was willing to damn a girl over the telephone, but could not forgo an argument with his supper.

"Very well then, doctor. I think that it is more than barbarous in a merely human sense to make that girl risk bearing such a child. I think such a thing is *essentially* barbarous. I think that the risk of any minute organism which the doctor might remove being human is ludicrously tiny. And on the basis of such a tiny or non-existent risk, I can't see that it's justified to chance the future ruin of both this *real* girl and any child she *may* bear. I'm sorry if this shocks you, doctor, and, as you say, you're the expert. But you wanted my opinion and that's it."

Everyone in the room had listened and now sucked it over. One of them said, "But that's very risky, James."

"Perhaps it is. I don't know. Thank God I don't have to think that sort of thing through."

"You can't," Costello told him, "enshrine a principle such as that the unborn foetus is sacred, and then chuck it out the door as soon as it looks edgy."

"She'd surely get the grace to bear this appalling thing," someone decided.

"It's hard," another said, "but a thing like that could make a woman a saint!"

Only vestigial good manners kept Maitland in the room.

Joe Quinlan, his cousin, had apparently been found bewildered among the pines, terraces, shrines and rockeries. By the time some student had brought him into the House and left him at Maitland's door, all the native dispassion he had shown that other afternoon had left him. Maitland found him on guard, sniffing the air, ready to run.

"Hell," Joe said. "What do you do for sunlight?"

So far out of his habitat, he seemed much more willing to be amenable. He said that Morna and the children were in the town below, doing the shops over. He leered and winked and said that he didn't want to upset the apple cart by bringing a good sort like Morna into the place. Maitland saw all this with nostalgia: the wink, the leer, the Saturday sports shirt and coat, the Saturday face ready for the pub, the races, the football or, more likely, the report of these things. Joe was a pungent reminder of Maitland's own father, of Saturdays when, since nothing ever happened, everything seemed possible.

"What I came to see you about, father, is these thieving swine."

He passed a newspaper advertisement to Maitland. It showed the family that Joe and Morna would like to become romping on a subdivided hill above a forest. You could have land on the hill for a hundred dollars down and fifty a month. Maitland had a vision of Joe and Morna arriving on the hill, Joe in his blatantly tatty sports coat, and being sirred and madamed all afternoon by some merciless agent; and going home feeling that they had gained a stake in the world.

Joe said, "I paid what they say there, and paid each month, and then I got a letter from them announcing as if I'd won the lottery, saying how I'd now qualified to take out a mortgage with some other company. Well, I went along to the mortgage company and they say I have to pay more than seventy dollars a month for the next seven years at a big interest rate. They say I signed to do it when I signed the first contract, but the bastard who sold us the land didn't tell us. You know. So we thought we'd be paying fifty a month for three years or so, but now we're paying seventy for seven years."

He shifted on his buttocks to say, just audibly, "Swine."

Maitland continued frowning over the advertisement. Joe pressed him.

"Well, it says fifty dollars a month at seven per cent, doesn't it?"

"Yes. It says from fifty dollars."

"*From,*" Joe hissed. He was startled that a preposition could, with so little apparent truculence, turn on a man. "It doesn't say seventy a month at twelve per cent. And it's a different type of per cent too."

"Flat?"

"That's right. In this *great* country!"

"It's wrong as can be," Maitland conceded. "Have you the contract you signed when you bought the land?"

Joe had it in his coat pocket. There were grease marks on it as if he and Morna had worried over it at meal-times.

"I tell you, that mortgage office, you've got no idea. Carpet like a Hilton hotel and them squiggle-paintings all over the walls and little tarts with short haircuts running all over the place with folders. And the whole place full of people whining because they've been had. Like me."

Maitland made a variety of promises. The following week, he took Joe's contract to a solicitor recommended by Egan. The solicitor sighed professionally as soon as he opened it, and then let it fall on the desk.

"I know this by heart," he said. "There's nothing can be done. People should never sign any contract in real estate until it's been sighted by a lawyer. It's the old story of fools and angels. This is a contract for fools."

Maitland told him, "There are people who have never seen a solicitor in their lives. They can't be expected to be absolutely wise with their unexpected windfalls. What I mean is, with all respect, joy is a more basic reaction than the urge to seek a solicitor."

114

"Oh, yes, yes, yes," the lawyer agreed shortly. "But the world we live in, the world. . . .!"

"What if he, my cousin, refuses to pay any more?"

"They can sue him for damages."

"They can. Will they?"

"At this stage, yes. I reckon that later on, after he's paid a good amount, they might let him go."

"A good amount is all this man owns in the world."

The lawyer sighed, opened the document, read a few lines, which confirmed all his sad wisdom, and shut both eyes migrainously.

"And the price of it, anyhow," Maitland murmured. "In this country. . . ."

At which flaccid comment the lawyer frowned even more deeply but kept his eyes largely closed.

"Oh," Maitland hurried to explain. "I've been away for some years. When I left, which was more than three years ago, that district must have been all poor scrub. . . ."

"Worth as little as six hundred dollars an acre. I know, father. But since then the happy day has dawned when it was declared non-rural and, behold, the companies knew—in fact, they'd been buying it up for months before, often through dummy buyers. Then in went the bulldozers and shaved the whole area—" he sketched razed downs with his hand— "engineers built roads that would fall into holes within two years, and another terrible suburb was born."

On Maitland's way downstairs, the lawyer's last sentence woke in him not only a barren anger but the memory of some lines of Ezra Pound's:

> With usura hath no man a house of good stone
> each block cut smooth and well fitting
> that design might cover their face.

It was a very rhetorical poem he used to recite while shaving in his room in Louvain. As he waited for a bus, he began to add his own riders to the poem. With usura, he decided, the land was made desert and tracked with—as the lawyer had said—minimum standard concrete; with usura the engineer was made futile, the seller forced to prey, the buyer harrowed, the usurer gorged with easy money; the short-haired tarts Joe spoke of served Moloch and did his cancerous paperwork. With usura.

The next day, one of these young ladies led him into the office of the Allied Projects Development Company's chief accountant. He was greeted in a manner he had come to hate by a man about forty. The greeting said, "We're all professional men together and know the price of fish. Besides which, some of my best friends are Catholics and Monsignor X has money invested in us. Your *company*, if I can call it that, and ours are two of the pillars that keep the sky up."

Maitland refused an offered cigarette. "I won't waste your time," he said. He told Joe's story. "I think he should be refunded his money, and if that isn't done, I shall warn people against your type of business from the pulpit or anywhere else available."

The accountant licked his lips, bemusedly, as if they were caked with that salt which is the salt of the earth.

"Come now, father. We're a respectable company, our prices are quite reasonable by comparison. Our auditor is a papal knight. . . ."

And the orderly clash of typewriters and comptometers in the office made Maitland suspect that he was lost with a grievance no one would understand. He would therefore need to stand by his first view of the matter; he would not cease to be angry. So he remained and kept saying his say; and was at length led across a floor peopled with clerks and long-legged girls who knew what they were hunting for in the steel cabinets and among ribboned deeds on the shelves. The inner Maitland shrank from their professionalism. Beyond them, through an avenue of abstracts, the managing director lived in a teak office.

He frowned all the time.

"No," he said to Maitland, "it would be very foolish to do that. We're well established and respected. Our auditor is a papal knight."

"That's the second time I've heard that, and it leaves me

singularly unimpressed. If I'm willing to accept that Pope Alexander the Sixth had a number of bastard children, I'm willing to accept that a papal knight would work with you. What is of basic importance is the weapon of deceit this advertisement is."

The accountant, leaning on the managing director's personal Chubb, was stung.

"Now, I don't think you should take advantage of your collar, father. I think there should be a gentlemen's agreement not to bandy insults."

"This is a weapon of deceit. When I say that I don't intend to insult *you* but to define *it*."

"Each profession has different standards," the managing director explained. There was a weariness about him that implied he had often given these same explanations, perhaps even to himself. "If a maker of toilet soap claims that by using his soap any girl can make men interested in her, no one objects. It's a convention of the trade. The same with our claims. No one would seriously think you could buy land on those terms."

"If no one would seriously think so, why make the claims."

"It's a convention. Besides, we say *from* a hundred dollars down, *from* seven per cent. That's the base line, the starting point. After one of our clients has demonstrated his reliability by adhering to these basic terms, he qualifies for a mortgage with a sister company of ours called Investment General Corp. Now, I'm sure our man-in-the-field explained all this to your cousin."

"Should he have?"

The managing director blinked. To Maitland he seemed distractingly honest, a man much put upon by the dodges of men-in-the-field. He said to the accountant, "We'll soon see. Have someone bring us our copy of the particular contract." He quoted a code from the document Maitland had dropped on the desk. "It will have the salesman's name. . . ."

Maitland managed the dourness to say, "Wait on. I don't want to see a salesman crucified."

"Now, father, melodrama. . . .!" the accountant told him.

"If he didn't tell my cousin about the mortgage, it's because he has permission or perhaps even orders not to do so."

"And if you weren't a priest, I'd have you shown out of the building."

"And if my priesthood has that much weight, I want my cousin released from his contract. I want you to give him his money back."

"Investment General own the land now."

"Surely the hand can speak to the glove."

"It's not so simple. Our contract is a legal one, theirs is a legal one. Why did your cousin sign them if he had doubts?"

"Perhaps it's just possible that marble and glass and aluminium and chrome—the works, in fact—and an acute air of professionalism can all hypnotize a man. I don't suppose you think so, though."

"I confess I don't."

The telephone burred, a soft and insidiously clean sound putting doubt on Maitland's crusade. The managing director excused himself and attended to it, moaning trade talk down it, frowning pitifully all the time. Some realtor's zealot could be heard barking back at him. He muffled it with a gentle hand.

"I trust you'll see the matter more clearly by Sunday, father. I'm very busy. . . ."

"Good morning," said Maitland, gratefully as a class released for a half-day, glad to have argued dutifully.

Now he felt intimidated by the outer office, and bolted down the fire-stairs, savouring their loneliness; bursting too athletically into an arcade of thrice-mortgaged coffee and lingerie shops and out among the sunlit mortgagees upon the pavements.

It was an expensive parish, but he couldn't help that. He was aware of faces pointed at him, seeming bland and coddled, or perhaps bracing themselves for another bland and coddling sermon. Their church was Spanish Mission in conception, but all the asperities of Spanish Mission had been softened with rare blonde brick. Costly-looking couples, risen from late beds,

118

dashed in through the porch and found seats while he gathered his notes. He assured himself that they wouldn't care, that Joe was an anachronism here. The proletariat, like vaudeville, was vanishing.

"The Church is criticized," he began, "for its neglect of social evils. And certainly we sometimes condemn an individual evil while we condone the social evil that bred it." *Sometimes?* It had rarely been otherwise. But one had to be careful with well-heeled congregations: they were always clericalist when it came to a pinch. "We condemn individual corruption but are not actively appalled by corruption on an international scale. We condemn family-planning but say little of the economic evils which make so many believe it so necessary."

And thus onto those evil sisters, Allied Projects and Investment General; though of course he did not name them.

"In this country," he called, shaking his manipled left hand in bafflement. "In *this* country!"

He remembered Ezra Pound:

> *"Usura rusteth the chisel*
> *It rusteth the craft and the craftsman*
> *It gnaweth the thread in the loom*
> *None learneth to weave gold in her pattern. . . .*
> *Usura slayeth the child in the womb*
> *It stayeth the young man's courting*
> *It hath brought palsey to bed, lyeth*
> *Between the young bride and her bride-groom. . . ."*

The orator's easy exaltation shook him; he was, for half a minute, drunk on the utter fitness of what he and Pound wanted to say, on the utter bane of Allied Projects and Investment General, all their thralled girls and all their works and pomps.

"In this illimitable country!" he said.

Unvesting sadly after Mass, emptied by the excesses of the pulpit, he tried to say the derobing prayers. Even more than normally they seemed to him shrines of words vacated by the deity. The question was whether it was necessarily due to a

119

fault in him, Maitland, the beadsman? Or was the shrine too old, too far gone, too long outgrown by whatever God it once held? He was down to his alb when someone knocked at the door. "Yes," he sang, without cause to sing. He expected a woman in a floral hat with a Mass offering, and she would expect him to be joyous, the Lord's skipping lamb down from the mountain.

What appeared was the smooth head-prefect face of Des Boyle, frowning.

Maitland rid himself of the alb and the room of acolytes.

"Father," Boyle said then, "it both *is* my business and *isn't* my business to say this. I think you're being very unwise."

"I see." Limp though he was, Maitland became fortuitously enraged to have his words accused of practical silliness when he had himself already accused them of moral folly. "I would have thought that with your involvement in charity you'd be pleased to see a social ill exposed."

Boyle fondled his fat missal, breathing deeply and devising an answer. At last he said, "I *am* able to appreciate irony, father. I caught all the irony you threw at me that night at the cathedral, even though His Grace, who's a better man than either of us, seemed to see none at all. You resent the Knights, don't you, father?"

Maitland had had time to be ashamed by now—short passion and long shame seemed to be the order of his life; and he began to give the vestments on the bench little evasive, housewifely tugs. He said, "I haven't any right to dislike anybody who doesn't do active harm. I merely thought Quinlan was outside your province."

"Now, father," Boyle insisted, "that wasn't all."

"No."

"As a Knight, I'd prefer you voiced your resentments."

"I don't like secret societies," Maitland granted. "I don't like the spirit of *Let's all get together and enjoy the unique dignity of being Catholics—*"

"As if that counted for nothing," Boyle murmured.

"—or worse still, *Let's all get together and pull strings better than those Masonic gents.*"

120

"I hope you know more about land-dealing than you do about the Knights, Dr Maitland. I would hate to see any priest made to look foolish."

"You have considerable powers of irony yourself, Mr Boyle."

"I mean what I say," the Knight emphasized. "I'd be very sorry. You see, every line of business has its own complexities and conventions. . . ."

"What I spoke of from the pulpit can't be explained away as a complexity or a convention."

"I say it can. I do the auditing for a development company, and—"

Maitland smacked his own cassocked thigh.

"You're *not* their much-vaunted Papal Knight?"

"Yes. The managing director telephoned me the other day to say that an angry young priest called Father Maitland had been in the office. He's not one of my closest friends, but I could tell he was nonplussed and a little shaken. When I found you here this morning, in the pulpit, in my own parish, I thought at first it might save embarrassment if I went outside. But a person still has an obligation to attend Mass."

"So you remained."

"Yes."

While a nun of the parish dashed into the sacristy to wash the wine and water cruets, the two men kept an unquiet silence. Maitland had leisure to see that he had dealt with Boyle as with an unbidden meddler. When the nun had the cruets dry and had gone off in search of further handmaidenly tasks, he announced, "You must forgive me if I sounded aggressive, Mr Boyle. I didn't quite realize your interest in the matter."

Boyle was generous enough to brush the apologies aside with the butt of his honest hand.

"It's a question of the conventions of the business. If you took the case of a toothpaste manufacturer—"

"But I took the case of a soap manufacturer with your managing director. I don't suppose it differs from the case of the toothpaste manufacturer?"

121

"Exaggerated claims and so on?"

"That's right. Mr Boyle, that argument is cant."

"Perhaps. We'll see later. There are economic reasons for the high price of land and I'll outline them first." Boyle's conscience was firm, he was himself both lucid and sure. A structure of costs prevailed in the community and, to fit this structure, it was necessary that land should cost what it cost. A development company had a responsibility to its staff and to other development companies and their staffs. Responsible behaviour towards a structure of prices rebounded to the employee as an increase in wages.

Even to Maitland it sounded dated—greed for my brothers' sakes. Yet it *was* believed by this decent man, it lived and did well under the brilliantined scalp, in the unimpeachable soul of Des Boyle.

"I had my crisis of conscience on this matter, don't you worry, father. So I took the question to one of the most renowned confessors in the archdiocese. He asked me whether their advertising told the conventional half-truths that are current in the profession. I said it did. He said, 'The sort of promise no one but the simple-minded takes seriously?' I said yes again. I also made it clear that I did not actually work for them, that I was a separate firm who merely did their auditing. He assured me that I need not worry. I then assured myself, for health's sake, that my conscience was correctly informed. I still believe that it is correctly informed. What say you, father?"

Maitland nodded. "Who am I to tell you otherwise?"

"You are a priest."

"Oh yes. . . ."

"Father, if you are going to be so certain in the pulpit, if you damn—out of conviction—people whom I'm bound to by contract, then you owe it to me to be certain now."

"You mean you want me to damn *you* too?"

"I want you to tell me what you think of my position."

"Your position isn't a simple one. All I know about is them. I don't know about you. I wouldn't have the presumption."

"But you have the grace of your state. Of Holy Orders."

122

"Don't bank on that."

Unwittingly, Maitland had been giving rope. There were sudden signs of anger in Boyle—he did not gesture with the missal, but his sober hands began to strangle it.

"You simply want to raise doubts but not to solve them. That's hardly fair, father."

"Oh, Mr Boyle." Maitland took the chalice and locked it away in a wall-safe. The move, which the priest made merely to fill a nasty hiatus in their interview, chastened the layman by giving a sight of a sacred vessel in a priestly hand.

Seeing this change in Boyle, Maitland said, "Your conscience isn't mediated to you by priests. You were sure I was wrong about *The Meanings of God*. Feel free to be sure I'm wrong now."

"After you were so convinced in the pulpit," Boyle once more maintained, "you owe me a judgment on how I stand."

Maitland shook his head. "Even if I'm right about *them*, it doesn't necessarily change how *you* stand. My conscience is no special conscience, just one man's. I can only judge the simple things. Like this."

And he placed on the bench, beside Boyle, the newspaper cutting Joe had given him.

"So you leave me uncertain?" Boyle rebuked him.

"Damn it all, it's good for a man to be uncertain. Certainty's only a front-end of a beast whose backside is bigotry. Look how bigoted I am about Allied Projects!"

So Des Boyle gave Maitland a look that meant, "We feed and clothe you and you give us certitude in return. That sublime contract is broken in you!"

He said, "I won't bother you any further, doctor."

One Sunday later, he preached the sermon again in what pastors delight in calling "a solid parish", among people who had what statemen persist in calling "a fair slice of the economic cake", yet who had also some affinity with the Joe Quinlans.

It was a funny world, Maitland afterwards thought, in which satellites were no longer news but sermons were. Per-

haps the odds against a sermon were greater than those satellites had to face—the press always cherishing the outsider who
comes home.

Knowing this, one of the congregation telephoned a daily
tabloid that dealt with religion in a becomingly sentimental
manner, and reported Maitland's vivid sermon.

"Regular mud-slinger, it seems," the duty editor told one of
his skeleton staff. "Do you think you can sit through the ten
o'clock Mass? We might be glad of it if that cyclone veers off
before Pago-Pago. And get a photograph."

The editor himself remained to wonder whether "Savona-
rola of the Suburbs!" was too literate a tag.

Maitland, stepping from the sacristy, was asked for a photograph, which was taken the next instant.

"We heard your sermon with great interest, father, and—"

"You can't print the sermon."

"Sermons are public property, father. Been that way since
the Lake of Galilee."

He argued and, as he did, another photograph was taken.

In this way Maitland's thirty-hour siege-by-telephone of the
cathedral presbytery began. Manners demanded that His
Grace be warned, but His Grace was not available for warning. The prelate had left to open a new wing at the Dominican
convent, and by the time the Dominican convent sent someone
to deal with Maitland's call, which must have rung in the
nuns' old wing for half the afternoon, His Grace was on his
way to Pontifical Vespers at a Benedictine monastery. The
Benedictines neglected their phone with a neglect quite
worthy of the Dominicans, and when some young monk
answered, the archbishop had gone five minutes, bound for a
Hibernian supper.

Later that evening His Grace was at home but reciting
matins and lauds. Suddenly, an hour came at which one didn't
telephone even people with whom one was on the cosiest of
terms.

His Grace's private secretary said, "You should get him
between eight-thirty and nine tomorrow."

Maitland respectfully split the time and chose a quarter to

124

nine. The archbishop had gone to present a sodality flag in the chapel of a girls' school. By mid-morning he was attending an aunt's sick-bed; he rested after lunch; but at three he baffled Maitland by answering the phone in person and, of course, listening tolerantly. The afternoon papers were, in any case, already on sale. Pago-Pago had been spared at Maitland's expense. There were no ninety-year-old sires that Monday, and Miss Associated Canneries had gone back to stoning peaches; their places had been filled by a frayed band-leader granted a decree nisi because his wife took her boxer (dog) to bed with her, and by Maitland himself, dubbed "A Power in the Pulpit" (a triumph for clarity over erudition).

Nolan met him in the corridor that evening and said something about the wisdom of young priests' keeping each week to the approved sermon topic as set down in the sermon list for that year.

The following day, the afternoon paper carried seven letters from people who had suffered under Investment General or its ilk. The third day, the managing director of Allied Projects made it known that the archdiocese owned shares in both itself and its mother-sister-company, Investment General.

Once more Maitland found out in the refectory. This time it was evening. One could hear the dark wind thudding at the windows and be solaced by the batteries of steaming teapots. The ritual went forward as before: Nolan seated in the sovereign chair with his closed face aimed at the reader, as if the Kingdom depended on enunciation; Costello striding in late, hatchet-man and ornament of grace, under his arm the evening paper to be dropped in passing on Maitland's dish.

Maitland sat forward, his hands clamped beneath the table, his legs trembling on tiptoe. The news was that that mammonish frowning gentleman, the managing director, had presumed that Dr Maitland had not meant to condemn Allied Projects especially since the archdiocese was one of the company's larger debenture holders. Three columns of comment stood beneath this basic information, but Maitland didn't care to read it now. He rose and felt exposed before the racket of cutlery and the reader's crisp evening voice. There was room for a thin man to move behind the line of chairs if it were done with care. A thin angry man could manage unprecedented things; such as to take the president by surprise, make him blink and drag the presidential chair, both hands on its seat, closer in to his spine. Maitland formulated to himself: "I am rampaging, the whole refectory must be able to see it. That sainted bastard. . . ." Who was by now seated and pouring mint sauce on roast meat. Aiming the rag neither at nor away from Costello's meal, he growled, "Thank you, doctor", began to feel silly edging past three other priests, all with dinners on their hands, his anger clinging to him like a morass. Free, he set his mouth, and his face admitted no guilt all down the length of the refectory.

He left the door of his room open, wanting Nolan and Costello to be able to find him. On his desk rested an old *Observer*—one of those corpses that occasionally surfaced there when masses of books or notes were shifted. He opened it straightaway to the potted cleverness of the stage and book reviews. They did not divert him. He would find himself holding the sane pages in clenched fists.

First came Costello. He took time to stand still and look dismayed. So Maitland snatched the first word.

He said, "Look, doctor, next time I make a gaffe, if that's what this is, I won't stand its being dropped on my plate."

"I *am* sorry." By which Costello meant that some people *were* edgy.

"Also you won't confront me at a time when I can't answer you in words."

"All right, all right." One worshipful hand was extended, conciliating the other. Maitland remembered that Costello might be archbishop one day, that that hand might have to be kissed. "But I have to say, we can get into terrible holes tackling social or economic matters. For one thing, society and economics aren't as simple as they were in the Middle Ages. You have to be trained to be clear on that sort of thing these days. It isn't as if there are howling inequalities any more. The country's happy."

126

Maitland remembered the Quinlans' suburb. "I wouldn't necessarily have noticed," he said.

"Oh, use your eyes, James. It's the patently artificial things a priest can safely attack. The mass media, materialism, advertising, the threat of Communism, paganism in the arts. Add all that to faith and morals and you've got enough for a lifetime of sermons." Costello snorted then, in self-effacement. "You don't mind, surely, my giving off all this? I mean, we're all equals and friends, let's hope. More than friends, brothers. I suppose a test of friendship is the amount of forced feeding of advice one friend is willing to take from another."

The patrician hand became an organ of friendship. Costello was a man of high personal standards, among which was included charity to the wrongdoer. Bound to defer to this ugly charity, Maitland shook the hand, saying, "I apologize if I've been rude. I'll remember it with embarrassment when you're a bishop—"

"Oh, that's the Holy Ghost's affair," Costello confessed spaciously.

"—however, if you attempt to *beard* me like that again, I'll be very angry."

"Of course you will." Costello looked mildly quizzical. "How quaint of you to be offended at that sort of thing. You should have warned me beforehand," said the eyes which were broad, bright, favourite-uncle's eyes.

An hour later, when Maitland, still unsoothed, had tried his breviary, his books, even, once more, his one copy of the *Observer*, Nolan arrived. His attitude paralleled Costello's. He entered apologetically, like one impinging on a tragedy. Old goat, thought Maitland.

"His Grace is on the downstairs phone, James." He stood back then, very morgue-attendant. "Enough said," said his face. On the dark stairs, the president told no one in particular, "His Grace is very upset about this. Upset and discountenanced." The antique word stuck abominably in Maitland's craw.

Just then the students were proceeding in a monastic

column-of-two's. Edmonds gave him a thumbs-up sign. He was glad there was a corridor to escape down.

"There," Nolan told him, and pointed to the booth, curtained, with an easy chair in it. Maitland glanced at its floral chumminess and felt abandoned.

"Your Grace?"

"This *does* put us squarely in the sights, doesn't it, James?"

"Your Grace, I am sorry."

"James, I detest this sort of embarrassment, you know, the type that gives hint that the Church is economically entrenched. My father was a French-polisher, and I know that he was far more genuinely shocked by a hint of the Church's wealth than he was by a dozen apostasies. Of course, there are still people who feel that way, who imagine that an archdiocese can be run without revenue, where an oil company can't."

Maitland could see Nolan, in attendance, halfway up the corridor. Not wishing to have the president miss the next sentence, he raised his voice.

"Your Grace," he said trembling, "is the archdiocese going to back me up by selling its holdings in both those companies?"

There was silence at His Grace's end, and Nolan had stirred from his shadows like a sentry from a box.

"My heaven, *that's* called turning the flank," His Grace decided, not without some hint of approval. "However, Mr Boyle, whom I've been speaking to, assures me that the companies are respectable and in no way depart from the norms of the business world."

"Your Grace, have you seen the way they advertise in the evening papers?"

"I don't read the evening papers. I have no interest in football or scatology."

Maitland closed his eyes, flying blind. He knew that as far as His Grace was concerned he had no right. . . . He said, "I know I have no right, but if you could judge their claims by your own standards. If you could make a comparison of what

128

these people *say* will happen to a buyer with what *does* happen to a buyer...."

He heard a flurry of sighs from the prelate.

"James, if I'd known you were attacking an established company, no fly-by-nighter, I would have been as angry on Monday as I am now."

"I see, Your Grace."

"The approved list of sermons exists precisely to safeguard young fellows like you from this very mistake. I'd be grateful if from now on you kept to it."

Maitland swallowed; there seemed to be a spur of dry bone at the base of his throat.

"Is that your command, Your Grace?"

After a silence, His Grace said in a voice that seemed to have been honed to a point. "I want you to do it willingly."

"Very well." But Maitland remembered, at that moment, the lawyer who had known Joe's contract by heart. "Your Grace, there's a lawyer...."

His Grace grudgingly took the lawyer's name.

The conversation finished; Nolan came near again. The unwelcome pity which bent his shoulder and made him obsequious as nurses are obsequious with the fantastically maimed, began to wake Maitland's anger again.

"James," said the president sentimentally, "I still have great faith in your future. Don't try to set the world on fire, though, that's my advice. We are expected to be men of the world." The head wagged, and the scalp and ancient hairstyle caught light from the corridor and mocked the man. "Our congregations don't expect violent social messages. We don't live in that sort of country. The Church is respected and has good standing without recourse to any of that sort of thing. That's why I recommended the approved list—and you mustn't resent my doing so. One can't very well open one's mouth too far by adhering to the list. Anyhow, it's cold here. Come upstairs."

On the stairs, Nolan's shoulders shivered. There was damp on the walls of the stairwell, damp enough to take glints from the lighted bottom landing. What it all threatened to the older, in fact, the *old* man, was croup, lumbago, neuralgia, rheumatism. If he had been a public servant he would have been retired by now, angrily scooping cut-worm out of his top-soiled lawn.

He turned to Maitland as they reached the first-floor landing. "Could I give you some advice?" he asked with a hint of timidity.

"Of course."

"Actually it's brief. You can't overdo orthodoxy. Conformity's a word people use a lot. Well, you can't overdo conformity when what you're conforming to is Christ's Vicar on earth. Now I see—and once more I'm sure you won't be pained—I see your (could we say?) *radical* attitude, your article on Luther, for example, and *this* disconcerting situation as connected. I don't think this would have happened if it hadn't been for your earlier recklessness."

"I don't think it would have happened if the Church had been more careful about whose dirty money it accepted."

Nolan shrugged. "Oh well, if you're going to talk heedless rot. . . ."

Maitland hastened to say, "I'm sorry. I'm vindictive, I suppose." His motive was that he played an incompatible Laertes to Nolan's Polonius and didn't want to hear any more.

"That's the third time you've been vindictive, James." The president had a memory for such things. "First, over those cousins of yours; secondly, over that Martin Luther article. I *have* some authority in this house, you know, and I'm getting tired of being paternal."

"I think I'd better simply apologize and go and do some work."

"Very well. Just let me say before you go—"

Maitland was in a panic of virulence. "I can't wait," he said. "I'm sorry. Good night."

In Maitland's room, Egan sat amid the clutter, not seeming at all alien to it. The *Observer* was in his hands and he had some undisclosed reason for gaiety—perhaps some decision regarding La Belle Tully. Standing up, he said, "A person misses out on some damned good films, eh?"

130

Maitland smiled dutifully. "I don't feel as guilty reading about films as I do going to see them."

"That's right. Especially when the bedroom scenes come on. You can feel people observing you—*I* can anyhow—and wondering what in the name of heaven you know about that sort of thing."

"Or musing on the orgies we traditionally have every second Monday with nuns."

"Or on priests' women," Egan suddenly said against himself and hung his head.

"Rubbish!" Maitland told him. "Besides, thou canst not have thy funeral tonight, Maurice lad, it being my turn in the graveyard."

All the time, Maitland exulted because Egan was there. Having a friend and knowing it went far towards filling his sparse needs.

"I came to see you about that," Egan admitted. "Would you like me to write to this rag saying that I uphold all your remarks?"

Maitland, not used to either greeting or having supporters, asked too gratefully, "Do *you* have something against these development people?"

"My dear James, I wouldn't know an acre from a rod, pole or perch."

"Then why. . . ? Not that you could involve yourself anyway. Not an official of the chancery."

"I trust your judgment, James. If you say these people are execrable, they are."

Nor was Maitland accustomed to having his judgment fêted. In carnival mood, he sat down to brew coffee for his friend.

On the following Monday, His Grace telephoned him once more and said, "I've sought advice, James." He kept on interrupting himself with short hacks of coughing and Maitland missed parts of sentences as the prelatial cold rumbled down the wires. ". . . consulted that lawyer fellow . . . meeting of the trustees and diocesan counsellors for tomorrow afternoon. I can take it for granted we'll be getting rid of that stock."

131

11

So that the next morning Maitland was firmly persona grata again. He was glad. To live in that grey elephant of a house on any other terms would have been a test of sanity he did not wish to undergo. Yet his success had its blemishes, as when Costello bombarded him with applause. Nolan, having carried so funereal a face on the question, kept clear. It was not until two mornings later, himself and Maitland passing vested for Mass and bearing chalices in the corridor behind the high altar, that Nolan smiled with an aged wistfulness and whispered, "So you talked His Grace round to your view of things."

During that brief springtime when Maitland seemed to bear His Grace's cachet, Costello came to him a second time and said, "It seems there's a nun in St Thomasine's College—that's across the city. She's apparently a little unorthodox, but the mother-superior has tended to be tolerant of her. However, two parents have complained now, and mother is shaken. His Grace is so far on your side over this other matter that he wants you to be one of the three members of a sort of informal inquiry."

Maitland, caught in his shirtsleeves and in contemplative mood, said, "I'm not a good inquisitor."

"It doesn't matter. I'll be there. I've done this sort of thing before. You just sit back and look as magisterial as all get-out and learn the ropes."

Moored on a hill against a high wind and vibrant south-easting clouds, St Thomasine's was neither as huge nor as Thomas Love Peacock as the House of Studies, yet fit to make hysterical any girl returning from summer holidays. Down to the last digit on its crass garden statuary, it seemed exemplary, the last place to harbour a radical nun. Inside was the browning winter light of institutions, waiting for them in the parlour like something they had been unsuccessful at leaving at home. Also waiting were Monsignor Fleming, the third member of the committee, and the mother-superior. Both were young sixty-year-olds. Their serge clothing lapped them about in unchallengeable snugness as they spoke of the signs of decline, angina and gall and kidneys, in old nuns and priests known to both of them. Introductions over, the mother-superior began to present the dossier on Sister Martin, the danger. She asked them to sit at the head of the table so that the thing would look judicial. She said reluctantly that she thought it had come to that.

"Sister Martin is a brilliant young woman, university-trained. If I say that I'm alarmed at her cynicism about questions of Church administration and history, you'll receive the wrong impression. She's gentle and pleasant and, practically speaking, docile. What I'm trying to say is this—I don't think that a Church history period should be an opportunity to describe how a medieval Pope was in such a hurry to go out hunting that he ordained some poor priest in a stable instead of a church. Nor to look into the lives of some of those Cardinals of pre-Reformation days."

Costello chuckled. "The sins of the fathers. . . ."

"Yes, doctor. But you see, one of the girls' parents complained. Two excellent Catholics. The mother is a member

133

of the Catholic Women's Guild committee, the father is an executive of the Knights of Saint Patrick. . . ."

Maitland blinked. He said, "Excuse me, mother. Not that it matters, but is the name of these people Boyle?"

The nun frowned as if an effort of memory were involved. "No . . . no. Not Boyle, father."

His sigh was too audible. He settled back to suffer the dull malaise that the brown light, the buffed pearliness of the oak table, the terrifying cleanliness-next-to-Godliness of the cedar floorboards, awoke in him. (The cobbler allergic to leather, the claustrophobic miner, were not more star-crossed than Maitland.) Beyond the window, girls yelped on the tennis courts; the resonance of nylon rackets came to him; and in some music room a child with a violin assaulted the jolly scarps of "Humoresque". None of it failed to add layers to his discomfort.

"They were very reluctant to complain," said the mother-superior of the exemplary parents. "They claim, however, that Sister Martin has criticized the traditional formulas of belief. Not violently. Firmly. I must make that clear to you. There is no arrogance in Sister Martin. Absolutely none."

"Have you questioned her about these matters?" Costello asked.

"Yes, doctor. That is how I know—not violent, but firm. She uses terms for almighty God which, it seems, were coined by Protestant theologians. She speaks of 'the ground of our being', although she has reservations about that term, as about all other terms."

Costello's eyes narrowed.

The nun said with a hint of pride, "I thought of letting old Father Royal speak to her, but the trouble is she'd run rings around him. Shall I fetch her now? Oh, her views on the sacraments are a little revolutionary." Her eyes dropped. She had the grace not to like what her conscience demanded, not to like giving up her sister to theologians.

"Before you go, mother. Did the parents complain on all these points?"

134

"No. Actually their sense of outrage centred mainly in that she'd called perpetual novenas magic."

"Did you ask her about that point, mother?" Monsignor Fleming said.

"Yes, Monsignor. She said that—well, that for her, magic wasn't necessarily a nasty word, that mankind deprived of magic wouldn't be the richer."

"You seem to be careful not to misquote her," Costello decided.

"Yes, I took notes of our interview and allowed her to reread and amend them. However, I am no expert, so I didn't think it quite just to burden you with them."

"You *have* been merciful, mother."

"She's a lovely girl. . . ."

"Sister Martin?"

"Yes, doctor."

Costello closed his eyes and made a harsh male sound with his sinuses. "There are questions, mother, on which we cannot yield an inch even to those we love." Maitland noticed for the first time that Costello had actually been taking notes of his own.

"I had better let her speak for herself," the reverend mother decided.

Waiting for Sister Martin, Costello and the monsignor sat up straight and ready, knowing that theology was a man's world and that here were men enough for the job. Maitland wished on the poor girl the guts of Joan of Arc, the wit of Héloise.

Costello told him, "James, we may not be able to observe all the amenities with this young lady."

"Why not?" Maitland was preparing to say. "She sounds civilized enough."

But then she came in; and in an attempt not to look judicial he took to playing with the cuff of his coat. It was impossible, though, massed at one end of a long table with an august theologian and a monsignor in purple stock, not to seem to be what he was. Which was, of all things, a judge.

She was young, with pale, fine-grained skin that reminded

135

him of Grete's. She said, "Good afternoon, monsignor, fathers," and waited like a schoolgirl to be invited to sit. Maitland blushed but lacked the courage; and in the end Costello glanced up and ordered her to take a seat. It was rudeness justified by the need for orthodoxy. Maitland became so angry at it that all he could do was sit on the rim of his chair and swallow. He thought, "One day, when you're a bishop, you'll be all worldly grace to the baggy wives of Q.C.'s."

As it was, the expanse of table between the three priests and Sister Martin too clearly imposed the status of culprit on the woman. The monsignor unexpectedly found it alien to his nature that it should be so, that the girl should be kept at such an inquisitorial distance. He pointed to the gas fire glinting inappositely under an antique mantelpiece.

"Bring your seat up where we can talk, sister."

The chair being massive, Maitland helped her shift it. "Here?" he asked, grounding it. "Thank you, father," she said. "Father" came out broken in two by a nervous lack of breath at the back of the throat. Maitland felt his profound lack of innocence. He was glad to return to Costello's side.

"What's all this then, sister?" Costello wanted to know. He smiled leniently, the sort of male leniency that provokes feminists. His fingers played sensitively with the edges of his notepaper. "Been scandalizing the parents?"

"It is possible for these things to be reported out of context by children," said the nun. "I believe I may have been reported a little out of context, father."

"Of course," the old monsignor said pacifically. "It happens."

Costello raised his voice. "Just the same, aren't some of the things you've said rather rash whether in or out of context?"

The nun told them, "When a class hasn't been fully prepared, it's unavoidable that something rash will be said."

"And you don't prepare your classes fully?" Costello asked her in a voice that only just managed to maintain basic human trust in her.

136

"We're very understaffed. It's impossible to prepare every class fully at the moment, father."

As a first principle to which he required her assent, Costello stated, "The teaching of the one true faith comes first, sister."

Seeing that she was not meant to win, "Of course," she said.

"Let us begin at the beginning," the doctor suggested. "I have always thought that God was God, sister, that we confuse the faithful by calling him by any tautological terms such as 'The ground of our being', and that other meaningless and downright blasphemous title, 'the God beyond God'."

Tautological terms such as 'Our father who art in heaven', Maitland thought. He began to wonder if he also were not the object of the inquiry—two anarchists for the price of one.

"Don't you agree, sister?" Costello persisted.

"When one spends all one's energies pursuing the vision of God, one is disturbed when people find it possible to say that God is dead."

"That God-is-dead business is just a university fashion."

"Partly, father, yes, but fashion is an extension of society. So that one is still alarmed."

The nun, her skin smooth with those cosmetics which Mother Church considered best for her—these being humility in argument, the seeing of God's will in the decrees of people such as Costello, modesty about the eyes—nevertheless managed her small ironies. Mainly by speaking to the tribunal as a whole, trusting to its joint good reason, using "father" in a collective sense. There was a marginal hint about her manner: that she did not trust entirely to Costello's good reason, that she did not consider him unqualifiedly as her father. This was so tenuous an implication that Costello would lose dignity by responding to it. Yet, while tenuous, it was also unmistakable. Maitland felt pleased with this nun. She underlined one of the few things he knew about women: that they were essentially ungovernable.

He himself broke in. "What do you think people mean when they say that God is dead, sister?"

"I hardly dare say," she answered immediately, but gave signs of being about to show considerable daring. "But human organizations limit God by identifying themselves with him. They express him in terms that accord with their nature and needs. Then the terms get old—like the organizations. The terms die." She glanced at Costello. "If I used the term 'God beyond God', which I can't really remember doing—but we're very busy—if I used it, it was to make the girls realize that no matter how old terms and organizations grow, the real God is still untouched and unknowable and speaks in silences."

Quickly she sat back, alarmed to discover herself eloquent before priests. She had, in fact, given the word "unknowable" a ring of triumph, of passion and blood. This helped bring all that was most arid to the forefront of Costello's mind.

"You say 'unknowable', sister," he observed. "What do you mean by unknowable?"

She tried to say, grimacing. "Words are a trap, father. Yet I suppose it is what you theologians would call unknowable in his essence."

That particular theologian became taut with delight.

"The first Vatican council rejected your opinion as heretical."

"Did they, father? It's so hard to express oneself, but then if one is a teacher one has to try. However, I'm sure we both ultimately agree, Vatican One and myself. So many of these theological squabbles are only matters of semantics."

"Are they, just?" said Costello.

"I was reading last week—" the girl began, and then, "Did you want me to continue speaking, father?"

"Why not? You're the informed member of the panel."

"Oh, no," she said softly. "I'm sorry. I realize how annoying it must be for a professional theologian to have to listen to me."

"At the moment you must speak. That is why we are here."

The monsignor smiled and assured her. "We're fair game."

For a second a small girl ran beneath the window taunting, "Boarders are getting cabbage for tea." The nun took her crucifix out of one place in her girdle and stabbed it back into another. Her flummoxed hands found this the first thing available for the doing.

138

"I was merely going to say that I read an article last week in an English review about Luther and Aquinas, that Luther meant by faith what Aquinas meant by hope, that Luther needn't have been excommunicated, and all that religious and political agony could have been prevented. The predicament we are in with words, you see. Now, when one speaks of God, one has to apologize for the poverty of words, one has to mistrust them. Yet we have to speak about the unspeakable, don't we?"

"Of course," old Monsignor Fleming said, as if for the sake of keeping well in the game. "But a teacher of the young has to be so careful, sister, so very careful. . . ."

In the meantime, Maitland, though not expert on legislation, decrees and anathemas, saw reason to suggest, "If I might correct an impression sister may have taken from what you said a moment ago, Doctor Costello. . . . I don't think that either yourself or the Vatican council intend to imply that Sister Martin is a heretic because she believes God is, as she says, untouched and ultimately unknowable."

Costello sighed. "Let me assure you, Dr Maitland, that that *is* what the Vatican council condemned."

"Of course, the relationship between man and God is personal and can't be legislated for," said Maitland. "All the council claims is that God can be known by reason. But surely not in his essence—whatever that word means."

"That is casuistry!" Costello cried out. He stared ahead of him. There was an unwonted pallor in the eye-pouch and cheek that Maitland could see. "How can something be known if it is not known in its essence?"

"Indeed," said the monsignor, who had none the less lost track of the hounds.

Costello announced, loudly but to no one in particular, "What I have said is aimed at proving the dangers of playing inexactly with theological terms."

Old Monsignor Fleming nodded. "It's done for many a good man. Look at the great Père Lammenais in nineteenth-century France. . . ."

But the other three had too much on hand to take this invitation.

"I must say in fairness to Sister Martin," Maitland enjoyed observing, "that she seems to have a profound sense of these dangers."

"No," said the nun herself, and meant it absolutely. "Not enough sense. Not enough."

"*Ipse dixit,*" said Costello. "Or should I say *ipsa*?"

There was a silence. The nun bowed her head, obviously accepting on it the blame for having spoken inexactly of the deity. Since this same guilt was shared by Moses, Augustine, John of the Cross, Teresa of Avila, Joan of Arc and an army of other master spirits, Maitland hoped she was proud of her crime. She gave no sign, however.

"And now, what about these sacraments?" Costello said, restored to victorious joviality.

After listening to Sister Martin on sacraments for a short time, and having watched that fool Maitland nodding his lean head, forbearing, perhaps even approving, Costello cut the drift of the girl's pleadings with one downward stroke of his hand. Passionless, breathing hard, he spoke.

"I have something to tell you, Sister Martin. I tell it without malice, merely with some sadness."

He once again made that sinusitic rumble already tested on the mother-superior. It sounded, and was almost certainly meant to be, male and harsh and mastering, gruff as a navvy's fart and, to Maitland's mind, even less creditable. "*You* are a modernist. And modernism is a heresy."

The woman sighed. *She* sounded feminine and soft as any deep waters; and indicted ever so slightly the vulgarity of the doctor's nasal cavities. "Do you wish to conclude I am a heretic, father?" she asked.

"Not yet." He waved his right hand spaciously. "We presume your good faith up to this moment. However, now that you have been warned. . . . I beg you, my daughter, in this hour of your extreme need, to prostrate yourself before Christ your Spouse and His Blessed Mother."

Maitland, speechless, battled for composure; as Monsignor

Fleming quoted, *"Woe unto him who scandalizeth a little one. . . ."* He was sure she had not merited millstones. But all those who dealt with the young had to be careful, so very careful.

Suddenly Costello became therapeutically kind. He said that he would draw up, prayerfully and with specific attention to her peril, a list of theology texts she was to con thoroughly. In the meantime, she should not teach the one true faith to children. After some months he would return and interview her once again. "Agreed?" he asked the monsignor, who certainly didn't want to seem severe, but thought that such a course was proper. Not that he didn't realize she did her level best. But until her small inaccuracies were cleared up. . . .

"Remember that you are the bride of Christ," Costello demanded of her, and shut his awe-struck lids.

Something began to pulse in Maitland's throat, and out of the pulse, full of the rhythms of his blood, grew unaccountably his voice. It swung across the room like a pendulum.

It said, "The bride does not need a formula for the bridegroom. Her knowledge of him surpasses formulas."

"That's all very well for the bride," Costello agreed after a silence.

"Exactly," said Maitland.

He told the nun, "I know each of the books Dr Costello has recommended to you. Let me say that you will find them alien, legalistic, sterile. None the less, perhaps mother-superior will order you to read them, and in that case you must not let them influence your life as a nun or give you despair."

The nun said, "I'd prefer you didn't continue, father."

"Ah, but preferences aren't your business. Dr Costello has made that clear enough. However, the only other thing I wanted to say was that I dissociate myself utterly from Dr Costello's concerted rudeness to you."

"Thank you," she told him with classroom firmness. "But, of course, I understood from the beginning that none of you was acting from spite."

As she was going, Maitland opened the door for her to pass

141

into the hall. Here the lights shone. Two barbarous statues, lollypop-coloured, postured across the void of carpet and stained boards, and, from a place where showers and taps ran, boarding students could be heard giggling towards cabbage time.

"Sister Martin," Maitland called after her from the door, "I haven't time to stand on ceremony. Have you—" He lost his temper at his powers of speech and ended in saying lamely, "Have you *seen* God?"

Behind them, at the far end of the parlour, Costello could be heard rumbling in judgment of this flourishing woman.

She smiled. "If I said yes, father, I could hardly blame you for calling me a liar."

"In this frantic world, how can a person be sure he isn't pursuing a nullity, or worse still, himself?"

"But what would you expect to be told, father? That you see God as you see a town clerk, at a given time on a given day? And as if by appointment?" She frowned. "Father, I don't think there's one being that pursues a nullity."

Costello coughed a summons to him. The nun formed a sudden resolve. She told him, "One knows by the results. Nothing is the same afterwards. Everything has a special . . . luminosity. You are able to see, well, *existence* shining in things." She shrugged, "Words again!" and seemed very sad.

"I have never experienced a more blatant attack on religious obedience," Costello told his notepaper softly as Maitland once more took the seat beside him. "If I were the type, I would count the number of times I have attempted to make you feel welcome in the happy brotherhood of this archdiocese. This is the second time I have been fanged as a result. I know that there'll be a seventh and eighth time. Therefore," and he made a large gesture of cancellation, "I wash my hands. Of course, I may relent. Christians are meant to be professional relenters. But I have rather genuine hope that once and for all, I have left you to your own juice."

The old monsignor chewed his lips and concentrated upon surviving the contretemps. Maitland did not make this task easier, contending, "No doubt, when the Holy Spirit sees fit

142

to raise you to the episcopate, you'll treat the society wives at charity openings with the same honest brutality you showed that girl."

"If ever it becomes necessary I will. Oh, what's the use of explaining old methods to novices? Do you know how to begin to rehabilitate a woman? Do you know what the basic step is? To make her weep. Once you have, the work can begin."

"That's barbarism."

"Ask any long-service husband," the doctor advised.

"Might I be excused? From the room, I mean. From the whole turn-out."

"You'd better wait till mother shows."

Costello kept working on the list of texts for Sister Martin and, when he was finished, showed it first to the monsignor, then to Maitland. In a short time, the mother-superior returned.

"Would a retreat be possible?" he asked her. "I believe that sister should make a retreat soon. There is a crisis of faith pending there, and it should be brought on quickly."

"My God!" Maitland said loudly.

"There are crises of faith in all directions," the doctor opined tangentially and gazed into the ordered depths of the gas fire.

Maitland stood and turned to the mother-superior. "Mother, thank you for having me. If I might be bold enough to say so, you gave signs earlier of thinking that perhaps you owned a jewel in Sister Martin. I concur utterly in your suspicions. Please don't burden her with those deathly books on Dr Costello's list."

"I don't think you can go that far, young fellow," the monsignor protested behind him.

"Believe me," said Costello, "he'll go all the way one of these days. All the way."

Maitland certainly went further there and then. "As for a retreat, silence can't hurt *her*. How far is it to the bus stop, please?"

"But surely Dr Costello would drive you. . . ?"

"Dr Costello is not safe at intersections," said Maitland. "Monsignor, it was a pleasure to meet you."

Outside, it was night in an avenued suburb. The leaves spoke elementally in the wind: you would never have known that they were all tame and pampered vegetables pollarded yearly by the municipal council. Maitland felt refreshed and free.

12

Egan kept at his work as earnestly as any earnest civil lawyer and plied the arcane rules-of-thumb of his trade. However implacably the climate of his court work and that of his regard for Nora must have mocked each other, his cheeks still were faultlessly barbered, the neat coat fell pat over his schoolboy hips. Only Maitland knew him as a man whose two poles were in opposite motion.

At the clerical pole, Costello's *Praelectiones* had been published. Its flight into the iron skies under which canon lawyers thought and functioned had been praised in all those journals that were professional meat and drink to Egan and Costello both. A colleague's success woke no jealousy in Egan; he did, however, suspect that he would never find *his* way into the beatitudes of the monthlies and quarterlies, against whom he had somehow sinned.

This void sense of unworthiness overtook him on the evening of Costello's further aggrandizement. Most of the staff had already come to table and were waiting to applaud the man's entry. A student, to whom not even Nolan listened tonight, read from the rostrum. As soon as the well-known meaty shoulder pushed the door open, and that head, which could rightly be called leonine, poked into the room, Nolan rose and rang the bell. Then all scraped back their chairs, stood and cheered Costello in. Egan, putting his hands together for his brother-priest, saw Maitland follow Costello through the door, to be transfixed by applause he could not understand. "Nobody has told him," thought Egan. "He is the only one in the entire house who does not know." And, aware now of what it was to be divorced inwardly from the striving of your peers, he spent his time in pity of Maitland's bemusement and hungry frame and poor soutane.

Meanwhile, Costello swam towards his seat through a miasma of applause. Unprecedentedly, Nolan made a gesture of largesse with his hand and gave the chief seat up to him. This prompted so solid a spate of acclaim that even Hurst's eyes were torn upward by it to rest on *that* face.

Maitland remained penned in the corner of the refectory, and began to blush for his intrusion on Costello's triumph. The doctor and he had said a merely polite good evening to each other, and Maitland offered no congratulations, in the corridor where two forty-watt bulbs had had no spare light to throw on Maitland's face and prove it honestly ignorant. Now he realized that he should acclaim whatever Costello had done—it was bound to be pretty impressive. He began to add his bit to the tail-end of the stamping, cheering, thumping approval. In the lull, while everyone found his seat, he tiptoed to his place at table. Passing Egan, he whispered, "Costello been nominated a bishop?" Egan nodded. "Three cheers for the Paraclete," said Maitland, and sat.

Nolan was waiting to speak and looked authentically humbled, like a man who has seen the mills of God grinding. He carried his head at just the right tilt to convey that this was another man's circus, not his.

"May I officially announce news of great joy," he said huskily. "It is news these consecrated walls were destined to hear

146

from the time a certain young man, more than twenty-five years ago, entered them as a brilliant student to become one of their finest products. The communication came from the Apostolic Delegate this afternoon that our respected colleague and mentor, Dr Costello, has been named by His Holiness the Pope as auxiliary bishop of this archdiocese and titular bishop of Umanes. *Te Deum laudamus.*"

Having meant every word of this, he closed his eyes and bowed his precise head. Everyone cheered rarely. And a long-disregarded viper, which had once whispered to him that he would be prince, stirred on a back branch of his brain-tree and forced him in conscience to smile fervently towards Costello; and go to excesses.

For he said, "It may be indecent in two ways to speculate on episcopal candidates as one speculates on racehorses. Firstly because they are sacred persons, secondly because one cannot make pious wishes concerning the future archbishop of a diocese without seeming to be casting the evil eye on the present holder of that sacred office. I am sure, however, that His Grace will forgive us tonight when I predict that His Lordship—as he soon will be—His Lordship Bishop Costello will one day be our archbishop and wear the red hat of a prince of the Church."

Maitland thought of Sister Martin and rejected the likelihood. He clapped, however, on the understanding that he was applauding Nolan for the valour of his guesswork.

"Reverend gentlemen," Monsignor Nolan called, his voice nearly expended in prophecy. "Reverend gentlemen, I present a new bishop."

There was such a raw and supreme joy in the Costello who rose then that Maitland's new resentment died utterly. It was impossible to be angry with anyone so powerless beneath an extreme happiness; it was largely impossible not to believe that a man of such blessed powerlessness would one day deserve a cardinal's hat.

"Gentlemen," Costello said, "this is a day that no man dare expect for himself. To be as frank as a man should be at such a moment, some people, our beloved president among them, have in the past told me that this was likely to come one day. Yet it is impossible to accept the basic fact, let alone imagine the overpowering sensation of election that a priest feels on hearing over the telephone that he will succeed the Twelve who sat at Christ's feet and heard infallible truth from his lips. I know that I stand here instead of better men. I know the time of crisis in which I have been chosen to lead. I do not flinch, because I am aware of your obedience and the strength of God. I know that I am able to depend on the truth of those words I have so often sung for other bishops. *Ideo iureiurando fecit illum Dominus crescere.* Therefore has God given His oath that he shall cause him to flourish. So may it be."

As he stared at the table-top, he, the pulpit orator, begging now for themes from the humble things of the table, the salt and condiments and the president's mustard-pot, the student Hurst rose pale and urgent from his seat and escaped the room.

Not having seen him go, Costello began again to speak.

"One wants to have the right words for an evening such as this. I believe I know what one of the right words is. Vigilance. Watch! *And* pray! Within the Church, tradition is under attack and, for the first time, the attackers are tolerated and, in some quarters, treated with leniency, even with favour. Our traditional theology is the object of scepticism, our traditional morality the butt of cynical raised eyebrows. Even the belief in a personal God is under attack."

One for Sister Martin and myself, thought Maitland, though he knew he flattered himself. Costello's just anxiety, like Costello's just happiness, was too universal for anyone to feel direct affront. But Maitland was grateful that the man had lost the nuptial air which, until a few seconds before, had exempted him from anything other than affection.

"The price we paid throughout centuries for this faith!" cried the speaker. "The price paid in Ireland, in England and Scotland and Germany and Holland! The price we have paid here! Our first priest a convict, political prisoner, shipped for months in a reeking hold, beaten in prison three hundred

148

times with a wire cat. If we are not vigilant within our own ranks, within our own minds, we will find that a great part of that price—the political persecution, the social opprobium our ancestors bore—will go for nothing. Our belief and moral code will grow indefinite and lose conviction; our structure of authority will be weakened to the point of chaos. Though we know that the Church will last for ever, we know also that it has at times grown sick almost to the point of extinction. This could happen again, within our life-span. For chaos can be bred at a thousand times the rate of order. And if chaos does come—and here I pledge my strength to see that it does not—it will not be due to assault from without. It will be caused by priests, above all by priests." In a hush, he said, "We are, or will be, priests. Will we be the so-called liberals, the so-called modernists, the so-called humanists, corrupted by expediencey, rotten with existentialism, at whose door will be laid the blame for the ruin of the Church as we know it?"

Every face seemed to shine with a negative. Even Maitland, who knew that the besetting sin of oratory was the sacrifice of the true for the glib, found it hard to remember that Costello had assumed that all the price which had been paid needed to be paid. It was a claim at least open to argument, though Maitland would not have liked to argue it tonight with this splendid, joyous, savage man.

The splendid man was saying, "I will be leaving you soon, leaving this house which has been my home, more often than not, for a quarter of a century. If I had one favour to ask of you before I go, it would be this. That you pledge your wit's end to prevent the ruin of which I have spoken. And the second thing is, remember me."

Perhaps, now that Hurst had galloped, only Egan and Maitland and a few others refrained, for their various reasons, from what is usually called heartfelt applause. Physically speaking, they clapped themselves dizzy, like the others.

Afterwards, in the parlour, liqueurs and coffee were drunk by the staff. Egan sat primly withdrawn, smiling at his cup of unlaced coffee, leaving the spadework of conviviality to the

149

drinkers. James waited with apologies on the fringe of Costello's vision. Tonight, when the air of the house was heavy with fruition, and the parlour smelt like an officer's mess, it was easy for the bishop-elect to keep a circle of priests laughing.

"That's the fellow," said Costello. "The little pansy fellow with gold-rimmed glasses. What's his name?"

"Monsignor Garossi," Maitland suggested in the peculiar desire to be recognized.

"That's him—Garossi. Well, when I went to the phone, I could hear him clear his voice like a contralto. Then he said, *'Hayc ayst Daylaygatio Apostoleecah.'*"

Everyone found this version of an Italian nobleman's Latin side-thumpingly funny.

"I said, 'Do you mean to say *Haec est Delegatio Apostolica*?' He said, 'Thatsa what Ia say. *Hayc ayst Daylaygatio Apostoleecah.*' I said, 'I see. But I thing I unnerstanna your English better.'"

Slack with brotherhood and emotion, Monsignor Nolan chuckled and felt his lids sting with tears. "It won't be the same without you, Cos," he called, and was convinced of it.

"He said, 'Dottore Cosatello. I haffa da grata plesser. *Permetta che io annoncio. Tu nominatus eras episcopus.* Da tellegrama she jost arife.' I said,'*Kyrie eleison.*'"

While his brothers laughed again, the coming man of God rolled a bitter-sweet sip of whisky around his mouth. Swallowing it, he sobered.

"I hope it happens to you all one day. God knows you all deserve its joy but not its terror. But, blessedly, it comes fast, without warning. Election descends as swiftly as death."

"And leaves one just as breathless, no doubt," ventured Nolan.

"Indeed. Indeed."

In the pause, while most took refuge in their cups, Maitland began to speak.

"Doctor," he said, "you must have thought that I deliberately neglected to congratulate you. You remember, when we met in the corridor tonight? The fact was that I must have

150

been the only one in the house who didn't know about the good news. I'd been working. . . ."

Costello frowned, saying gently, "There's no need, there's no need. . . ." One way or another, Maitland's excuses came close to making him wince. Perhaps he was as disquieted by Maitland's good faith as Maitland had occasionally been by his.

"You'll notice now," someone said, "that all the ambitious men on the staff will take to print."

"If we can't do anything better, we'll write novels."

"Or some of this new poetry," Nolan decided. When he said "new poetry", he meant Ezra Pound. "And how that Gerard Manley Hopkins could write all that barbaric verse and then approach the altar of a morning. . . ."

"The man had verbal diarrhoea," said a Scripture scholar. "I was never brave enough to say so in my youth. But one is less scared of fashions as one gets older."

"The man was a Jesuit," Costello muttered, and solved the question with laughter. "All those poor Protestant youths who have to decipher him in the universities! It pays them back for the Reformation."

When he raised his cup to his lips then, a third of those in the room did likewise. But it was a feint on Costello's part; rather than drink, he extended his half-smoked cigarette towards Maitland. "Would you mind getting rid of that for me, James?"

Nor did this seem too exorbitant a toll for anyone to pay to the man's ease tonight. Not only did Maitland almost accept the butt, but no one in the room weighed the request and found it strange until Maitland shook his head. He could see in Costello's sovereign-looking cheeks the assumption that no one could refuse him anything so simple, decent and do-able as this. There was even the assumption that no one could refuse him anything so simple, and not become a pariah.

The other priests were becoming aware of the new bishop's hand stretched out in this strange way, the gesture of an instant given too long an existence because Maitland stood resisting. They were all men who had their pride, yet they would not forget this refusal. "When I am sent away from here," Maitland knew, "this will be quoted as one of my final indecencies."

He said softly, "It is your *episcopal* ring that I am supposed to kiss, My Lord."

Which left him one thing to do: put down his cup and flee.

It was a night so clear that Maitland could see in the Milky Way the stars within stars within stars. Under worlds that flew free of diocesan strife, he went walking, felt the smooth air part and let his head, disembodied by pique, forward into successive planes of starlight. He followed the terraces and hedges. A quarter of a mile away the sea moved, scaled by the lights of the House of Studies. Down there the scales broke on a lovers' beach where a girl had once been murdered for love, for not being a tepid and equivocating being like Dr Maitland.

One level of the gardens brought him, thinking kindly of the girl, to a long grassed platform, a chalky surface shining dully between tussocks. This, the sea and the clarity of things, reminded him of the Adriatic coast, visited two European summers past. He stood imagining himself parish priest of some Balkans-facing village; a moon-dream after anger, incised two minutes later by a metallic bark from his left.

He saw at once that this was a place where any Alsatian would be pleased to wander at night, and his ankles cringed since he feared big dogs. The ravening noise came again, revoking the temperate climate of the platform, producing the feel of Dartmoor. Then, however, Maitland could see a face of luminous pallor, perhaps fifteen yards to his right; and as he stared at it, the bark rose but extended itself to a clatter. He was so pleased to forgo the Alsatian that he called good night and went to see. In a small bowl of grey earth, the student called Hurst had a hole dug and seemed to be burying the cutlery.

Maitland said, "Good night. What in the name of. . . .?"

He could see the blemishes around Hurst's mouth, which

was open and gulped. It was not a face suited to digging.

It said, between struggles for breath, "I'm not mad."

Hurst stared into the hole he had dug. At the bottom lay a drawer of dinner-knives.

"I don't suppose it will do any good to bury these."

"No, I don't think it could."

He peered violently at Maitland, then back at the cutlery. "My God," he said. "What have I been doing?"

"Never mind. Do you want me to help you? Getting them back to the kitchen, I mean."

The young man held his breath to convulsive lengths and let it go in sobs.

"I'm not mad. These things were a direct occasion of sin to me. You know. It *sounds* mad, but. . . ."

Maitland slid into the hole, thinking, Another triumph for Western Christianity. He asked Hurst, "Did you get much dirt in them?"

"I don't know. Not much."

"Well, we can just slip them back into the kitchen."

He scrabbled his hand in under the corner of the thing. Hurst watched, jabbing at tears, warning, "It's very heavy."

It was, in fact, as heavy as a strong-box and, when first edged from its bed, growled like an animal. Maitland laughed and told Hurst, "When I heard that noise a moment ago, I thought it was an Alsatian. Come on."

They made a coffin-bearing silhouette against the clear heaven, but there was no one to see them, and the nuns had gone from the kitchen to their early night-prayers. As his arms began to feel the strain, Maitland grew improperly angry. He could remember leaving his room at night, a God-struck eighteen-year-old, to roll drums of tar, used for path-mending, off this very platform, lest his brethren stumble over them on their evening walks. Now as the memory of himself at eighteen, performing moral idiocies in the moonlight, nettled him, so did Hurst. There was something particularly insufferable about grunting indoors to find that someone, as if to underline Hurst's fatuity, had left a honed kitchen-knife on the chopping board.

"I'm supposed to be at study," Hurst said, rapidly espousing the sanity of timetables.

"No, I think you need a bit of supper. Come upstairs."

"I'm not mad, doctor. I simply don't want you to jump to conclusions."

But he followed Maitland. It was not yet time to ask what grudge he bore cutlery. He was still in a state where he took it for granted that many a good life and mind had been ruined by an improper attachment to table-knives. Within twenty minutes, though, breathing into a cup of coffee in Maitland's room, he was able to speak about his strange anguish as about a symptom. So Maitland, eleven years past, having rolled drums half the night, strode into the lecture hall at nine the next morning and explained Leibniz's theory of monads with utter lucidity.

"Used you confess this sort of thing?" Maitland asked him.

He used. Usually once every two or three days.

"What used your confessor say?"

Hurst gave an outline.

"My God!" Maitland called out. "Why did you keep on patronizing him?"

"He seemed so—self-contained."

Maitland said, "Believe me, for your sanity's sake, he gave you some benighted advice."

"Did he?" begged Hurst, grimacing with an effort of hope. "I thought I was the benighted one." And, within a few seconds, thought it again. "It's impossible, Dr Maitland. You heard the brilliant sort of thing he said tonight. Look, his—composure stood out so clearly I felt I had to get out of the refectory."

"I saw you go." Maitland squinted in a futile effort not to ask, "You're not speaking of Dr Costello?"

"Yes. He's my confessor."

Despite layers of insouciance and a passable acquaintance with the history of the Church, Maitland was still appalled to find that Rome had chosen badly. He decided to be rash.

"You've got only your own and my word for it, and you'll probably find out that Costello resents me perhaps more than

154

I resent him. But believe me, you have been perilously advised."

Hurst stared into his tranquil coffee again, and addressed it as if reading Costello's features there.

"His motives were good. He didn't want me to seek treatment because he thought the whole business would pass. And he thought it might endanger my chances of ever becoming a priest. As you know, a person needs Monsignor Nolan's vote to be ordained priest. And you can't go to a psychiatrist without his permission, and he never seems to forgive anyone who does so. So," Hurst ended hopelessly, "there you are."

"And it's bloody infantile."

"Just the same, I want to be ordained a priest."

"As if it were your fault and not theirs!"

"Perhaps it is mine, doctor. It was impossible, listening to Costello tonight, to think of him as a man at fault."

"Even if he threatened to put his episcopal boot up your. . . .? Pardon me, Hurst, I was already angry with the man when I met you this evening."

"It's strange," Hurst admitted, "but I've always found him oddly disgruntling." He raised his eyes tentatively and smiled. "Isn't it strange how often you want to be like people you don't even like?"

"I suppose it is."

Since Costello's spirit filled the house to splitting, these two men who had scores against him were bound to brotherhood of a kind; two members of an underground. In celebration of their freemasonry, Hurst's sight kept taking small excursions along Maitland's bookshelves. He seemed expectant, this young man of twenty-two who had felt called by the devil to gut clerics and by God to bury the cutlery. He was twenty-two and innocent, a believer in books, a believer in the Incarnation, Christ's light yoke, moral theology, and his own fundamental depravity. Now he rested in the certainties and in the false peace that follows excess or exposure.

Considering whether he should turn the matter over to Costello's discretion, for the man could not be a thorough fool and had never had for guidance the potent sight of Hurst actually interring the knife drawer, Maitland rose and plugged in the hot-water jug once more. This stood on two volumes of Migne's *Patrology*, probably the two most valuable books he owned. He thought, "If I brew up coffee on Migne, can I pretend to outraged sanity when faced with Hurst's exploit?"

Hurst said, "I want to see a doctor. And I want to be ordained a priest."

Maitland nodded. "Let me tell you this. In a camp for suicide pilots, the prime goal in life for all personnel would be to successfully and at all costs kill oneself. Here it is to manage at all costs to be ordained priest. So that you may think that a mad priest—we'll let the word stand—is less mad because of his priesthood than the mad gas-fitter or clerk or short-order cook. You may think too that the torment of a sick priest is more desirable and consecrated than the torment of a sick anybody. As they say in the films, 'Forget it, Buster!' "

"I know," Hurst said, sounding hurt.

"I'm sorry. No doubt you're full up of being advised floridly by your elders. But being a priest isn't everything."

"Did you think so, at my age?"

"It doesn't make you of a different race. The basic duties are human ones, surely. To get back your—"

"Sanity?" Hurst suggested.

"Equilibrium," said Maitland with relief, after thumbing through the poor *Roget's* of his mind. "Which is a different thing altogether from merely avoiding going mad. Am I being too dogmatic. . . .?"

"You make my prospects sound remote," Hurst accused him, and Maitland was overcome with peevishness at this boy so willing to swallow all Costello's pietistic guff, so resistant to basics.

"The trouble is, you want to be comforted, but comfort won't take you any distance. You want the same old ineffectual elixir. To be told that you must immerse yourself in God, submit yourself with an utter submission on all levels of your being. To be told, too, to stop worrying about the compulsion

156

to cut peoples' balls out—" Hurst quickly shut his eyes—"and leave the onus of the matter on God."

The boy, who had gone grey with quiet anger, asked, "Isn't it all the truth?"

"Of course it's all true. But you can't do any of it. Neither can I. And when we can do it, we'll be more or less perfect. We'll taste God face-to-face and dive into death like a trout."

"That'll never happen. And whose fault is it?"

"Without being maudlin, I think we're two good lads ruined by the poisonous old idea that will-power will get you anything." Maitland raised his hand and outlined the words he spoke, as if they were bannered in carnival-sized letters across the room. *"You can be a saint this month if you want to be! Suppress the wild provinces of the spirit! Put a lid on the stew!"*

The jug began to shudder, and Maitland spooned into Hurst's cup the cheap coffee powder he bought each week. Every time he intended to ask for something that tasted less like granulated cardboard, but always concluded, once he breasted the grocer's counter, that a brain-clot might finish him any old night and make inane the quest for a better coffee.

He said, "Yes, you can be a saint if you want. But then, what's the use of the idea of the divine, what's the use of mystery, rite, myth, the whole caboose, if you can be the man you want to be?" He poured the hot water. "In another sense, Hurst, we *are* the men we wanted to be. Except that we've gone off on ourselves, like time-bombs or something. The old explosive idea of God went off in our faces. You, Hurst, are the maimed laboratory worker, and the management won't be happy. God damn them!"

Hurst was still angry. "God," he said, "provides the grace that vivifies the will."

"Don't make me sick! Here, drink this. I'm not very kind, am I?"

"Nothing to worry about."

"As a matter of fact, there's all the hope in the world for you."

"Is there all the hope in the world of becoming a priest?"

Hurst's mouth, which seemed never to have emerged from adolescence, quivered with yearnings bred on ordination speeches, treatises on the priesthood, Lacordaire's sermon. There was an almost feminine, and therefore—to Maitland—alarming quality of sorrow in that mouth ringed with scars of boyhood pimples not yet quite outgrown.

Maitland lied to a face that begged lies. "Why not?" he said.

In that case, said Hurst, binding him, would Dr Maitland consider arranging a visit for him to a doctor. If they had expert opinion, they'd know better how to approach Dr Nolan without damaging the good chances Dr Maitland had just assured Hurst he had.

"I could slip out one afternoon."

" 'One' is the word," Maitland said. Nervously. A person got inured to the tone of the house and thought of his standing. And found it not too grotesque that adults should be required to abstain from psychiatrists; psychiatrists being usurpers of Nolan's overlordship of spirits. "After one visit I do the Herod and soap act. Then it's up to you, God, and Nolan."

He would have thought that breakfast was to be a trial, to sit and suffer that frigid attentiveness by which the outrageous are passed the sugar and salt without delay. So it was that the bacon dish came to him from Nolan like a symbol of isolation. Yet one of the younger priests leant and whispered to him, "I enjoyed that. If Cos has one fault it's that he's a little bit lordly. It isn't good for bishops to be lordly."

So Maitland forgot himself and had a good breakfast.

After morning thanksgiving in chapel, Egan, who could have strolled down the hall with the president and the bishop-elect, chose to talk to Maitland, chose to be openly companionable.

"What do the staff think?" Maitland asked him.

"I'll be frank, James. They thought you could have been a whit less pungent."

158

Maitland laughed gently and without malice at the small priest's courtly choice of words.

"However," Egan pursued, "if our honoured friend has any fault...."

"Oh, I think that's established," said Maitland. "I've seen him exercising a fault or two."

"Indeed. And his faults all stem from a certain pomposity of temperament."

"I couldn't have said it better."

"I think it will do him nothing but good."

Maitland saw that the certainty with which a *defensor vinculi* should lay down his judgments shone in Egan this morning.

Maitland whispered, "You seem very much at one with the world this morning."

Egan rolled his eyes, meaning, "There are reasons." Taking Maitland's elbow, he guided him through the traffic of break-fasted students and cornered him against one of the appalling fluted pilasters. It was, besides decisive, an extravagant gesture for Egan, and James saw now a hard excitement, not completely joyous, in the man's eyes.

"Nora is flying to London in two weeks' time. Thank God she has the money."

"It will be better for you then, won't it?" Maitland said.

Egan hissed, "Yes. Yes. It's our salvation. Nothing less."

"I suppose there are ways in which it causes you—" he shrugged; he was ill-acquainted with lovers' terms—"heart-burn."

"Oh, no," said Maurice swallowing. "Well, yes, I suppose. But heartburn doesn't count. She has the money to do it and she's doing it." He laughed in brittle joviality. "The rich certainly have the advantage on the poor when it comes to avoiding the occasions of—of sin. The rich can do it by inter-national jet."

Suddenly he was so proud of Nora's background that he let James out of the corner and they walked on. "Did you know that Nora and Celia and their brother own between them thirty-five thousand acres of grazing, the very best hotel in half a dozen country towns, and three or four racehorses? The brother manages the property and Celia manages the racehorses. He has told me stories of things Celia has done to jockeys that would fill you with pity for the poor fellows."

"That's not hard to believe," Maitland told him.

"No. Whereas Nora has a talent for—what do they call it? They have professorships in it these days. Yes, hotel administration. She managed the premier hotel in W——."

Once more the native name that Nora had spoken while drunk evoked red peppercorns, red earth, and jagged atoms of light; and the desire to catch a train to these things.

"That was before her sickness. It serves to show you that before her sickness she was very capable, very even in temperament."

"Speaking of sickness, Maurice, do you know the name of a good psychiatrist? I think he'd need to be a Catholic, but not party-line. Someone who has a jovial contempt for that cockeyed organ known as the Catholic conscience."

Egan laughed. "You're very unorthodox, James." He looked sly. "I have just the man," he said.

13

Maitland had not yet finished having adventures with newspapers.

It was an opulent winter afternoon. Light lay on the eye like a veneer of the best quality, and the indoor dimness of the house seemed enriched to mahogony. Maitland was seated at his desk, stifling the urge to sleep or go out strolling, when Nolan came in without knocking.

The president was a known after-lunch napper. He was, at that moment, stripped to black trousers, slippers and flannel shirt. The shirt, like everything else about Nolan, spoke to Maitland of a lost and naïve age, of sombre flannel-shirted fathers standing before a basin of water set down on a black-butt stump, ritually washing red grime and sawdust from their arms. Nolan's paternity within the house was of this flannel-shirt era—strong and remote, and so piquantly old-fashioned that it could not fail to convince those who survived it that it had been what every young cleric needs.

The monsignor's Adam's-apple, chicken-fleshed from the

161

work of cut-throat razor and anno Domini, jiggled as he swallowed back the bitter juices of his late lunch.

"I knew you shouldn't have touched that land business," he told Maitland.

"I beg your pardon."

"That land business. It's not our sphere. As I warned you."

Nolan's anger seemed to Maitland to have emerged unexpectedly from the president's pre-nap musings, to have moved so powerfully in him as to make him rise and tramp down the hall to chastise the difficult young man.

Maitland shrugged, "I simply thought it was my sphere."

"You have a cousin involved in all this? Some post-office employee?"

"Some post-office employee." Maitland nodded.

"Yes. Water's thicker than blood with him."

"I beg your pardon."

"He's not backing you up in this matter. There are some people downstairs to see you. From the press. I think you should speak to them. Your cousin has."

Maitland could have kicked a chair or pounded the wall or even Nolan. The way in which his petty adventures in benevolence returned to their dead-letter office in this stale old man was, for the moment, intolerable.

"There's no need to dress," said the stale old man.

Which prompted Maitland to put on his soutane; to show that he was not racked by curiosity and that the pleasure of being effectively mum and augurial all the way downstairs would not be Nolan's. Similarly, he took the time to fit his collar on.

"Hurry," Nolan said.

In the vestibule, Maurice Egan seemed to be holding back a tide. One of the leaves of the double door was held open with a firm pink fist, the other pushed shut with the shoulder. He stood so heroically that it might have been the Goths or Charles V's German mercenaries or some other raucous body of anti-clericals that he opposed there. In fact the only raised voice was Egan's own.

"No, no," he was saying. "It isn't my place to ask you in, I'm sorry. It's Dr Maitland's affair."

"Do you know they've gone to the trouble of sending a photographer?" Nolan was provoked into asking as they traversed the arms of the marble cross inlaid in the vestibule floor.

Beyond the door a polite blonde showed no desire to force an entry. A photographer stood by her, frowning over his flash.

"Good afternoon," Maitland called to them over the pudgy stanchion that was Egan's left arm.

The girl said quietly, "Dr Maitland, I'm sorry to worry you. But the editor thought it only fair that you be given a chance to comment."

"Comment? Excuse me, Maurice." He edged around Egan's shepherding form and onto the porch. "Comment?"

The girl sighed and handed Maitland a folded galley proof.

"I wonder could you hurry, father? We have no more than forty minutes to get your reply into copy."

Maitland read that Allied Projects were seeking legal advice over accusations recently made against the company "from a pulpit in this city". It was believed that the managing director of the company had been referring to Dr James Maitland, a Catholic priest, who had recently made a withering attack on land-developers. No one more thoroughly respected the clergy than the managing director, but. . . .

"And here's something volunteered by your cousin." The girl offered another proof.

Joe had said that he was amazed by his cousin's attack on Allied Projects. Joe had merely outlined the details of his contract to his cousin and found that his cousin had become very angry and threatened to preach against land-developers. There had been a misunderstanding; Joe himself was satisfied with the deal he had made with Allied Projects.

"None of this would be of any value," the girl explained, "if so many people hadn't taken an interest in Monday's feature on yourself. Do you think we could have another photograph? We may not use it, but it's editorial policy. They like to be able to put, 'Today's picture of So-and-so'. As if it made any difference."

"It does make a difference. People will study it by the thousands to see if they can find lines of fanaticism in it. Just the same, no, I'd rather you didn't take another."

"I applaud that decision," Nolan muttered.

"Please," the girl said, "it would make things so much easier for me."

"If you have to," sighed Maitland, and composed himself. The camera sparkled once in the dusk of the porch.

"Could you stand against that bit of stained glass, father."

Maitland obeyed and smiled radiantly, a regular Bing Crosby of a priest. In fact Allied Projects' legal advice, the hint of law suits, Joe's denial, all stimulated him to a mild gaiety. The photograph was taken and, as he moved back to the debate, another unexpected one. After which the photographer seemed to be having trouble with one of his camera's attachments.

"You see, I've put a curse on that thing."

"Instead of acting the fool," the president hissed at his back, "why don't you say you didn't mean any particular company? Why don't you draw attention away from yourself by saying you didn't mean this crowd . . . whatever their name is?"

"Did you want your cousin's money back for any particular purpose?" the girl said.

"Did he imply I wanted it as a votive offering?"

"He implied you might have wanted him to give some of it to a church fund."

"See," Maitland told Nolan, "I'm not a complete write-off yet." He said to the girl, "Something like a new refrigerator for the good nuns at the orphanage, who haven't even got anything to keep their beer cold?"

The girl sighed.

"I began interfering in this matter at Joe's request," Maitland claimed, "But you mustn't say so."

Nolan said, "That's just what you should say. You interfered at your cousin's request, but you didn't mean to offend any particular—"

"Why would your cousin take the trouble to come forward and say this?" She tapped the appropriate galley.

"He must have been induced. He's married, you see. And if I were as married as he is, I'd be easily induced too. But of course you mustn't say that, either."

"What are we to say?"

"That I stand by my sermon, I suppose. That's about all I can say."

"You could say that you didn't mean. . . ." Nolan suggested a third time.

"But they're obviously contemplating a libel suit," the girl told Maitland.

"That's all there is to say."

"I see." The girl closed her notebook and smoothed the front of her long hair with one hand. Even to Maitland's celibate eye, it looked an unmistakably fishwifely gesture and would one day signify the last chance of at least one good man.

Maitland said, "Joe is lying. I congratulate whoever it is made him lie. I wish him well of any spoils and advise him strongly against shame, which is the curse of his breed. . . ."

"That sort of stuff is useless," the photographer ventured—reasonably, lest one of Maitland's deep Latin malisons extend the curse to his exposure-meter.

"I suppose so. Perhaps I should give your readers a tip for the three-thirty."

The president knuckled Maitland in the back. "You have a responsibility to this house."

"Well, come on, Glenda," the photographer said.

Already their special car stood idling beneath the stairs; all that proud metal and cylinder-capacity waiting their grumbling, at great expense to the company, simply so that today's unsatisfactory statement by Dr Maitland could be got into the hands of the four-thirty masses.

Glenda gave them a steely good-day. Egan closed the door tenderly. The afternoon light shelved through the shut door

165

and the windows peopled with Irish saints, and Nolan's flannel shirt was spotted with the gay eczema of stained glass.

"You could have faced the accusations far more firmly," said Nolan, unaware that his old working-class shirt had been glorified. "You didn't even *try* to maintain a responsible attitude."

"I sulked," said Maitland still touched by unseasonable glee.

"Don't joke, James. *Sulk* is almost exactly what you did do."

Egan had an opinion. Not one to take sides, he stared at the middle distance and looked disturbingly like that rare creature, the informed observer.

"I think Dr Maitland demonstrated that he would not play the game on their ground. I think that was the correct thing to do. As if that piece with the blonde hair has a right to extend or withhold her mercy. . . ."

"That's very well by individual standards," Nolan spat at them. "But the priest isn't an individual. He's a corporate being with duties to the rest of us. I don't believe you have fulfilled these duties, James, as seriously as you might have. 'Perhaps your readers would like a tip for the three-thirty.' Is that the proper way to face dangerous possibilities?"

"It *is* my dangerous possibility, monsignor. I believe I sufficiently own it to do what I will with it."

The president said, presidentially woeful, "I shall telephone the archbishop."

"Not before I do."

"I beg your pardon?"

"You aren't to telephone before I do. It's my place. . . ."

Nolan gestured widely through the stone walls at the vanished reporters. "When they were here, you didn't seem to know what your place was."

"Just the same, I'm not so corporate that I need other people to make my telephone calls."

The president pretended an interest in his left, perhaps arthritic, priestly hand. There were blotches of blue on it the size of coins.

"By all means, contact His Grace first if you want to. Perhaps there is still time for you to emerge with credit—though I can't see it. Let me know when the line is free."

The old man left. Keeping to the walls of the stairwell, he stopped halfway up to huff beneath a glacial window where St Brendan eyed the Atlantic and a boat full of his deathless sailor-monks. The president bowed his head for a second here, and Egan and Maitland, watching from below, saw the two captains, who each knew what it was to have one unruly tar in the crew, seem to commune.

On the other hand, His Grace was merely sad; with a sadness that implied a fault, no more, but a definite boyish fault in Maitland. Maitland, not seeing any reason why he should apologize, yet did apologize at length.

It proved, later in the day, that the blonde had been moderate with him. She got into print that he stood firmly behind his sermon; and this in a paper that did not run much to adverbs.

14

Egan began again to insist that he should confess to Maitland. It was as if he wanted to add sacramental dimensions to the bare human fact that they shared a secret.

"Bless me, father, for I have sinned," Egan muttered. "It is five days since my last confession."

Maitland, sitting stoled at the prie-dieu where Egan knelt, blushed at the formalities. But to Egan a confession was a confession, that is, a sacrament and a tribunal. He would take no liberties with the judge, whatever the judge intended.

"Why I came tonight, father—James—is that now Nora is going, I see that my motives for continuing to meet her over the past months, and in a variety of places, were not always for the best, for her sanity or mine."

Maitland, keeping his head averted, said, "Come off it, Maurice! Do you really see yourself as guilty? Or do you simply want to talk things out?"

"I see myself as guilty," Maurice insisted.

"Very well. I'll absolve you. That's simple. I wish that idiot would quieten down."

Once more the sound of the broadcasting van that had plagued the suburb downhill for the past half-hour, penetrated the ill-fitting windows; the sound of gear-changing, and of spoken but indistinct things to do with some fête or festival or fair. The loudspeaker pulsed with the excitement of hoop-las and merry-go-rounds, though the individual banalities could not be heard. All the more reason for them to assume that it was summer and a season of promise at the bottom of the hill and to wonder at how even *their* innocence had gone hollow.

Egan said, "I very nearly went to see Nora tonight. I could easily persuade her not to leave. Now, there's no ignoring the fact that it's an exciting business for any man to have that sort of power. A heady thing, James. Quite genuinely, I need the grace of the sacrament."

The broadcast voice receded with its undisclosed wonders.

"How long before she goes?"

"Thursday morning. Three days. If I saw her again, it would be impossible to hide, even from myself, that I'd be doing critical harm to both of us."

The sober skull nodded inarticulately, in a way that left Maitland convinced that Egan was not merely playing at guilt.

"Perhaps it mightn't be as deadly as all that," Maitland said. He went on lamely and compulsively, as one speaks to the bereaved. "Just the same, if you've decided, both of you, that it's best for her to go to Europe, you're probably wise not to visit."

"I know," Maurice contended. "If I visited her, it would be the end." By "the end" he meant something unspeakable, uncanonical. "I've already done unlimited damage at numerous times over the past year. Mainly by convincing myself, or letting myself be convinced, that I mustn't give her up to this Celia, that I was performing a necessary charity. Now I see it was probably never necessary. It's certainly done her no benefit."

Mentally he surveyed this hard decision, and then reasserted it. "Yes, not the least benefit that I can count. I don't know

169

how guilty I have been, James, but there's always guilt in a case like mine."

Maitland readjusted the stole about his neck, as if it chafed. "You've no right to decide that. I'm the judge and I haven't got the right either."

"You *are* the judge, James. Just the same, I'm a man who has always lived by principle until now, and I have always expected others to live by principle. On the basis of principle, I haven't shrunk from telling women that they can't use contraceptives no matter how much trouble their husbands make. I have advised lovers to abandon their beloved rather than marry against the prescriptions of the Church, and ordered policemen not to take subtly disguised bribes. All on principle. On principle, I've commanded ordinary people, who have no stake in the divine, to do exceptionally brave things. On principle, and in the name of a higher mercy. But when I met Nora I forgot principle and the higher mercy. I decided what was better and best for the poor girl. Events proved me wrong. But once you act against principle, you're at the mercy of sentiment. Principle is what I've always preached and enforced—except in my own case."

Maitland said, "Come on now, I'm the referee. Self-abuse is out. And I don't mean onanism."

The unlikely and true lover chuckled dutifully. "Isn't humanity a sad, sad case? I'm the type of priest people joke about. The type Christ was angry with. But I must assure you, for Nora's sake and your own, that our relationship was —at least in the conventional sense—blameless."

"For God's sake, I know that."

"You don't know anything of the sort," Egan almost barked. "You think that just because I'm *your* friend, I couldn't have committed what is for us practically the ultimate."

"It's not that, only. . . ."

But Egan could not be dissuaded from presuming Maitland's callow pride. "Well, let me tell you, James, something you are likely to find out for yourself one day. That the distance between innocence and guilt, in *these* matters, is a hair's-breadth."

170

"I know. It's simply that you don't seem a hair's-breadth sort of character to me."

Egan snorted so heavily that he might well have learnt it from Costello. "I have to confess something that would make any priest ashamed. If there was nothing blameless, I believe it was due, under God, to Nora."

"I see."

Egan kept silence for fifteen seconds, a long time for a judge as uncomfortable as Maitland, not knowing what came next. The *defensor*, who knelt on the edge of Maitland's vision, had grown reticent, and there was a hint in the reticence. The hint was that Egan wanted to tell the history of Nora and himself, but did not feel self-lenient enough to begin.

"Tell me, Maurice," Maitland supplied, "how did you meet her?"

It took a few more seconds for Egan to gather his notes. "We were the court of appeal from Nora's first trial. The *defensor vinculi* in W—— appealed against the decision of the court of his diocese, which had declared the marriage unconsummated and therefore capable of being nullified. Remember, I told you that Nora managed the Imperial Hotel in W——. She had been married about six years before she began to take steps to have the marriage nullified. It seems that the time went quickly. She had a great deal to do. They had a dozen permanent guests and constantly put up businessmen and graziers and people of that kidney. She supervised the public bar and the lounge." Again Maitland looked on the sober, nodding intensity of the little teetotalling priest, reciting by heart the duties of his capable country girl in those years before she had recourse to canon law. "She kept a dining-room," he announced as her ultimate distinction, "of twenty-four tables. It was no small feat for a girl of, say, twenty-seven years."

Maitland confessed, "I'm sure I couldn't do it."

"Neither could I. No one is as capable, James, as a capable woman."

Perhaps Egan's most luxurious daydream was of himself

serving on any front—the lounge, the dining-room, the reception office; taking brute loads off the chatelaine's shoulders.

"Anyhow," he said, after an abstracted while, "the husband was a problem. Their marriage did not prosper. He drank."

"And was impotent, you say."

"Yes." The penitent closed his eyes. It seemed that the thought of that grotesque discovery, that stale joke of impotency whose butt was Nora, provided his sight with a problem of focus. "And he drank a great deal and molested the guests, so that he ended by giving what was virtually his own hotel a bad name. Celia, whom you would expect to know her canon law and anything else to her advantage, told Nora that she was sure the marriage could be annulled in the Church courts. Nora wouldn't consent—she had a terror of doctors. It was only when he cornered Nora and three guests with a fire-axe in the lounge after closing-time one night, that she decided to approach the bishop and see what could be done. She says it was for his sanity as well as her own. I believe her. You see, he used to accuse her of liaisons with perfectly respectable guests."

"Poor fellow," said Maitland.

"Yes," Egan said, "poor fellow. The man himself changed his mind a number of times about whether he was impotent or not. He changed his mind both in the W——— trial and in the one held in this archdiocese. By the time I met him he seemed clearly a case for psychiatric care. It was quite a game to follow the turns his mind took. His depositions were often given in the most obscene way imaginable, so that we had a terrible time cleaning them up for use in court. When I say we, I mean the *promotor justitiae* also, Doctor Costello, who was very kind to Nora. I was, of course, the villain. It was my duty to do all I could to preserve this impossible marriage."

"Would you like to sit up, Maurice?"

"No. Oh no! I'd never tell anyone else, James, but my knees are like bark from prayer, especially these last months. At least I spend a long time on my knees, and priests who do that are not supposed to behave as foolishly as I have. Good heavens, I even get infections in the cracked knee-pads." He

172

lifted a knee and rubbed it, one bursitic knee-cap ruined by love and piety. He uttered in despair his clerkly small cough. In the circumstances, it smacked of hysteria.

"Perhaps if you did sit up for a second—" insisted Maitland.

But Egan would not again enter into the subject of knees. He said, "I don't know if you have ever had any contact with the Church courts, James. But in marriage cases most of the evidence is taken outside the court, privately as it were. After I had interviewed Nora at the cathedral nearly two years ago —privately, though there was another priest present, of course, acting as notary—she came back after the notary had left and begged me not to make her face our *periti*."

"*Periti?*"

"I forget that there are even priests who do not understand these terms, whereas they're my bread and butter. *Periti* are the Catholic doctors who perform medical examinations for us. There were reasons—all to do with her husband's producing so-called new evidence—why an examination had to take place. It was a matter of law. I told her so. She began to shudder so much that I began to wish the notary hadn't gone. She cried in fits and starts, and every time she stopped she put her wet handkerchief away. I remember that I didn't feel particularly patient and wanted to tell her to keep the thing handy until she had wept herself dry. I told her that the *periti* were chosen for their uprightness and that there would be an *honesta matrona*, an honest matron, present. I actually thought, James, that that should satisfy her."

"But if the husband was quite clearly unbalanced—" Maitland began, realizing too late that Egan must often have had this debate with himself.

"I had no one but myself to consult. At the time, I thought to myself that I owed it to my colleague in W———, to the bond of marriage, which is surely sacred—"

"Of course it's sacred."

"—and to the church itself. I'd had very little experience of women. In any case, I seemed well and truly bound."

"Was it as bad as she expected?"

"Nobody concocts these things for the torment of humans.

173

Not even canon lawyers." His eyes, freighted with discovery, sought Maitland's. "The conflict between law and charity, James, is sometimes insoluble."

This, though no great news, Egan had reached his mid-thirties before suspecting. Maitland felt that he owed it to his friend to say dubiously, like a young man who has not yet seen the inside of the crucible, "I suppose so."

"Nora ended the examination in a state of hysterics. Some weeks later, a decree of inconsummation was issued. That meant that Nora was free of her husband, free to marry again."

James smiled. "I *do* know that much canon law."

"Nora entered a psychiatric hospital then. I didn't know— she was on the mend before I knew. You see, one afternoon I was stopped by Celia at a charity bazaar and accused at top note of destroying her sister. People all round me were absolutely transfixed listening to Celia calling on the divine mercy to strike me down. She doesn't care whom she embarrasses, that Celia."

"Jockeys and priests," James murmured.

"I visited Nora and asked forgiveness. That was as extraordinary a thing to do as it would be for a doctor to apologize for causing pain. But this is the essence of the affair, James, this is what I could never make other confessors swallow; I had been too willing to apply the law in her case. One likes too much to be able to depend on a blanket law, one likes to be able to apply it without consideration of individuals. It is one of the dangers of our work."

Maitland affirmed, "Someone has to be *defensor vinculi*"; and thought, "Who would, superficially, seem more suited than neat Maurice Egan?"

"I was so used to being inflexible," Egan further explained. "I was surrounded by men who were used to being inflexible. So that whenever I confessed my part in Nora's breakdown they always said what you have just said; that it was my duty. The difference is that they were sure of it, whereas you are only being kind."

Maitland disagreed.

"Oh no, you're what they call a humanist, James." Satire was apparent on the thin lips. "Even Dr Costello says so."

"Go to hell."

"Seriously, James. You are what they call a loner. You are impatient of law, and the reason is that if all men were like you, there would not need to be any laws."

"Hell!" said James. "Stick to sarcasm, will you?"

Without ceremony, Egan reverted to Nora. "I was very busy then, but somehow I found time to visit her again. She was so polite to me, and at the same time continuously afraid. Not of me, though. We walked around the grounds, but kept returning to the front of the building so that she could see whether her doctor's car was there. He wasn't due there that day, in any case, but she would hold herself very stiffly until she was sure that he hadn't arrived. Then she would let herself go limp and would begin to smile and chat again. It was —well, a terrible smile in the circumstances. She would be too full of joy. Then we'd stroll away again, around the gardens. Within five minutes she would want to assure herself again that the doctor hadn't come. It was so strange. She attributed unlimited powers of deception to that poor man, and yet she actually considered me as some sort of protector. She had no doubt that he intended to violate her, as she believed the *periti* had done."

"My God!" Maitland called out sincerely, seeing that a dilemma of classic proportions had overtaken this far-from-classic little priest.

"Perhaps my intentions were bad. I don't know. But it seemed to me—not that there was anything I could do—however, it seemed that I must come back and keep track, more or less, of her return to health."

"Yes," Maitland said, "that seems an honest decision to me. And I'm the one wearing the stole."

"But we get so used from childhood to making our decisions seem honest. I can remember how in my last year at high school we had a teacher who taught us literature. He was an enthusiast, but somehow he seemed to bore the boys. At the end of the year he told us that he was very sorry and that it was his own fault, but we were going to fail the literature section in great numbers. He said that each time he thought of giving us a critical exercise, he remembered how little we knew and decided that he would wait until he had given us another two or three essential ideas. And he would give us the two or three essential ideas, during which we would doze or do our mathematics."

"You doze? I can't imagine little Maurice Egan dozing in class."

"Little Maurice Egan was destined to become *defensor vinculi*," said Egan in seemly but unmistakable self-hatred. "I speak of the class as a whole. In any case the teacher was right, and more than not failed, because he couldn't release their minds long enough to let them have their own say, however clumsy. It has been exactly the same case with myself and Nora. The time when I could say good-bye to Nora was always two or three weeks away."

He came to an end of eloquence, lowered his head and said, "Advise me, James."

Maitland protested. "Come on now, Maurice. You're a better man than I am, Gunga Din. Especially at this kind of lark."

"Don't say that. You're the confessor. Don't you believe that the grace of the sacrament could make you wiser than yourself?"

The question made Maitland self-conscious and betrayed him into a silence that couldn't help but be sceptical.

For his part, Egan was betrayed into peevishness. "Sometimes," he announced, "one can sense a particularly annoying quality about you, James—in the way you consistently refuse to be impressed by old ways, old habits of thought. In case you didn't know, that is precisely why Nolan and Costello always expect the worst of you."

"It must be very annoying. However, where would they be without someone to expect the worst of?"

"Don't waste your time turning the other cheek," Egan began, but slapped the top of his own head in mid-petulance, causing the hair to rise in brilliantined spikes. "Forgive me, James. I must seem laughable enough to you, a middle-aged priest seeking marriage."

So, holding in his lap his consecrated hands, cupped as if damaged, he began to stare at them in a secretive manner, and saw the irony of his thirty-six holy years and of his not having dozed in the literature classes and failed like the honest majority. Maitland chanced putting a long, inept hand on his friend's shoulder. He said, "I'm sure some solution can be found," forgetting that a solution had been found, that Nora was due to cross the world within days and leave Egan inviolate.

Then, still wearing the confessional-stole, but failing to recollect that the sacrament was still in progress, he went to the volumes of Migne and absently switched on the electric jug. He felt repelled by that Egan who sat benumbed, too much like a shocked child. So hard he stared at the harmless, yellow jug that he might have been able to see the murderous watts moving in it like sharks in an aquarium.

"Well, James, what do you think?"

Harried, Maitland demanded, "How do you mean?"

"About my guilt."

"Are you seriously asking me to—"

"Yes. You are priest and judge."

Maitland weaved his head. "Oh hell, Maurice. . . ."

"You must want to ask me questions."

Maitland snorted. "All right. An obvious question. Did you ever try to stop seeing Nora?"

"I was always telling her she seemed so much better and that this would be the last time we would meet. When I say always telling her, I mean about half a dozen times in the last year. Each time I meant it. Or at least I thought I meant it."

"What happened then?" Maitland said almost brutally.

"You must remember, James, that Nora was not a melodramatic woman. But each time, she'd say, 'I don't know whether I could stand it!' "

"Your departure?"

"Yes. She wasn't the sort of woman to make such claims

lightly. I learnt that much from her encounter with the *periti*."

"So you think she wouldn't have been able to stand a breaking of the ties."

Maitland's hostility had begun to wash off on the penitent, who said, "Is that a question I had a right to ask myself, James? I mean to say, one would not risk the mental balance of one's worst enemy."

All desire to probe Egan's blind side died now, leaving Maitland both ashamed and very grateful that the girl was having recourse, not to novenas, but to international airlines.

The two of them were unaccountably tired, as if they had wrestled with each other—a spiritual round or two for a pound or two which had not done anyone any good.

"If she said she couldn't stand it," Egan murmured, "it was the truth."

"The whole blame is yours?"

"Practically."

"It's a bit Asian, friend Egan, to assume that someone is to blame for every human situation."

Egan sighed. "This isn't a bit like a confession. You owe me a judgment."

"Well I don't damn-well want to give one. Do you want me to say 'not guilty' just for the sake of comforting you? I said it at the start and I still say it. *Not Guilty*. And now I think you should let the subject lie."

There was an absolution, which Egan accepted with disconsolate bowed head.

A minute or so later, nibbling a biscuit, he said, "Anyhow, perhaps Nora will meet someone on her—journey." He laid the word down like lead on the brittle hope. "Some businessman or grazier from this side of things. They say London's full of them." He could have been talking of forests full of tigers.

Just as Maitland's contest with Allied Projects began, he had been following an absorbing line of research at the public library. He was suddenly exalted to find that much of the material he had gathered demanded to be treated in some ex-

178

tended form; in fact, in a dangerous form for any priest—the novel. So his working-day became a short creative fever in the reading-room, encompassed by those waste levels of time in which he occupied a place at table, taught, timed his meditations, and had the Egan conscience forced on him.

"We just have time, James," Egan said on a crucial morning. "Please. It seems indecent not to be there for this."

"But I have a class at eleven."

"We'll be there no more than ten minutes."

"But listen, Maurice. What if the thing is held up and we have to leave before it goes? That would be worse than inconclusive."

"Please, James," was all that Egan said.

Maitland drove Egan's small car. Within half a mile of the airport, creeping among tankers and busfuls of travellers, assailed by hoardings offering foreign cities and the wine and girls of foreign cities, Maitland began to suffer the sick sense of being alien to his native city. What he was especially grateful for was that he did not dress well—his badly worn shoes did not look like those of a man who could afford a ticket to London; his old coat at least gave him some specious claim to representing eternal values. He would otherwise not be able to move in the terminal building without being challenged by eyes.

Transitory then, but compelling gazes as much as any eternal value, stood the London-bound jet.

"We mustn't meet them," Egan said. "There's some sort of veranda upstairs."

Maitland laughed, and said in a voice like a municipal alderman's. "In this day and age, we call them observation decks."

"Very well," hissed Egan, and pounced at the staircase as if fleeing loreleis in the lounge.

Upstairs, the wind tugging at their forlorn black hats, Maitland had some advice for his friend. "Anyone who has ever said good-bye to someone—"

"I am not *saying* good-bye," Egan insisted.

"Anyhow, they say this is the most difficult to accept. These jets climb into the sun and vanish within a minute. People feel it's improper to have friends taken so quickly. I thought I should warn you."

"Thank you," Egan said.

He made Maitland hide behind a family of wealthy Italians as the passengers appeared from the terminal doorway. There was Nora in a rich check coat, long- and full-legged in claret-coloured stockings. She turned once to wave cursorily in the direction from which she had come. It was a gesture like a blessing given by a priest who is sick of his priesthood. As she entered the plane, Egan said, "She could see us from a window, James. I'm sorry. We must go back downstairs."

They sheltered in a bus bay, listened to the machine snarl, felt its exhaust heat their faces like an indefinable reproach, saw it trundle away, turn and, gathering all its inevitable knots per hour compactly behind its wings, rise and vanish. Maitland had been right; decency demanded more ceremony: the streamers, say, that are strung between wharf and inching liner.

Egan said desperately, "It's amazing how they can get those monstrous things up."

The incompleteness of the good-bye kept them waiting in silence in the bay for two or three minutes. As they looked down the vacant runway shining with a light that was nearly crystalline, Maitland sensed that his friend's composure was so cliff-edge that even a pat on the shoulder would disturb it. At last Egan sniffed drily.

"Well, there doesn't seem to be anything else happening."

But, of course, Celia also had waited, absorbed in an empty sky. Convinced at the same time as Egan that, however expansive, it would produce nothing, she emerged at the terminal front door when the two priests were twenty yards away. On seeing them, she mopped tears off her cheeks with two fast swipes of a tissue.

"It's beloved Maurice," she said in full voice. She wore the enamel, corsets-are-killing-me smile of the professional entertainer. Both priests cringed. Both wondered whether her high-calibre tongue had their retreat to the parking-area covered;

180

both decided that, as with pythons and tigers, the best chance was utter immobility. "And James, the friend of the alcoholic." Other bon-voyagers, coming out of doors chewing over their inadequate farewells, caught the suggestion of a scene in her voice, glimpsed the two Roman collars, and bolted. "She whom thou seekest is not here," said Celia in a venomous parody. "She is risen, *Alleluia*. She is gone before you into Chelsea where dwelleth her pub-owning aunt, Mrs Beatrice Flanigan."

Egan said, "She hasn't gone before me. She's simply gone."

"Surely you can get a discount trip out of some pious wop airline."

"I wouldn't want to. She's far better off without the two of us."

Maitland ventured to say, "I think this is only going to cause pain to both of you. Perhaps if you—"

"Not in mufti today, father?" Celia observed cursorily, and then, "Maurice, did you happen to see the wave my grateful sister gave me? You would have thought she was brushing scurf off her shoulder. That bloody dry-wife of yours. . . . A flap of the hand. I think we've both been used by that sweet child. One day, when she's sitting in her flat with some extreme form of male—she's got a talent for extreme forms—priest and eunuch so far—when she's sitting there with her next freak, she'll mention off-handedly that she once was involved with a *defensor vinculi*. She'll say, 'Do you know what a *defensor vinculi* is, darling?' And he, out of the special insight given him by his having only one leg or one eye or a really elegant hare-lip, will say—"

What, Maitland did not hear, because Egan, with a bunched fist, struck her on the cheek. It was more, even, than she had hoped for.

Having to lead her away and soothe her, having to lead an Egan who hid his face in his hands three hundred yards to the car, Maitland became even more intensely grateful for his unworldly shoes.

While Maitland drove, Egan sat solving the simultaneous

equations: *A man who strikes a woman is an utter coward* and *Maurice Egan, not thought to be an utter coward, has yet struck a woman.* By the time they parked in the stone bay behind the House he was still limp and far from a solution; and, behind any solution, lay the untouched mass of his grief.

15

Distrust of Maitland characterized Hurst over the following week. Three days after he had been due to visit the doctor, Maitland had still not heard if he had kept the appointment. Maitland, approaching, would see him flit into doorways and up staircases. It was when you wanted to speak to somebody who didn't want to speak to you that you realized how some Victorian architect, of talents stolid as plum-duff, had constructed without trying a house fit for the chase sequence of a Marx Brothers' comedy.

Maitland ran him down by accident. It was a weekday morning and a High Mass was, for some liturgical reason, being intoned in the chapel. James, on his way upstairs from saying his own Mass, stopped by in the downstairs toilet and found Hurst, stock-still in surplice, soutane and biretta, staring at his own anguish in the mirror above the basins. Seeing Maitland, he jumped back and stood at bay.

"Good morning," called Maitland, breezing up to a urinal. "Good morning, doctor."

"Go to the doctor?"

"Yes."

"Good. What did he say?"

"He said I was letting myself be bluffed by this—you know—compulsion."

"Yes, but that's easily said, isn't it? Although they say he knows a lot about priests and religious, that doctor."

"Yes. He doesn't like the way we're trained. He thinks it's anti-human."

"Well, of course," Maitland said, buttoning his fly, "that's no secret."

"He agrees with you about the will," Hurst announced, opting for academic questions so that personal ones should not be raised. "He says that we are taught that the will can conquer anything and that we wear our will out by trying not to—in my case—maim people."

"But he doesn't exactly believe that one should give in, does he?" Maitland asked sunnily. "Give in and cut away?"

Hurst winced. "No. He thinks that other methods should be used. Utter serenity."

"My God! If you were capable of utter serenity you wouldn't have troubled him."

"He gave me some pills and I'm to go back in a week."

Hurst wanted, with every pore of his unsunned flesh, that that should be the end of the interview.

"Are you any better?" Maitland asked him.

"Yes. I have these pills."

"What about the letter he gave you?" It had to be asked bluntly. "Surely he gave you a letter for me?"

"Oh, no." Hurst began to comb the tassels of the biretta with his fingers. It was the type of gesture that goes with not-too-artful lying or, on the other hand, with complete guilelessness. "He didn't seem to think that I was any sort of serious case. Only bluffed, as I said."

"Could I do anything?"

"No. It's very kind of you to have taken this much interest."

Maitland laughed as kindly as he could and patted the boy's shoulder. "You're not mad, Hurst, but you have to take yourself seriously. I actually found you burying the cutlery. Polite terms like 'very kind of you to take this much interest' don't enter into it. Now, did he give you a letter?"

"No," Hurst said, hardly friendly, and gripped the three-peaked hat in both fists.

Maitland already felt disgusted by the tone of annoyance that seemed native to his dealing with Hurst. He said, "Please trust me. If I sound angry, it's because futile sicknesses *do* make one angry."

"Of course, doctor." Hurst was still a gentleman; he woefully lacked the desperation that brings man to a cure. "And I *will* keep you informed of the treatment."

At the same time Egan too was using every facility the house offered for the avoidance of Maitland. They seemed to meet only in places where silence or near-silence was the rule—noticeably, as before, in the passageway behind the high altar. Each nodded to the other over the chalice he bore; two liturgical denizens in green or white or scarlet chasubles. No doubt Egan suspected Maitland of thinking along juridical lines: here is a man who punched a woman; what right has he to don a chasuble over that atrocity? Maitland, whose atrocity was that he belonged to nothing and agonized for no one, could have boxed Egan's blunt little ears.

Meanwhile, loss, guilt and regeneration brought to that bland face the delayed puberty of a frown.

One eleven o'clock, returning from the classroom, Maitland caught sight of Egan's boyish coat-tails making the short dash from the end stairs to the back door. Maitland ran after him, cassock whooping like bellows. The quarry was still palely fiddling with car keys when James caught him among the vehicles.

"Heard from Celia or Nora, Maurice?" Maitland asked, invoking Celia's name purely as a reprisal.

"The plane arrived safely."

"They mainly do these days."

He thought: One thing about being vengeful; you know you're alive. It's wine. It's a drug.

185

"James," said Egan, "James, I'd prefer it if we both forgot those two names."

"Oh. Now you're back to the stable life, you want to forget your old friends?"

"Never, James. I'll never forget what you've done. But. . . ."

"Never forget what I've done? You sound as if you're going away."

"No. No." He raised his elbows as if under suspicion of carrying a change of clothing beneath the armpits.

Maitland said, "Listen, Maurice, if you want to be quit of me because I'm associated in your mind with given acts of valour of yours, such as clocking a certain fishwife, hereinafter anonymous, to her own and my intense delight—if you want to be quit of me because I'm some sort of living emblem of your sins, or what you consider to be sins, then just tell me."

Egan turned over his keys one by one as if they carried apt quotations from Ecclesiastes or St Augustine.

"Well," Maitland insisted, "tell me!"

"That's not the problem. What sort of man do you think I am?"

"If you think when we pass in that bloody dismal tunnel behind the altar that I wonder whether you're saying Mass 'in the state of sin' "—he gestured two handfuls of inverted commas either side of the time-worn expression—"then you're a great damned fool offering the worst damned insult that ever I've suffered."

"That's not the problem either."

"My God," called Maitland, with a further gesture which the books of piety would have described as inordinate. "You *are* a tortuous bastard!"

"You're a young priest, Maitland. How old are you?"

"Full twenty-nine years have I," Maitland said, still petulant.

"Full thirty-seven have I," Egan announced without enthusiasm. "Like all older priests, I owe you an example. I owe you some edification. In fact, I have given you not a thing other than certain cynical insights—"

186

"Oh God. Now I can't even take the credit for my own cynicism!"

"You're right to be angry."

"Oh, stop pretending to humility. It resolves itself down to this. Either you do me the credit of letting me decide for myself whether you're such an old reprobate that I shouldn't mix with you, or else we stop all pretence at acquaintanceship. One more curt nod at table and you can get someone else to dole out your secrets to."

Then, under the influence of a strange spasm, the desire to top Egan's guilt, Maitland went on, "If you think you're the only one with a sizeable shame, let me tell you about mine."

And although it was no sort of enormity to him that he had published without ecclesiastical permission, it was and always would be a genuine enormity to Egan, being for him part of that inalienable citadel of the conscience which even murderers have, the things one would never do. So Maitland told him about *The Meanings of God*, and watched him.

"My goodness!"

"Go on, then. Treat me as a leper."

"Don't talk rot."

"Ah!" said Maitland. "That is my very point. Either we take the rot as read, or else."

"That book," said Egan. "James, that's a superb book. And it was written by a priest, as the publisher claimed."

Maitland laughed. "You mean that if a Catholic wrote it there may be some truth in it?"

"I mean that it's a superb book. You really are a very bright young fellow for twenty-nine."

"Jump at yourself, Reverend Egan."

Maurice, on the brunt of Maitland's information, had managed to open the door of his small car. Then he stood up straight and put out his hand. "Rot as read?" he said.

"I beg your pardon."

"We'll take the rot as read?"

"Oh yes."

"Really, a marvellous book, James. Do you intend doing anything about it?"

"My opus?" Maitland asked. "Let it die without recriminations."

When Joe Quinlan telephoned him, Maitland—for the first time since the blonde reporter had come visiting—suffered a momentary sense of betrayal. He said into the receiver, "Want another loan, Joe?" So, with abject ease, he made a mock of any forbearance he might have practised in the past or might practise in the future. Not that forbearance itself hadn't been abjectly easy. He had awarded the money to someone who meant nothing to him, who was, by conventional standards, totally undeserving. These were the conditions he had set himself, and by its nature, the very giving was an insult and deserved traducing.

"I wanted to talk to you," Joe said painfully. "I wanted to apologize."

And if Maitland now felt a panic rush to reassure Joe, and if he said nothing, it was because his brand of reassurance was likely to be taken for sarcasm.

"If you could come tonight, father?" wondered Joe. "You won't be able to come home because they're trying their best to get us out of the place, but I could meet you at the busstop. We could have a talk. You know."

The electronic mysteries of a telephone exchange crackled in the pause, while Maitland weighed the tensions of creation, demanding release, at the back of his brain. For though he had not yet attacked that rampantly gentile beast called the novel, he had yet begun taking notes (upstairs, only seven yards distant from the nearest Couraigne painting, only fifteen yards from the nearest moral theologian) which were nearly the real thing. Balancing their claims against Joe's, he heard Joe say, "By Jesus, I'm sorry."

"It's not that, Joe. It's just that you live so far away."

"Not any more," Joe said. The Quinlans lived in a new place, only *they* were trying to get them out of it. Joe's *they* was that terrible pronoun of the working class, embracing the cabinet, the insurance companies, organized Christianity, the price-control board, the breweries. Maitland suffered a second's

188

fluorescent vision of his own father waiting grey with loss outside a casualty ward, telling the skinny theological student who Maitland once was, "*They* won't let us have her. *They* say there's got to be an autopsy."

He flinched. "I suppose," he decided, full of proletarian tenderness, "I could catch the bus."

An hour later he found Joe hunched against a locked and blazing appliance store. They were both cold and, without overcoats, seemed outdated in the glare of that new shopping-centre. Still, it was Maitland's business not to blend into the landscape of new suburbs. All the rebuke of the lit galleries was on Joe's tweedy shoulders.

As Maitland came up, Joe let his shivers run mad so that he would not be forced to notice the mockery or other-cheekness of Maitland's extended hand. They asked after each other's health, while the wind stropped itself on acres of plate glass and filleted the two of them in their corner.

"Shout you a cup of coffee?" suggested Maitland. He blushed for being in the right, and found it impossible to look at Joe's face, which was trying to cope with its own problems. He stared therefore at the display window behind them, and read the chrome badge of an automatic washing-machine, read its labelled buttons, its citation of red cardboard, its blue arrow indicating the spinner that was "Tarzan-tough and Galahad-tender". The influence of G. M. Hopkins on advertising, Maitland thought. If Costello were a woman, he—she—would own that machine.

"I just left the table," Joe said. Morna's table, stew and one pumpkin-stained little boy.

"Come on," Maitland commanded.

The Hungarian proprietor was glad to have a reverend client, or any client, this raw night. Both cousins felt a shy access of cheerfulness as they sat down under his smile and the insinuating smells of his coffee machine.

"I'm sorry I couldn't take you home," Joe said again, as he had on the telephone. "But they call sometimes of a night, and if they called while you were there, Morna'd throw a fit."

"Who are *they*?"

"The people from Allied Projects. They say that Clark had no right to offer us the house."

"Clark?"

"That manager bloke."

"Clark offered you a house?" Maitland could not stop smiling sideways. Paris is worth a Mass, he thought, Maitland is worth a three-bedroom brick cottage with shingle roof.

"Rent-free like."

"A good house?"

Joe put his face in his hands. "I wish to Christ it was ours," he said.

"They're trying to break their promise?"

"They say he had no right. When I telephoned him he said it was out of his hands, that he's retiring in September."

"Typical of *them*," James murmured, aligning himself with his dead father and with Joe.

Joe said, "It was hard enough to say them things about you. . . . ."

"I know." Maitland quashed the melodrama by slapping his right knee a number of times. Then he said softly, "I know. Bad enough, without all this."

"Don't you mind what I said?"

Maitland smiled gingerly while the proprietor himself, and not his acned cashier, laid down two coffees as tenderly as kittens before them.

"Thank you," Maitland said to the man's departing and gratified buttocks; and to Joe, "I know you'll always take a serious view of the affair, Joe. But you see, I'm not a career priest, so I can't be hurt in that way. They aren't sweating on me to turn forty just so that they can give me a cardinal's hat."

They both laughed, still very shy. But Joe went sombre without warning. "We really needed a place of our own. You know."

Slapping his leg again, Maitland said, "I know, I know." If only people would take their motives as read. But neither Egan nor Hurst nor Joe Quinlan would. The malice of betrayal might essentially be that it prevented two men from

190

taking an easy cup of coffee with each other. "Joe, you didn't do me any harm. All I wish is that *they* let you enjoy the spoils in peace."

"The spoils?" Joe asked.

"The—house."

"Oh yeah."

And it was immediately appalling how such a small and comic-opera betrayal could become freighted with such terror of loss as now made Joe Quinlan's eyes seem to bulge.

"It's built on a downhill plot, there's a garage underneath and a spiral staircase going up to the front patio. There's french winders from the lounge-room onto the patio. . . ."

Maitland nodded. French windows, which are glass and wood to those who can manage to afford them, can be a formula of salvation, a certificate of ownership of the winter sun, to those who have lived all their lives in plaster-board.

"No chance of buying it?"

"You'd need to be an accountant or somebody to own this one."

Maitland almost explained that he didn't have the money, but knew that that had not been Joe's point. Then what is Joe's point? he wondered.

Joe said, "They reckon they're going to make us pay a big rent from next fortnight onwards. They want us to take some money and get out. . . ."

"But you don't want to go back to the old places?"

Joe shrugged. "Morna bawls her eyes out," he explained.

Maitland looked away, his frightened eyes landing on the proprietor's face by the cash register. The proprietor smiled a smile that said, "Another cup?" It was an unequal contest. Maitland gave in at once, nodded, held up two fingers.

He said, "Joe, I don't think you're telling me this for the sake of getting help from me."

Joe perished the thought. "Oh, Christ no!"

"Why are you telling me then?"

"Well, I thought you'd be pretty crooked on me and that you'd like to know."

"How do you mean like to know."

"That the thing didn't pay off for me. Like."

So Joe Quinlan, in tatty sports-coat at a laminated table, made a medieval obeisance of the head. Before Maitland could say something worthy of the man, the Hungarian was beside them, insinuating two coffees, creamed and nutmegged, between them.

16

Now Egan was chatty as a fishwife, called at Maitland's jumbled room at all hours, kept him from the public library and the utter luxury of taking notes for the novel. Maitland ended in all manner of stratagems to leave time free for this work. Behind the catalogue file in the House of Studies library there was a desk that could not be seen from the door, and Maitland would put his notes there before meals and hide there himself immediately after. But the severe spaces of the room were hostile to the private exhilarations of his imagination. Next he took to leaving his street clothes in the downstairs lavatory before lunch and changing into them immediately after, skipping to the ferry while the others were still giving thanks in the chapel. He still felt himself bound to stop work by seven and return across the bay to make his ear available to Egan.

One such night he found his friend already waiting for him, seated like a suspect in an alien gendarmerie, his hands on his knees, not prying into the significance of any of Maitland's mess of notes.

"She's coming back," Maurice announced.

"Back?" asked Maitland and, suspecting that the ham sandwiches he had bought for their supper had somehow become superseded, dropped them on the table.

"Back here. Back home, she says. She says she misses Celia and myself."

"It's not kind of her to say that. To say that she misses *you.*"

"I have never been very kind to her."

His brow was focused, cross-eyed, on some ultimate intention.

The generations of men had found that the only cure for love of this nature was not to put a hemisphere between the lovers but to sink them in a blessed calyx of red-brick or oregon, on its own land close to bus and shops. Yet it seemed impossible that a *defensor vinculi* should come to the same conclusion.

Maitland could hardly help asking, "What will you do?"

Egan said, "I am used to confessing unlikely things to you, James. I also know how long these things take to pass through the normal channels. I intend therefore to write directly to the Supreme Pontiff, asking him, beseeching him as from the fires of hell, to save two souls by reducing me to the lay state and dispensing me from celibacy."

The idea possessed magnitude even by Maitland's standards, and reverence for it imposed a ten-second silence.

"What do you think?" Egan invited.

"One of the functions of a public service is to prevent letters getting to the top man. The Church has its public service. How can a priest get a letter straight to the Pope without its having been screened by bureaucrats in Roman collars?"

Egan smiled. "I have a friend who is one of these bureaucrats in Roman collars. He's an American, and we studied together. He is a member of the Holy Office and he can arrange to be at some private audience and pass the letter directly to the Holy Father."

Simultaneously, both men shook their heads, for the scheme induced its own vertigo. And on this same account Maitland

194

refrained, for the time, from raising problems.

"The thing to do," Egan said, "is to convince him that when I speak of two souls who will otherwise be lost, I mean it literally." He took his eyes from the Vatican, at which he had been gazing through the walls and around the curves of hemispheres. "I can tell you're shocked, Maitland. But you yourself told me to take any attempts at coddling you as read."

"I'm *not* shocked," Maitland said, and went hunting in the sandwich bag to prove it. He had not had his evening meal. "I have to be honest. I don't know whether it's a good idea." He stared at the innards of the sandwich to make sure that the lady in the delicatessen had done the right thing by him.

"It is *not* a good idea, no. It is the only idea I have left. No doubt you wonder how I will get on without the Mass."

Maitland slammed the sandwich down on a study of seventeenth-century Spanish diplomacy.

"For God's sake, stop confusing me with some sort of vocation-poster priest. There are thousands of priests who could get by without their Mass, just as there are thousands of husbands who could get by without their wives."

"I'll miss the active life of the priesthood."

"Of course you would. But if a person left a Chinese laundry after giving it twenty of his earthly years, he'd miss it."

"I myself have no doubts, James. It *is* a question of salvation."

"Are you sure it's as basic as all that?" asked Maitland, like a born counsellor, like a chancery sharp-shooter.

"Do you think I use such terms lightly? Speak up, Maitland. What's your objection?"

Maitland felt his beard, the long bristles around his Adam's apple which his razor missed, often for a week at a time. "Firstly, if I had to forget that I was a priest, I could with ease do so. But *you* could never forget. The second thing is that perhaps when a person has suffered as Nora has—I only say *perhaps*—he or she gets used to abnormal situations, becomes addicted to them. All I would say is that you should make sure she would want you as a mere citizen, as a spouse."

"I *am* sure," the little man said slowly, and sat contemplatively for some time before losing his temper so thoroughly that he saw no false plea in asking, "What sort of priest do you think I am?"

Maitland said, "You must realize, Maurice, that this is a suggestion and not an accusation. In fact, the usual cowardly claptrap." To show his mundane faith and his lack of high-flown malice, he retrieved the sandwich and began to eat.

Egan, a man who had patience now only for accusations, bounced to his feet. "Sometimes you behave as if you deserved everyone's hostility, James. You have no sense of fitness, no sense of time or place."

By the skin of his teeth, Maitland managed to be mean enough to say, "This is my time and place, mate. I've had no lunch and no dinner."

"Don't let me be the one to keep you from your bun-bag. Besides, I have a letter to write."

Maitland intercepted the small angry man at the door.

"Forgive me, Maurice. Eating sandwiches in front of you at a time like this." But the stupid thing was still in his hand, half-eaten. He went on, "There are considerations, human and otherwise . . . I suppose you've taken them all into account."

The little priest shook his head, not as a negative, but to dismiss his own profitless anger.

"I have," he said. "I was stupid enough to ask for advice I didn't want. But if a young radical like yourself knows that there are considerations, James, all the more so an old stuffed-shirt like me." He smiled. "I exempt you from the obligation of cataloguing the things I have already taken into account. I thank you for your attention. And I do have a letter to write."

He passed Maitland and emerged in the seedy faubourg of the hall, a stranger who had to take his bearings by one of the economy bulbs.

Maitland hissed at him from the ante-room, "Maurice, I must say it. It's hard to see you succeeding."

There was something of the vehemence of his scheme in the little priest's voice as he said, "I refuse for the moment to consider the possibility of failure. Of sacrifice, obedience and mercy, I know which one is the most perfect. I cannot believe that a Supreme Pontiff does not also know." He rubbed his paws and gathered his shoulders like a man already seated at a desk writing what he wants to. He paused before telling Maitland valedictorily, "In any case, you are one of those people whom I feel I can never repay."

On the appropriate morning, Maitland cornered Hurst after breakfast and told him that this was his day to return to the psychiatrist.

"I don't know whether I need it," Hurst said, though his eyes, pallid and moon-struck, were symptoms in themselves.

For once, Maitland went gently with him. "You're feeling better?"

"Much."

"Well. Nothing lost by going today. It's only etiquette, you know. I'm afraid I must insist."

"Very well, doctor."

"And don't be seen catching the ferry, eh? Oh, and please, if he writes a letter—"

"Of course."

"I said earlier that I'd abandon you after your first visit."

"Yes. But it takes time to decide what has to be done."

What had to be done, so far as Hurst had decided, was that he must confess the psychiatrist's findings and deliver the psychiatrist's letter to Costello, on whom the Spirit had breathed, and not to this inept outsider.

Meanwhile, Costello was as full of business as any bride with an outside chance of happiness. He kept tailors busy on his episcopal robes, goldsmiths busy on his pectoral cross and ring designed by himself. Often bishops inherited the insignia of deceased prelates; but that *was* a risk, to depend on the taste of a dead man. He booked his air passage to Rome for his *ad liminal* visit, could be seen in Asiatic pyjamas limping the passageway after inoculations, made after-dinner speeches, and lovingly prepared his autobiography for the secular and religious press.

Morning and night in the chapel, the prayers for a newly elected bishop were said; and Nolan spoke, prayed and effervesced about the coming consecration as fervently as an ugly bridesmaid who knows not only that she will never reach the altar on her own merits but that it has occurred to all the wedding-guests that she never will.

While Maitland was trying to corner Hurst a third time and considering telephoning the doctor, Costello brought home three tailor's boxes full of modish pontificals—a cassock with cape and piping, a chimer, a *zucchetto* and biretta. The big man, clad in them before his mirror, would have been seen as touching and lovable if anyone had happened in. Though the robes seemed extremely new and incomplete without his overdue pectoral, he stood immobile in them for some minutes and murmured three times before disrobing, "For He that is mighty has done great things to me. . . ." So he hung them in the wardrobe and went down to dinner.

While he ate, the students' dinner ended and Hurst came to the bishop-elect's room to admit two visits to the psychiatrist. Hurst had noticed that Costello had not been at table at the beginning of the meal, but he had then been once more consumed in a spirit-to-spirit struggle with the bread-knife. That wedge of inimical black that was His fulfilled Lordship entering no more than nudged the outer edges of his vision. So now, believing Costello to be *in*, his frightened veins, freighted with blood-lust, jumped as he waited for an answer to his knock. He thought he heard the bishop ask him in, though it was only a window grating in the wind. When visibly exercising patience, His Lordship did sound like a window grating in the wind; and now paid the penalty. For Hurst, desperate though well-mannered, opened the door to see immediately the robes, empty but ineradicably suggestive of the princely bulk of Costello. At the same time he wondered whether Costello's teak letter-knife, which he had often eyed during confessions, was on the desk.

The paper-knife served only for making triangular rents in the cassock, but his hands could do the rest of the work. Tittering through introverted lips like Charlie Chaplin's, he sat on the purple biretta that lay on the bed. After that, confident that he could explain the prank away, he went upstairs and took enough tablets to give him a good sleep short of the final one. He took, in all, four days' supply of sedative.

Maitland himself found Costello stumbling as never under the influence of smallpox injections. The mouth was forced towards one corner of the face. He was hissing.

"What is it?" Maitland had to ask.

Costello tried first to gather the pace to brush past, but then stopped dead.

"You *might* ask!" In contravention of his years of sober deep-breathing, he champed a mouthful of air. "No, not even you could have done this."

"Are you sure, My Lord?" Maitland asked boisterously.

The bishop leant against the wall. "Oh God!" he said.

Maitland took hold of Costello's elbow. "What is it?"

"Just you come and see!"

Across Costello's room lay his shredded robes. He said, "A hundred and seventy dollars' worth", and punched the wall with his fist, and began to weep, neither for the money nor for the fist.

"I'm terribly sorry, Costello. It's barbarous," Maitland told him, and saw the paper-knife lying near the wardrobe.

"Who in the name of heaven did this poisonous thing?" Costello called to him.

"No one who merely dislikes you." He struggled uselessly with the temptation to suggest, "Someone with disappointed hopes—"

"Don't be insane. If you think Monsignor Nolan would—"

"Of course not. I wasn't naming names."

Costello found the chair by his prie-dieu. "It's so disgusting," he said, and stared at his cassock with as much horror as if blowflies had been drinking at its wounds. He seemed nauseated, and his large hands just managed to control themselves.

But where was Hurst and what was Hurst doing?

As a pretext, Maitland said, "I'll go and get you something for the way you feel."

199

Upstairs, on a floor where he had lived as a student, a bunch of young clerics stood finding nought for their comfort beneath a dim bulb. The remembered dinginess struck him, even in his present hurry, with an odious nostalgia. He asked them where Hurst's room was and left them with such urgency when they'd told him that their eyes followed him and then, off-handedly, as if going to their rooms, they followed too.

Hurst was asleep and his person innocent of blood. After trying to rouse him, Maitland could not resist taking the boy's slack jaw in his hand and shutting and opening it fluidly, like the jaw of a sambo money-box. Even in those muscles that traditionally resisted and gave the alarm, Hurst slept. Without pain and dreary interviews with Nolan, he had eased himself out of the priestly life.

The pulse, Maitland found, was low but strong.

"You've managed it," he told the utterly reposeful form. "You're out of limbo." A bungalow and seven mortal and miserable thousand a year for Hurst; and offspring, smelling of wet, milk and talc, in his arms. So Maitland hoped.

Nolan was not so happy.

"Poor boy. Is it an attempt at suicide?" he asked, blinking at the livid sleeper.

"Monsignor," said Maitland, "he'd hardly know what you were talking about."

And he felt a genuine hatred of the president, who began to tidy up the affair from a sacramental point of view by raising his right hand and muttering an absolution.

"Conditional absolution I hope, monsignor. I mean to say, he may not have passed out in the state of grace."

The president mistook the derision for alarm. "Of course, conditional," he reassured Maitland. "Of course, James." And he began the absolution again.

"Whatever possessed him?" said Nolan, waiting for the ambulance. "Demons," Maitland informed him. "Demons for a start."

Nolan boggled at the thought of exorcisms.

Furious at his own negligence, Maitland talked turkey.

"Demons first off. And carelessness topped it off. If you're

200

wondering whose, then mine in the last instance, Costello's in the second. Yours ultimately."

Demands of Nolan, explanations of Maitland, sleep of Hurst, all continued in the ambulance.

"Yes, yours!" Maitland was contending. "For a variety of reasons."

"I'd be interested to hear."

"For one thing, monsignor, making it hard for those you expose to your high-geared system of kibosh to see a doctor and ask him why the hell they can't sleep of nights and want to mutilate people."

"Did Hurst want to mutilate people?"

"Let him tell you."

Nolan snorted and inspected the boy, whose jaw was still deliciously slack.

"Your inimical attitude, James—" he began.

"That's not the point," said Maitland. "Hurst is the point."

The attendant, who kept taking Hurst's pulse, smirked at the blossoming wrangle. Nolan murmured, "Maitland, don't vulgarize *this* affair. Not everyone—" he waggled his eyebrows towards the attendant—"is in sympathy with us."

"Me for one," Maitland admitted. "Now Costello! If Costello had known one end of a human being from another, he would have got Hurst to a doctor months ago. Instead he told him to pray to Our Lady of Victories."

"You surely wouldn't quarrel with that advice."

"Only with its utter ineptitude."

The ambulance man, frowning over Hurst, seemed disappointed by the veer the conversation had taken towards theological debate.

"As a matter of fact," Nolan announced, "Dr Costello did approach me some weeks back about a student who spoke of seeing a doctor. No doubt the student was Hurst, because Dr Costello is Hurst's spiritual director. Now, you don't realize how much these doctors interfere. We had three students with stomach ulcers last year, and before I knew it the guild of Catholic doctors wrote to me recommending that students should have both a small morning tea and a small supper. I

201

put their recommendation into practice, for all the good it's done. . . ."

"It's done no good for Hurst. He doesn't have a stomach ulcer."

Nolan raised his voice. "Maitland, if you think I owe you any of these explanations. . . ." But he went on giving them; the presence of Hurst actually compelled him. "There had already been a dozen students to psychiatrists in the first half of the year. Psychiatrists are the last people we want to have butting into our affairs. I asked Dr Costello was it urgent, and he assured me that he thought not. Now, I happen to feel honoured that Dr Costello is a member of my staff. He is, like most men, fallible, but he is never stupidly fallible, and he lacks both a pride and a malice that are prominent in your own make-up, James. I honestly cannot envisage any future for you in the House of Studies."

"May it assist you in your orisons, monsignor, to know that it depressed the tripes out of me as a student and gives me the gorblimeys as an adult?"

The ambulance and the debate stopped, and the doors swung open on a neon sign saying "Casualty" as merrily as any sign ever said "Ladies Lounge" or "Wine and Dine". A tired resident, who had been playing Rugby all afternoon, was the first to take delivery of poor Hurst; but by the time the pumps were manned, nuns of high rank were arranging supper and inside information for distinguished Monsignor Nolan. The inside information was that Hurst, apart from the necessary discomfort of the treatment, was quite safe.

"Did I hear you admit, James," Nolan asked drolly after a time, "that you actually hold yourself partially to blame for what has overtaken Hurst?"

"Indeed," Maitland showed some enthusiasm in admitting. "I sent him off to the doctor but didn't take the trouble to find out exactly what the doctor said. As they say at tennis classes, my execution was good but my follow-through lacked strength."

"Has it occurred to you then that Hurst could not have put himself in this state if you had not violated my authority?"

202

"I shouldn't be surprised," Maitland said, "if you find in Hurst's room a letter from the doctor telling you or me or whom it may concern that Hurst should be immediately hospitalized."

"Yes," said Nolan, smiling after a hard victory. "You refuse to answer my question." He sat back saying, "Obedience, James, obedience is better than any other thing on the earth."

17

In July there were to be examinations for the students. It was certain now that Maitland, once he had his history papers corrected, would be sent into some parish accustomed to rugged fund-raising clergy who trained the youth organization football team to a grand-final pitch and held boxing evenings. For himself, Maitland felt afraid; but he was sorry also for the salt-of-the-earth people on whom his few half-learned uncertainties were soon to be foisted.

He thought it discreet to stay away from the meeting in the parlour held annually to decide, by vote, whether each student be allowed to go on to a higher grade of Orders. No one accused Maitland for his absence. No one except Edmonds ever spoke of it.

Edmonds had come to say good-bye.

"Good-bye?" Maitland asked.

"They'll never admit me to Orders. This is the second year the vote has gone against me. Even an Edmonds comes to understand in the end."

Maitland said nothing.

"No condolences?" Edmonds wanted to know.

204

"No. If you have a reason to go, thank God and go. Sit down."

Edmonds slung himself indolently into a chair. Already he seemed to be back with the sweet life—debenture issues, Niagaras of whisky.

"There's a rumour you weren't there at the vote."

"That's right."

Maitland could see that Edmonds half-considered the absence as a merely secondary form of treachery.

"What keeps you here, doctor?"

"In this college?"

"In the cloth."

"Listen, if I had gone to the meeting I would have spoken up for you. And that would have merely confirmed them in their intentions. They would have rejected you with even greater certainty."

"Why do you stay, though?"

Maitland wound up his alarm clock which had stopped two days before at some insignificant hour.

"It's my life."

"Is it?" Edmonds doubted that.

"I'm an institutional being. I have been from childhood. My one hope is to wait for my institution to re-establish some contact with the . . . living truth again, that's all. Some individuals—mystics, prophets, saints—outgrow institutions. But I never will, unless I become a mystic or prophet or saint. And there aren't any indications." He laughed. "I suppose you think it's a funny thing that I call myself an institutional being. After all the trouble I've caused here."

Edmonds said, "I know what you mean." But, immune now, he dared to say, "You're a waste, though."

Maitland shook the reawakened clock and agreed negligently. "Almost entirely. But I have to wait for the revelation within this framework. I wouldn't be any less of a waste anywhere else." He set the clock down. That much was a small triumph. He'd felt sure it was broken. "I have to wait and see."

"And what do you suppose you'll see? Costello made an archbishop?"

"No, I don't think that will happen. Perhaps, though, I'm waiting to be endowed with the type of certainty that Costello has. But that won't happen either."

Edmonds nodded. He was no longer as recklessly bitter as he had been when he first walked in. "Just the same," he said, "you and I . . . we've been ghosts here, we've scarcely existed. And no one is bound to remain a ghost."

"Yes," Maitland said, "we've been pallid beings. We've nothing to set up against their dogmas. And I find I can't even resent them effectively. I can be angry, I have been. But it doesn't last. I'm prejudiced against myself in that way. I judge *them* good because they're sure. I feel that being sure is a superior moral state, the sort of state a person should be relatively humble in front of."

"We all feel that way. It's the upbringing."

At the sink for a glass of water, Maitland was moved to Antarctic imagery. "I'm like Shackleton caught in the pack-ice. All I can do is wait for a lead, an indication. Sometimes I almost believe that I'll be damned for not going into a South American slum and sitting down merely to share death with the people. But there's never a strong enough indication in that direction."

"And why a South American slum? There are pretty presentable half-caste slums within drive of most of our towns. You can share things somewhat less glorious than death in those places."

"Long live the financial columnist," Maitland laughed. "The cure for romance."

"Besides, you can't sit down in any hovel. Because you're wed to a bishop and bound by canon law not to be absent from your parish."

"Ah, the administrative ironies of the Church! In any case, I've a whale of a suspicion that a man must find his way within his own civilization. That it's no use going off imposing your destiny in alien places."

206

Edmonds said, "What about Xavier? What about Albert Schweitzer?"

"I don't know them," Maitland told him arbitrarily.

They shook hands, making doomed promises to meet at a later date.

It was the safer of two unsafe courses to keep Egan's secret limited to Egan, Egan's American, the Supreme Pontiff, and himself, Maitland.

What Maitland went to Nolan for was to offer to pay for some of Hurst's medical expenses. Hurst was now in what Maitland's parents used to call a nerve hospital. Under a strong drug that smelt like ether, he had tossed and spoken of nothing but the evils of inordinate castration, had sweated, railed, begged God, spoken of suicide as of a safe harbour, repented of this, begged God again. All other areas of the young cleric slept, except these that accused, were barbarous, or feared God. Whose God?

No matter whose. Hurst would be in hospital for months.

Maitland made the offer. He was especially anxious that his wish to save the archdiocese an expensive medical bill should not be misread as an attempt at buying a reprieve for the remainder of the year. He said contentiously, "I feel I have a large *but not exclusive* part in Hurst's present state."

"I understand that your motives are of the highest order, James," the monsignor conceded. "But I can't allow it."

"Can't allow?"

Maitland decided that Nolan hadn't understood the offer. Or was he now such a pariah in the archdiocese that his money could not be accepted by an organization which, to be frank, would accept nearly anybody's money? He explained the proposal once more and saw the tenderness, traditional to the face, drain like a tide. Maitland stared at the two hard nodules of cheek-bones left high and dry by the old man's anger.

"It's no use trying to argue it, James. Your offer is against policy. If you or any of us paid for Hurst, the family of every

207

young man who fell sick here would expect payment from us."

Maitland squinted from Nolan to the desk, to the typewriter advertised and caressed by nubile blondes in international magazines.

"Do you mean the archdiocese does not intend to pay for Hurst's care?"

"James, the archdiocese has problems of its own."

"Hurst *is* the archdiocese's problem."

"Look, James, thinking out of tune with the rest of us is a speciality of yours. The truth is that Hurst's ecclesiastical education is at an end through no fault of ours, or should I say, through no fault of the organization as a whole. The archdiocese cannot pay. And if it doesn't, would you expect individual members of the staff to do so?"

"Yes. Though I suppose I'm old-fashioned."

Nolan said slowly. "Let me assure you, James, that you are not anything like old-fashioned."

"It seems I've come to the wrong agency."

"Yes. And, James, I am not a superior in the monastic sense. You are not bound to obey me as a monk obeys his abbot. But let me warn you that if you do contribute to Hurst, you are setting a dangerous precedent for the members of the staff, who—"

"Have enough on their hands," supplied Maitland, "buying six-cylinder cars, Gregory Peck pontificals and typewriters favoured by blondes."

Nolan's hand strayed onto the keyboard of the impugned machine.

"Besides," Maitland added, fairly alight, "I think you underestimate the pride of people."

"I don't think I can devote any more time to you, James," Nolan said.

Not being a monk, and having the contempt of the young for that middle-aged fear of setting precedents, Maitland found Hurst's address and wrote a letter to his family. He wrote, "Every priest is a man who believes, one way or another, in retribution. I am partly to blame, by neglect, for your son's present state, and therefore face the retribution. If you could afford me the luxury of forgiving me and accepting this contribution. . . ." He knew that if they were anything like his father there was no way of convincing them that they shouldn't hurl it back in his face.

Within a week, a polite note came by registered mail setting down the family's gratitude but returning the four hundred dollars. He thought then, for a crazed second, that he might contact some famed hotel, might hire a reception room called "Conquistador" or "Alhambra" and there gather the outsiders he had met that year, his cousins Brendan and Grete, Egan, Hurst, Sister Martin, Joe Quinlan and Morna, even Edmonds and Nolan's sister, Mrs Clark. Yet the next day, feeling defeat in every bone, he was at the bank to re-deposit his money.

He climbed the hill home, thinking warmly of his notebooks.

Costello, the vessel of election, beamed throughout June. He had his ring and pectoral cross now. These things were shown off of an evening in the staff parlour, where Maitland came each night to drink one cup of coffee. The mere and relentless courtesy of the other priests, who all knew that he was culpable over Hurst—had even admitted so—could not quench him. What came close to quenching Maitland were the more and more thinly disguised spasms of hope in which Egan spent whatever days were not given over to resentment—resentment of those who would be sure in the future to question his wisdom and his motives. Within the *defensor*, extremes were developing of such a size as made it wholly necessary and wholly impossible to deflate him.

"Nora is very well, *and* very hopeful," Egan would say on a typical morning of hope. "She is making a novena for the success of our petition. That rather destroys your criticism, James."

"I made no criticism," Maitland would say, putting down his pen, for he would not get anything done for some time. "I merely suggested a possibility."

"Don't worry," Egan would chuckle. "You're forgiven."

"Maurice, what are you going to do with yourself? That's what I can't help asking."

This would make no mark on Egan's enamelled visions.

"I don't know, exactly. I could manage one of the hotels." He would laugh and Maitland couldn't help but laugh too at the vision of Egan controlling spreeing fettlers in the saloon bar. "I might take an interest in grazing." Maitland would not give room to the barbarous urge to laugh a second time. But Egan, down for the wool sales in big sheepman's hat and the best of tweeds (from which the Sacred Thirst badge would be removed) also tickled the fancy.

Then Maitland, wriggling in his seat and shaking his long head, would be bound to ask Egan not to be so sanguine, and Egan would take it as a judgment and rush to his room, where some days, curiously weakened and hollowed, he would sleep as much as fourteen hours. The staff guessed uncertainly that he was sickening for one of those sane diseases which are the only ones canon lawyers are prone to. Maitland, keeping a close watch, found that his friend had taken to two unhabitual things—napping in the daytime—napping in the daytime in devoutly creased shirt and black suit-trousers.

Always he would return to speak with Maitland in the end, and would say with the sham jauntiness of the man just managing to conceal seasickness, "I know you have no sympathy for my little expedient, James. However, I want you to know that I will never cease to have a special regard. . . ."

So, trapped in yet another man's incipient madness, Maitland even considered handing his friend into Nolan's care. It was the equivalent of choosing a short death for lingering kith. But Egan was a choice lambkin, a chancery priest; and Nolan would take a narrow view, infect His Grace with it, have Egan doing penance in a monastery and ending in some *ne plus ultra* parish.

18

One midday, at the dinner-table, Egan handed Maitland a
note. It said, "Don't you *dare* try to escape via a lavatory after
this meal. As you can imagine, I must see you. I shall wait in
my room as I prefer the uncluttered surroundings. I anticipate
you will not be such a coward as to avoid this interview."

It was the sort of note that comes to Holmes in Baker Street
during mist, fog or downpour, and James looked up smiling.
He saw that Egan merely sat taking savage mouthfuls of soup,
swallowing it in retaliation. Soon the entire staff would begin
to notice clefts in the man whose face and body looked like a
fair attempt at a formula for sanity but who left the table
after half a plateful of vegetable soup.

Maitland, too, left before dessert. He might have time to
deal with Egan and still catch the quarter-to-two boat. Over
the House of Studies the sky was closing in, all the windows
full of Irish saints and Christian symbols had lost their radiance and gone the gross colours of boiled lollies. On the stairs
where he and Egan had toted Nora, the gloom was still thick
enough for any escapade.

Striding his room from desk to window, Egan had become out of tune with the rational pastel walls and curtains genial as chance acquaintance. He said, immediately Maitland entered, "If I didn't mention that that business about the letter was confidential, Dr Maitland, it was only because I thought you might realize that much for yourself."

"Of course," said Maitland.

"Oh? Did you have a late growth of conscience then? People such as Monsignor Nolan will be gratified to know."

"I don't understand you, Maurice."

"His Grace has asked me to go into retreat for ten days at some friary—to give sober consideration to the requests I made of His Holiness."

"My God."

Egan stood as still as a priest arrived at the turning-point of a rite. He said fervently, "I only hope it was a matter of conscience with you, James, and not simply malice. . . ."

"You mean you consider that—"

Egan latched both his fists onto the desk, and bellowed, "Don't temporize! I am willing to believe that it *was* a matter of conscience with you, because your conscience was outraged from the start by the very thought. If you're not malicious, you're a . . . bloody fool. But Nolan has suspected that much from the start. No mean judge of men, Nolan."

"I told nobody," Maitland said.

"Who then? The Holy Father? My friend wouldn't have had time to see him as yet. Perhaps Nora did."

"Perhaps," Maitland assented.

Egan went, making noises of disgust, to the curtains and peered illusively at the grey face of the chapel. "Just allow me to say," he begged in a wafer of a voice, "before you go, that with full composure and deliberate malice—you see, I don't fear to announce these things aloud—I intend to give them *your* secret. I want you to know what it is to have to explain the unexplainable to people such as His Grace."

This is what it is to be between Gods, thought Maitland, between the defined, tabbed and codified God of corporations and the indefinable, untabbed, uncodified God of Sister Martin. You lose friends and don't care, you lose secrets without fearing the loss, and are accused without its interesting you. Because accusation cannot make you feel any more estranged than you already are.

"I didn't tell anyone," he said for the sake of form, because Egan was expending so much on the interview that it would have been unfair not to show some vigour. "If you want to tell Nolan or His Grace anything I told you in confidence, feel free. But I can't imagine you behaving out of character to that extent."

"Wait and see!"

"Secondly, you should consider the possibility of Nora's being the culprit."

"When I was about fifteen I found half the senior football team smoking in the dressing-sheds. I was appalled to find the flower of the physical side of the school puffing weed. But worse still, the captain glowered at me and yelled, 'Crap off!' I am indebted to that forgotten hero for enriching my grasp of the language, because I can't put it better than 'Crap off, Maitland!' And have your explanations ready for His Grace."

All the way downhill Maitland could see the moored ferry at the pier and was engrossed in catching it. Going on short sprints and pulling up broken-gaitedly whenever his breath gave, he wondered how a man could be damned or saved in any traditional sense when, on a given afternoon, the catching of the quarter-to-two ferry could seem the ultimate, while a book of notes could omit a radiance like a divine person.

He missed the ferry, none the less.

Now he was sobered by the poor alternatives the half-hour wait offered him. He could buy an American malted from a sad Greek or stroll along the wintering fun parlours or see sluggish monsters in the aquarium. None of this emitted a radiance like a divine person. He had time now and space in which to see the danger. *They* would force him out of that great scandalous body, that infamous but mystical corporation they called the Church. And, convinced on the infamy, unaware of the mystery, he would find it easy to oblige and go. The question was whether a man was justified in leaving because he didn't care. Was that an adequate or human motive? To go on the basis of a vacancy—because he didn't care and Costello and Nolan did? If ever he proceeded to take a wife and teach in good Protestant schools, it would need to be by his own decision, not by command of those two odious Brahmins.

He found a telephone. It was answered by some student.

"Yes, doctor. He's in the president's office."

"Tell him I said he *must* come to the phone on the instant. Please. *Must.* An emergency."

There was a silence of some minutes before anyone came again.

"James. Dr Costello here. The president would like you to come home. Immediately."

"Home? What do you mean, *home?*"

"*Home!* Unless you have to dine with your publishers."

"No. But I'll be home towards nine."

"Now, James, that's hardly immediately. This is of massive importance—"

"I know. You want to make me Dean of Studies. But I'll be *home*, as you so fetchingly call it, at nine. Also, go gently with Egan."

He said good-bye and hung up. In fact he wanted vengeance, was tempted to jab at the stanchions that held the pier together.

He came back with lovers and the crapulous in the half-past-eight boat.

Egan could be seen straying up and down the cold pier, like an Angus Wilson clergyman with an eye out for little boys. When he saw Maitland he started to weep.

"You must forgive me," he gurgled.

"Looks that way, doesn't it?" Maitland said, a little too reminiscently of some big-hearted American hero taking his joys and betrayals with half a pint of bourbon.

Egan pressed into his hands a blue airmail letter. With the contrariness of such things, it presented its finish first. Maitland saw, "Your brother in Christ the King, Henry."

214

"Please read it."

"My dear Maurie," it began, as if a diminutive could soothe, "I find it hard to believe that you fully intended the commission you have given me to do and which—I'm sure you'll be willing to believe—I will perform at any personal cost if that is what you want. Just the same, I'm sure that if I tried to negotiate the difficult business which you have decided on, I'd be very glad of a chance to reconsider the course I was taking. I feel that the one to help you reconsider, Maurie, is your own archbishop . . ."

"As this man himself would say," Maitland muttered, "that's rich."

". . . I feel that questions of confidence don't enter into the relationship between a priest and his bishop, and I hear that yours is a very enlightened man, so that he'd be aware of what a high-quality product one Maurie Egan is. I am writing him by the same mail as I am sending this . . ."

"A good old chancellery fascist, this boy!" said Maitland.

". . . and will be willing to perform anything that you and he work out in concert. Rest assured, Maurice, I shall remember you at the altar of sacrifice each morning. . . ."

"I've ruined you for nothing."

"No one ruins what isn't." He found it hard to be disturbed that the crisis had come.

"I was mad, James." That being preferable to a fall from grace. "I was mad. A good friend, a good friend. . . ."

Maitland forced him into the back seat of his little coupé and drove him back to the House of Studies. Later in the evening Nolan called in a discreet Catholic doctor to inject sedative into Egan. To Almighty God via the almighty knock-out drop, thought Maitland, although he was glad to see his friend sink to sleep, and only the super-righteous presence of Nolan and Costello moved him to irony.

Later, Costello cornered him. "The president and I, we've been reviewing the time you've spent here. We find it hard to believe that you want to remain a priest."

Maitland was shaken. He said, "It's essential that I stay."

215

"Essential? You mean, for your salvation?"

Maitland agreed. "Yes, for that."

Costello sighed. "With your record, James, and taking that book into consideration . . . it becomes impossible for anyone to tell whether what you say is merely an exercise in sarcasm."

19

Nora, who coyly remembered her drunkenness of some months back, fluttered, but insisted that Maitland come in.

"Maurice asked me to visit you," he explained, and his eyes wavered towards the bay-windowed prow of the living-room on his left. "Is your sister in?"

"She is." But Nora foresaw no difficulty on that count. "Please come in, father. We've just made tea."

He followed her inside; where she kept remembering in a quavering way to perform little politenesses, such as to take his hat and point the way. He sensed, not altogether trusting the sense, that she was rushing him indoors; and found it beyond him to cut into her vein of ditheriness and force a conference in the hall. Full of complex dismay, they shuffled in the doorway of the living-room, both yielding the way, both beginning to move but yielding again. Within sat Celia, possessed by an acrid calm. She glanced over her shoulder at Maitland's entry and sat forward almost politely, her raised left hand begging silence. Beside her, a race broadcast gurgled towards its upshot.

"Sit here, father," Nora whispered. She was suddenly more expansive; even her shoulders were not as hunched.

Maitland sat in what was obviously her chair, at the sunny end of the room near Celia. Now the horses were into the straight, and Celia swallowed. Living for the culmination, dressed in a long floral frock that made her seem proportionate or, better still, lovely, she woke large and cordial sensualities in Maitland's belly. But the habit of celibacy asserted itself. *He who rides a tiger*, he thought. . . .

By which time the winners had been semaphored. Celia's indolent hand turned the volume merely down, being satisfied when the ranting voice sounded like people arguing four or five gardens away.

Immediately Maitland told them that Egan had gone to hospital. They heard him soberly. There was no yell of jubilee from Celia, no breast-beating from Nora, who looked unfathomably from Celia to Maitland to Celia again.

Celia asked what the trouble was with Egan, and found a Dresden china teacup for Maitland while he told her of Egan's nervous collapse. An acute anxiety state, he admitted.

Nothing was said as tea was handed round; though Maitland could hear some harsh breathing from Nora. Yet, through silences that begged to be broken with tears, she did not weep. Rather, eyes down, Maitland began to feel that he was being stared at and, glancing at last, saw the two sisters, far from engrossed in him, totally distracted from him. Out of inert faces they peered at each other; raw, level, irrefragable communion. He wondered how Maurice Egan, with or without the Pope's consent, would have dealt with this sisterhood deep as the womb.

"What hospital?" asked Nora, putting down her cup and straying towards the windows.

Maitland told her. "He said he will write fully when he's able. They have him drugged almost continuously."

"Poor, poor Maurice." Her voice gave. "Can he tell people apart?"

"Oh, yes. It's like a perpetual state of drunkenness, that's all."

218

Though he bit his clumsy lip, neither woman saw need to impute spite to him.

"We must go and see him as soon as possible, Celia. Are you using the car tomorrow?"

Maitland tried to say, "There's no chance—"

"If you'd like the outing yourself," Nora suggested, "you could drive me up there."

"I might, too. It's superb country. On a clear day you can get a view right to the sea."

Nora held her hands out for the afternoon sun to rinse. Saying "Poor, poor Maurice" more resolutely this time. She stared at the moored yachts across the street, and the pottering yachtsmen.

"We could take a picnic lunch," Celia proposed.

"He's probably not up to eating much. But we could take that chicken, in case. And then there are the giblets."

"Giblet broth."

"I was thinking the same thing. We might—"

Maitland, close to panic-stricken, made a clatter with his cup, a brutal noise for Dresden. Picnic plans withered on the stem.

He said. "Nora, you can't see him."

With perhaps a sneer, Celia murmured, "My goodness, he *must* be ill. . . ."

Maitland persisted. "It isn't that he's too ill. Nora, I wonder could I speak to you in private?"

The woman had gone sallow, but she said with a ferocity akin to Celia's, "I want my sister to be here."

"Sit down, Nora," Celia prescribed and was obeyed.

She made a good convenor. She said, "It seems you have something to tell us, father."

Just as he felt certain that these two women were sufficient to each other, he felt certain now that Nora would weep affectingly, temperately. In view of what he had to tell her, he hoped that these hastily founded certainties were valid. And it was not only the talk of giblet broth, nor their relish at the thought of nursemaiding the broken priest that gave him hope. Rather that Nora had not convinced him, when he had come in a state that could largely be called *willing to be convinced*. His instincts hinted that, having suffered, she had become inured to living off the stored fat of her agonies, was growing, like her sister, into a professional wronged-woman.

"He wanted me to let you know," Maitland began, "that he can't see you again, not even once. He'll write, as I said, but he isn't capable of writing or telephoning yet, and the message couldn't wait."

Nora wept affectingly, temperately, yet credibly enough to alarm Maitland.

He thought, "So much for certainties! This may be the real McCoy, eternal widowhood for Nora Tully." Yet he could not manage to believe it.

Celia could. She had risen, and stood chafing Nora's shoulders. Since to go on lolling and to intervene both seemed improper, Maitland sat tight, waiting to give details. But Celia began first. The tragedy, or whatever it was, had at least muted her.

"He decides when to terminate the affair, eh? When *he* feels the bite? Ask him what about the girl he's kept bloody enthralled for two years."

"Well, it wasn't his own decision."

"I suppose his spiritual director told him. Lop off the limb of Satan! She won't feel it. It'll only damn-well kill her, that's all. Spiritual directors! Illiterate disrespecters of human decency—"

"His archbishop told him to cut the connection."

"His archbishop?"

"*The* archbishop. It was a command." He tried to speak directly to Nora. "He could never have given the system up. It would have killed him to do it. He would have been no use to you as an apostate, or whatever they call them."

"I suppose you think God is honoured by all this?" said Celia.

"I don't know. I'm the type who could leave tomorrow without my old vows poisoning me, turning to gangrene, if you like. But Maurice isn't."

"Well, Nora doesn't happen to be interested in you."

"I know. It wasn't a proposal."

Nora asked, her small voice caught in clenched fists, "The Pope didn't grant him his petition?"

"Some minor official returned the letter to His Grace. It was an impossible plan, Nora. If Maurice hadn't been so wrought-up he would have seen how impossible it was."

"She's just the type to take a lot of notice of archbishops," Celia judged of her sister.

"So is Maurice," Maitland told her.

"Oh, damn Maurice. Celibacy is only a high form of sex-titillation. An attack on women from a more exalted level. You read the psychologists!" she recommended.

"I don't think Maurice is getting much fun out of it, Miss Tully."

"*Mrs* Crosley, however abandoned." She bent and made soothing noises close to Nora's ear. Egan's dark girl, bereaved by a prelate, laid her head on the arm of her lounge chair and locked it down with her slim tragic fingers. Bolstered by such grief, Celia glowered at the priest.

"It must be convenient to be attached to God via an arch-bishop. You play about with a girl until the human toll begins to mount. Then you let your archbishop know that you have been ensnared by some unscrupulous woman. He commands 'Cut the connection!' You tell the girl, 'I'm sorry, but I'm bound in conscience. It's the will of God and I'll always pray for you, etc.' Isn't that the perfect male fiddle? No male with the normal endowment of brains in his backside could think of a better one."

Maitland sighed. "If you're trying to tell me that church-men are dishonest, I know that already. The question is smaller—Maurice and Nora. They believe in archbishops, they be-lieve in canon law. There's no hope for them."

He saw that the quivering Nora was listening. He whis-pered to Celia, "Arguments about the turpitude of churchmen and Church won't have any bearing. You must help her—"

"Oh, Christ!" roared Celia, and pranced away into the win-dow area. Maitland blushed for sounding like a stage parson, and swallowed as she swept back down on him, strutting, her glorious breasts bobbing visibly. "Will you perhaps send me roneo'd notes on how to do it? Arrogance in the best traditions of Holy Mother Church! Maitland's balm for the sin-sick soul!"

Solitary now, Nora mourned and skirted some of the milder borders of hysteria. Maitland felt bound to stay until the girl had been calmed; yet calm might take as long as a birth or a death. He was pleased to see that Celia was intent now on making it quick.

"Come over here with me and sit in the sun."

Helped to hobble to the window-seat, Nora indomitably rasped, "You don't want to miss Regal Fred's race."

"No. No. We'll listen together. We won't miss it. No. Some more tea?"

They seemed again to have forgotten Maitland. Celia stroked Nora's dark hair for some minutes and held her watch up to the light once. It must have been some time after four. The bay was going slowly molten, and the windscreens of a luxury launch blazed miraculously. At length she turned to him, her hair and shoulders glowing in the prismatic light of advanced afternoon.

Completely lacking in ardour: "You can get out," she told Maitland.

20

On a night in early July, Maitland came—to sit before an inquiry—to the door marked *Sapientia* at the cathedral presbytery; and was taken without delay to the council room where he had dealt so unprofitably with His Grace and Des Boyle some months before. There the fire went well, the table glinted like port wine. Recognized now by Maitland as an old acquaintance, St Sebastian still exercised his terrible heroism in the window behind His Grace.

On the archbishop's right sat Costello, within a day or two to enter retreat and reduce his life to order for consecration as a bishop. Already he looked quaint in his black, caped priest's cassock; his presence was a prelatial one, and that he should still be wearing simple black looked like a deliberate and poorly staged act of public humility.

Monsignor Nolan sat on the left of the head of the table, and occasionally fuelled the fire. Before him lay a thin sheaf of typewritten notes, but the copious note-paper in front of Costello and His Grace had not been touched.

For Maitland, a chair had been placed to Nolan's side of the room. The table seemed even more suited to dramatizing the gulf between judges and judged than did the one at Sister Martin's inquiry, and His Grace had wanted to avoid overtones of trial: he sensed that Maitland's case was too important to be dressed up in formal ways. So Maitland, treated again to that upside-down consideration which was his right as a wrong'un, would sit at least as close to the fire as would his judges, and on the edge of a chair made for fireside dozing. He wondered whether, if he had murdered Nolan, they'd have given him a chaise-longue.

Nevertheless, he would be throughout badly exposed to the tribunal behind their oak ramparts.

"You still don't have an overcoat, James?" asked His Grace, mostly in accusation, partly in something that was indulgent.

"He earns enough," Nolan asserted.

As Maitland looked shamefaced and moved along the table to kneel before His Grace, the archbishop sat and warded him off with both hands.

"Is this your idea of satire, James? I know you probably squirm and think it medieval, so I'd rather you didn't."

Maitland said softly, "It's a polite gesture, Your Grace. If I can't be polite to my own bishop. . . ."

"Isn't that by way of being the point?" Costello asked.

"Sit down, James."

But then the sight of this thin and ascetic trouble-maker stooping to sit piqued His Grace.

"You must know that I would be quite justified in suspending you without so much as speaking to you."

Maitland nodded.

"You'll notice, Dr Maitland," said Costello, "there is no clerk-of-court here. Conscience is, we hope, clerk-of-court and sanctioner. There is no notary. Conscience keeps the book. All right?"

His Grace took up the thread. "Why I have chosen to consult you, James, is that I want explanations. And it's not only a matter of this book. There are other failures—*failures*, note! —of yours which will work against you all your life unless you

224

answer for them here. It will be necessary to impose a penalty on you. I want—I'd even say I plead with you—to accept it and remain my priest."

Maitland said indefinitely and with some embarrassment, "Yes, yes. Certainly."

His Grace nodded at Nolan, who scanned the details of the first complaint. "It seems, Dr Maitland, that within a month of your being appointed to the staff of the House of Studies, you gave a sermon at a most peculiar Mass, in which you applied to priests the dictum, 'Because they love nobody they imagine that they love God.' "

"Well, James?"

"Of course I didn't apply it to priests as such, Your Grace. It was used to outline a danger, nothing more. What I said that evening was a plea for tolerance for priests."

Costello smiled. "It's kind of you to be concerned for us, Dr Maitland, but people seem to tolerate us to a quite satisfactory degree."

"It's a nasty quotation, James," the prelate murmured. "You say you were outlining a danger. A danger for priests, I suppose you mean?"

"Yes."

"Don't you think lay people have sufficient problems of their own without being let into ours."

Maitland took a risk. He said, "I don't want to seem flippant, Your Grace. Least of all tonight. But the Mass in question was said for a society of graduates. To many of them, *we* are one of the major problems."

"My nephew, Mrs Lamotte's son, who attended the Mass, found the dictum in bad taste," Nolan claimed.

"If His Grace questioned priests about every sermon that individual Catholics found distasteful. . . ."

"I would find such a statement in bad taste whether in or out of context. I would find it so, not by the standards of some individual quirk, but by absolute standards."

"Oh, monsignor," James protested, "we've never been friends, let alone admirers. Isn't it natural we'd find each

225

other distasteful by absolute standards. That's what resentment's all about."

There was a silence. Then His Grace said, "Maitland, you're not here to make proverbs."

Maitland admitted this. There was a further silence, broken, without a trace of gall, by Nolan.

"Your Grace, the quotation came from a French poet called Charles Péguy."

His Grace, who harmlessly fancied his own French, went sorting names in his mind. "Péguy . . . Péguy. . . ."

"He was a nominal Catholic, a violent anti-clerical, and he didn't attend Mass."

"Monsignor, that has no bearing on wisdom or its lack." Maitland longed to say something specious but ironic about Abraham and David, robust non-Mass-goers. But His Grace intervened loudly.

"*James!* It seems you have to be told you're not here either to make proverbs *or* to argue as the equal of any other person in the room."

Apologies had to be made a second time, and the proper silences again to be observed. The archbishop was frowning.

"James, you say, 'because they love nobody. . . .' But don't you believe that Costello and Nolan and myself love our brothers for the love of the good God?"

"Yes," said Maitland. "Yes, I know you do." For their God was a kinsman, not an absolute, not a void in the heart.

"Then can you name any priest who fits the statement made by this Péguy?"

He knew that he would be badgered with it in future conflicts, yet it had to be admitted now. "Yes," he stated. "Myself."

Fairly covertly, the judges eyed each other.

"Come now, James," His Grace said, "you desire to behold God, don't you?"

"Yes."

"Well, that desire is love."

"I don't know if that sort of love suffices. Half the evil

226

things done on the earth are love-offerings, from someone to someone. I don't know if I. . . ."

"My God!" Costello made his classic sinus noise. "He's gone all Dostoevski on us now."

Questions proliferated, and when they were finished, the three were satisfied that, within the limits of the theological definitions, Maitland loved God. Throughout, Maitland wanted to announce, "But we're not talking about the same entity!" But that would merely have initiated a parallel line of questioning.

Then Brendan and Grete were raised by Nolan, apologized for by Maitland, commentated on by His Grace, and forgotten.

Third in the president's notes, but bracketed by two red question-marks, was a digest of the strange theological opinions avowed by Dr Maitland during discussions among the members of staff in the downstairs parlour. But His Grace did not want a doctrinal showdown, not until *The Meanings of God* was brought up.

No question-marks flanked the names of Hurst and Egan, two unstable men, the secret of whose instability had been too well kept by Maitland.

Nolan at length neared the end of a long annotation on Hurst's case.

". . . went so far as to arrange interviews with a psychiatrist for Hurst. Entirely without reference to me or to the young man's spiritual director. If I stood on ceremony, I could manage to resent profoundly the bad manners. But what I most resent is the danger to the priesthood involved in such bad manners."

"Of course you do. James, I have to tell you yet another thing. You've got no sense of belonging to an institution. You'd better hurry up and acquire some, that's all. No explanations?"

"I couldn't explain without seeming to accuse, Your Grace. I plead guilty to beginning something I shouldn't have begun, and then treating Hurst negligently. Just the same, the person who has been harmed at my hands is Hurst, not Dr Nolan."

Nolan appealed to His Grace. "You see?"

"In any case," Costello said urbanely, "I'd like to see you attempt to accuse."

"I'd prefer merely to let my apologies stand."

"Ah, the beginning of wisdom!"

"Then there's Maurice Egan," murmured His Grace; and, more loudly, "Maurice Egan. Once more the problem of institutional sense. Or its lack."

Maitland affirmed, "Maurice's case would have confused the wise. . . ."

Nolan made an axiom. "With a priest, wisdom is obligatory."

"James, you realized that his letter to the Supreme Pontiff was a mistake. Why wasn't I warned of it? Do you think I'm beneath trust?"

The young priest gave a negative shrug. "You're absolutely right. You should have been warned in Egan's case. But Maurice had a career in the Church and . . . well, I feared a disintegration. Which has happened in any case."

"You say, in *Egan's* case," Costello observed.

"I beg your pardon?"

"You emphasized, in *Egan's* case. As if it wouldn't have been better in any case to bring the problem straight to His Grace."

"There was no special malice in my saying *in Egan's case*. But even a priest surely has the right to give or keep secrets. The archdiocese is not a police state."

"Enough rhetoric, thank you, James."

"In Egan's case in particular I should have appealed immediately to you, Your Grace. Maurice lived by the book, and the book said that there is no appeal to Rome except through your bishop. I don't want to sound portentous, especially since I've already been warned against such things. But those who live by the book—and it's an enviable way to live—have to be saved in terms of the book. It was an unbalanced thing for him to have written that letter. I should have used the fact of the letter to gauge his condition."

228

"I see," said Costello, "no mention of any vow of celibacy the fellow might have had."

"What I said was only another way of putting it."

Now it was well after nine, and His Grace, fuddled by the exchange of shots between Costello and Maitland, looked to the central question of *The Meanings of God* affair to show quickly and finally the precise quality of Maitland's revolt. To conclude all minor matters, he asked Maitland whether by daring to mistrust authority he had saved Egan or Hurst from anything.

Maitland said, "I saved them from nothing."

There were reasons, though he didn't broach them. It was in general as impossible to help two people who are impacted in a given structure as it was to dig the eyes out of a whale and demand that they still focus. He had saved them from nothing. At that moment they both still slept, stubble growing on both unlikely faces. Egan nearly had a beard, his face made vagabond by it, a child's face, gratified with wonder drugs, fallen asleep with its pirate's mask still on.

His Grace had said something to Nolan, who dissentiently pursed his lips and put aside the typewritten notes.

The archbishop began. "Are you aware yet, James, of the provisions of Canon 1386, the law governing publication of books by priests?"

"I know that I've broken the law by publishing *The Meanings of God* without permission from yourself or one of the other bishops the law nominates."

"It was a book," testified Costello, "that required censorship as well as permission."

"I don't believe that it required censorship because I don't believe that it put forward theological opinion."

"The pseudonym seems to indicate that you suspected it did."

His Grace mediated, saying firmly, "Now it's Maitland's mind on the matter that alarms me and that I must be certain about."

"I knew there must have been some provision of law by

229

which I had to seek permission to publish. I am absolutely guilty of not making sure what the provision was."

"Oh come, Dr Maitland," Costello said, "I taught you when you were a student. I have regularly spent eight lectures every two years on this very topic, permission and censorship. Now I'd put my money on you to remember the details of the Dried Fruit Trading Act till your dying day if you'd listened to one or two, let alone *eight* lectures on the subject. How is it you don't remember the details of Canon 1386?"

"I wouldn't dare say. . . ."

"Please do."

"Well, I suppose it all arises out of the human capacity to forget odious laws."

"So you think this is an odious law?"

"I can't pretend I don't. All I can do is give my word to keep it in future. Until it's revoked, of course."

"And if it's never revoked, James?" His Grace wanted to know.

"I *will* keep it, Your Grace. Ironically, all that's essential is that I should remain within the Church."

Costello whistled, casting question on the word "ironically".

Maitland went on, "You say you wanted to know my mind. There are many priests in Europe who ignore that Canon 13. . . ."

"1386," Costello supplied.

"Many of them use the expedient I used, and publish under a different name. They speak about the right to free expression being more basic than the rights of bishops, and all the rest of it. However, I didn't do what I did on philosophic grounds. Far from it. I suppose I have to say my behaviour arose from a . . . native laxity."

"But this has no bearing on your breaking the law," said Costello.

"That's quite right. I know it's not the thing a judge can take notice of. But a bishop may be more pleased to hear of it than of outright rebellion."

"Not this bishop," said His Grace, "not particularly pleased. I remember a charade of some weeks back, Des Boyle, your-

230

self, myself. You discussing this same book as if it were somebody else's. No, I'm not particularly pleased."

"Books live as long as cicadas, Your Grace. I thought—conscientiously—that it was best to let mine die. The pseudonym I used was a matter of . . . well, bashfulness. If Dr Costello wants a word he can laugh at."

"I'll laugh at it, certainly. And I'll also say that if ignorance were a defence against the law, etiquette should still have bound you."

"Yes," Maitland said. Though there were higher interests than etiquette. Throwing a grenade was not etiquette, but it was possible to think of occasions when it might be necessary. He wisely kept that image to himself.

Nolan said, "But we must return to the central controversy. Of course, your book *is* a book of theology."

"No."

"Does it or doesn't it put forward a *logos* about *Theos*, ideas about God?" Costello asked.

"Not about God in himself. It puts forward ideas about the ideas men have about God." Even to Maitland it sounded a little specious.

"James, if I ordered you to recant some specified ideas from your book," His Grace proposed, "would you?"

Maitland said nothing. Costello didn't mind admitting, "Nolan and I both believe that your book runs counter to a number of Papal decrees on the nature of God. I am not afraid of confessing that I raised the question to His Grace."

"The recantation would never be made public, of course," the archbishop explained. "It would be secret to the three of us and to yourself. And to my successor as well."

After some time Maitland said, "Not that this has anything to do with it, but what would be the penalty if I didn't."

"I won't speak about penalties. Not at this stage."

"Your Grace, I could recant if I came to hold different opinions. But a man can't decide in five minutes to hold different opinions."

Costello suggested, "Give it a try."

"None of the book's reviewers thought it heretical."

231

"Do you have copies of reviews, James? By Catholic scholars, I mean."

"Yes."

Another long, conscientious silence fell. At last Maitland said, "I'm no enemy of doctrine. But if you want to get rid of me, the book will serve."

"The implication is an insult, James."

"I ask you not to make me recant."

Costello made a wry nasal noise. "Please don't punish me, judge. It could make me an enemy of society."

Someone, proving to be the Irish spinster who had solaced Maitland with cocoa some weeks before, then knocked at the door. She announced a trunk call for His Grace, who left to take it in his office. This was the unkindest ruse that events could manage—to leave judges with nothing to do but chat with the accused. Nolan and Costello at first tried to elude speaking with Maitland and spoke in whispers. But Maitland's apparent equality with them, his closeness to the hearth, the easiness of his easy chair, all incited them to give him unofficial advice, peer to peer.

Nolan said, "Pride or Church now, James, pride or Church." And, more cryptically, "Remember the night of the Couraigne prize?"

Costello said, "James, if I've been baiting you it's because you're a provocative young man. But you must make the humble decision, not the resentful one. Resentment can only harm yourself. The Church can't lose either way."

Suddenly Maitland became, if not acutely resentful, acutely angry.

"The Church!" he called out. "You think of the Church as Christ's young bride already come into the fullness of beauty. I think of her as a scruffy old eyesore with half her tats drawn who's whored around too much with politicians."

"That is a sustaining vision, that is!" Costello hooted.

"And I don't mean to be driven out to satisfy your sense of fitness."

"Dr Costello will be archbishop of this diocese one day," Nolan claimed. "His sense of fitness will bind you then."

232

"I may die, he may die, we both may. He may even fail to make it."

Costello was jovial about the odds against him. "Indeed, indeed," he laughed. "All I say is, don't jump the wrong way because you resent Nolan and myself. We are inadequate grounds."

"You really mean to be kind, don't you?"

"Of course."

"Then don't plant this recantation idea in his head."

"That is a matter of conscience with us," Nolan explained.

No one was ungrateful when His Grace returned; all three stood with hearty reverence. But the prelate stayed in the doorway, holding the door ajar.

He said, "As far as I'm concerned, everything has been said. Except this: James, when you say the Credo during the Mass, can you say it with an honest heart?"

"Yes."

"Wait in the front parlour on your left."

"I won't recant, Your Grace."

"And I won't be bullied, James."

"I wasn't bullying. I was pleading."

"Molly will bring you some supper."

An hour passed in that front parlour. He was emotionally languorous but mentally aware of being under a more pervasive danger than ever before. He was, as he had told Edmonds, an institutional being. He must develop, however achingly, within the structure; and he had an intuitive certainty that unseen development was proceeding. Random death—at an intersection say, in Costello's car—could render this growth inconsequent. But being cast out would make it void and leave him a nomad.

Yet his alarm was of the cooler, mental variety. He had leisure to regret the absence of books. He learnt the family tree of the Benedictine order, framed on one wall, and achieved a working grasp of the map on the other; of the red arrows (migrations of priests) emanating from Ireland and spearing into the heart of the Americas, of Eurasia, of Oceania.

Then there was the life of St Kevin in the stained-glass window, with a summary in Gothic-print Latin at the bottom. An untranslatable gerundive in this inscription kept him busy for ten minutes.

At a quarter to eleven the baffled Molly called for him.

"You sitting for an exam, father?" she asked.

"You could say that, Molly."

"Then God bless. That Joseph of Cupertino is the feller for exams. Look, I have him in the kitchen, and I'll say the prayer while you're in there."

"You're very kind."

But she said no, she had a pledge to spread the devotion.

Dirtied cups and fouled ashtrays occupied the judicial end of the table.

Maitland took comfort from its looking like a decision-makers' mess: as if some arduous soul-searching had taken place. But he got little time to gather omens. The archbishop told him to sit. The big plush chair attempted to coddle him as no accused about to hear sentence would ever want to be.

"First," His Grace said, "you assure me that you can say the Credo with honesty?"

Maitland said he could.

"Now it's hard to *make* you recant. No one knows you wrote the thing. We don't *want* anyone to know you wrote the thing. You understand?"

"Yes."

"I've decided to suspend you for three months. You will neither say the Mass and administer sacraments under my jurisdiction, nor seek to do so under any other bishop's. You will write to me at length during each week of your suspension. You will occupy the first month with a period of recollection in a monastery I shall name to you later."

A month's quiet would, in itself, be a delight. But Maitland knew that there would be some attempt to read daily the level of his rivers of perversity.

Sure enough: "You will confess regularly, follow out the life of the community as best you can, and speak for at least half an hour daily with a spiritual director whom, once again, I shall name to you later."

"I could have hoped for more freedom, Your Grace."

"This *is* a penance, James. You've already exploited all the freedom you're likely to get. Do you submit?"

"Yes." He had begun to colour. He said through tight lips, "But I believe my book was a valid book. Even a good book."

His Grace sighed. "We'll come to that. You submit, though, without argument?"

"Yes."

Costello said gently, "Our prayers shall keep pace. Neck and neck."

Maitland came close to blushing, and all three judges bowed their heads imperceptibly for the pious thought.

His Grace said, "I would have suspended you for much longer, James, but we have a grave shortage of priests. Just the same, I trust that this first part of your penalty is a greater blow to you than the second. Because you are a priest, you exist for that, and now you cannot be a priest, in any active sense, for some time. Secondary to that, then, you will publish nothing in my lifetime, James, although *you are free to ask* me to relax this ruling in individual cases. But unless the individual case has exceptional validity, you will not publish."

Maitland felt a vacancy half an inch from his heart, in the small and incandescent space filled, up to the moment, by the notion of his novel. But terms such as "exceptional validity" were vague and could be argued in their time.

"Do you accept this, James?" His Grace wanted to know.

21

Egan had become very possessive about his hospital. Stark-eyed, he led Maitland through the ground-plan, displaying the stucco and the monstrosities in the incurables' section with equal pride. Sixty years past, the house had belonged to a pastoralist, had begun its life as one family's stone bungalow, with tower. It had suited the departed sheep king's swank; and it suited the present dwellers, all suffering classically named diseases, that Jason striving should hold up the balustrade, that lumpy girls labelled Hebe and Nike should stand in the stained-glass windows, or Apollo and Daphne languish asexually above the main door. The humble brothers of a Hospitaller order passed with bed-pans and white mixture.

"There's a priest here who never speaks," Egan boasted. "Never. Not for months. And they can't let him say Mass because he's liable to fling something, even the chalice, at his altar-server. It's happened."

The small priest, sedated to a level where he could rejoice even in chalice-hurling, chattered on as he and Maitland

236

emerged on a veranda of red tiles with an inlaid Celtic snake swallowing his tail in the porch. It was impossible to believe in the serpent's elegant distress, but the grounds crawled with credibly morose patients.

Egan chattered on. "Well, my second day here, I woke for an hour or two, and I saw this priest in the ward and asked him how he was. He glared at me as if I'd called him a foul name, and then they gave me some more drugs and I slept for three days or so."

They sat on a garden seat, Maitland remembering just in time to remove a new paperback from his hip pocket. Before them was a conservatory, and beyond it orange orchards ran downhill to mudflats possessed by grazing cows. The river ran quietly, but flicked its thighs in the sun to cross a sandbank.

"When I woke, the priest was beside me. I thought that he'd been there all the time, while I slept, but that wasn't possible. Anyhow, he looked at me, full of hate. I thought he might murder me. All he said was, 'Mind your own bloody business!' Imagine!" Egan giggled. "It isn't funny, of course, but the man in the bed next to mine told me that the poor fellow had visited me each morning while I was drugged and waited for me to wake up, and when I didn't, said, 'Mind your own bloody business!' with plenty of venom, and then marched away." In the same hard-pressed breath, he asked, "How are things with you, James?"

"Very well. I'm boarding in a friary, theoretically under supervision, but the friars are better sports than Nolan. I have a good monastic breakfast, spend no less than five hours a day in the archives at the public library, chant the evening office with the community. I sleep like a just man." After thought, he admitted, "I miss the Mass. I miss it very acutely. It's a surprise."

How deep a one he didn't say; but the rite he had learnt at twenty-two out of a yellow book, with a chalice made of half a jam-tin, he fretted for now with a trenchancy he had thought himself beyond.

He said, "It's a matter of what you've been bred to."

237

"I suppose if my mad letter had succeeded, I'd have missed the Mass, too."

Maitland's eyes slewed away towards the blue distances of the river, but he said in the end, "You're sure to have, Maurice."

Egan wept feverishly, like an unhappy drunk. Maitland ignored him.

"Listen, Maurice, I've taken a cottage at a little beach town along the coast for the last month of my suspension. Some of the paperback royalties on my infamous book will pay for the rent. It isn't a very luxurious place. Outside toilets. Cans."

"Well, they were good enough for Duns Scotus and Aquinas and Peter Abelard," Egan said, rubbing his eyes.

"So they were," Maitland said. "I was wondering, would you like to come with me? You can see the beach from the cottage and there's a whopping cone-shaped headland. We can run over it every morning. Like a couple of Legion of Mary boys trying to sublimate our lower urges."

Egan chuckled and kept shedding tears, though happily.

"Then we'll go for a swim and have lunch. Then you can have a rest and I'll work on my new book. . . ."

"New book?" Egan asked like the old Egan, the *defensor vinculi*.

"It's a novel. But there's little chance of its being published. Not while His Grace rules."

"They're going to make bishops retire in their seventies. So I won't have you saying there's no hope."

"How old is His Grace?"

"Sixty-one." For the first time since infancy, on the face of things and before another human, Egan, fallen cherub, leered. "Coronary age," he hissed.

They took the cottage. Each morning Maitland bullied Egan across the conical headland and taught him to catch small fish in the surf. Tired himself, he worked four hours each afternoon and wrote up to fifteen hundred words on most days. Egan napped and read, waking to find Maitland half-satisfied at dusk with his day's work.

238

"How's the conscienceless man?" Egan would ask, for Maitland's novel was the record of an obscure Edwardian who had entirely lacked moral imagination.

While the novelist said his office, Egan made the evening meal. At the town pub, they had the snooker table booked for a quarter past eight every night, and if no one had booked it for nine they would play on till closing-time—Egan squinting toutishly at hard lies and letting his beer go flat on the mantelpiece. Every first morning, he slept until nine because of the pills. Every second morning, they drove in his car to the main town, and he said a Mass which Maitland served. The ceremony had its poignancies for both of them; but neither gave a hint, except that, climbing back into the car one day, Egan said, "You say your office and I say Mass every second morning. Between us, we are nearly one whole priest."

They were sent a few letters. The graduate society for whom he had said Mass on a headland one autumn Saturday wrote to Maitland and asked if he would say Mass for them in three weeks' time, the very day he would be given his faculties back by the archbishop. He replied pleasantly, accepting.

There was a letter from his publisher with a cheque for the American edition of *The Meanings of God*. Since the contract had been signed ten months previously, Maitland had no choice but to accept the money. That night they drank liqueurs over their snooker.

What did the most damage was the letters from the chancery.

"I didn't know you two gentlemen were doctors," the lady at the post-office told Maitland. "It's handy to have a doctor here. A girl who was mauled by a shark here three years back had to be taken thirteen miles to the doctor."

"Oh, but we're doctors of minerology," Maitland said.

Egan had already gone outside and opened the formal envelope in the shade of the telephone booth, as if it must be kept secret from the few strolling housewives. As Maitland came up, the old pallor returned to Egan, who handed the letter across rather than speak of it. So Maitland read it before reading his own. It consigned Egan to an industrial parish and said that the work load was light there. Maitland imagined the little man among the factories: the schoolboy face and the prim body and the set diction. He clicked his tongue but could not afford to be angry, for Egan's sake. Instead he dealt with his own letter truculently, read it quickly, and rammed it into the pocket of his shorts. He was to go as a curate to a parish in the mountains. His lot was sleet and sodalities. He told Egan.

"They say that the parish system is dead, a relic in an age of technology," he said. "Let's be two jolly maggots."

They dawdled home. For Egan, reality had drained out of the conical mountain, the sea and the fish in the sea. He dreaded the iron realities of a priesthood which three out of four men did not believe in, but which he could not forbear believing in. He was the unwise virgin of the modern advertisement, bound to the use of the non-majority soap.

"I suppose we could arrange to take this cottage again next year," he proposed, and the small mouth set when Maitland said yes. But it did little good.

On a Saturday, Maitland was received by His Grace. That same evening he said Mass on a cliff-top above a flooded valley. Mist nudged the ragged plateau across the gorge, and a wind made his chasuble fly. Somebody again placed a truck to the weather side of the altar. Maitland, unsure for the moment, did not preach.

240